Any minute n
cuss

But to his shock and dismay, she only smiled and allowed those remarkably thick dark lashes to sweep over her chestnut eyes once again.

"As you say, Brooks," she agreed demurely. "I do stick out like a sore thumb here in New York, part Irish and part Indian—a cat's whisker from being a barbarian, wouldn't you say?"

Missy—brave, blunt, wonderful Missy was still beneath the lonely veneer.

"No, I wouldn't call you a barbarian and neither would anyone else within my hearing, I assure you—*Marisa.*" A sudden burst of possessiveness flared inside him. All he wanted to do was enjoy her company alone and keep other men from looking at her with hungry eyes.

Their gazes locked. Heat rose between them like fog on a warm April morning.

Breathe, you idiot, a voice inside his head screamed....

Dear Reader,

This holiday season, we've selected books that are sure to warm your heart—all with heroes who redefine the phrase "the gift of giving." Since Linda Castle's first book, *Fearless Hearts,* appeared in our 1995 March Madness Promotion, she has been inundated with letters from fans asking for more. *Territorial Bride* is that long-awaited sequel. Now cowgirl Missy O'Bannion is all grown-up—and she's bound and determined to become a *lady* to impress Eastern rogue Brooks James, who's already shown her he can be a real cowboy. In this darling "opposites attract" romance, their love is tested on many levels, especially when Missy is seriously injured.

Rising talent Sharon Schulze returns this month with *The Shielded Heart,* a stirring tale set in eighteenth-century England about a warrior who learns to accept his special psychic gift as he teaches an enamel artisan about life and love. And award-winning Cheryl Reavis is back with another of her sensational Civil War stories. *Harrigan's Bride* features a soldier who chivalrously marries the bedridden daugher of his late godmother. Don't miss it!

Rounding out the month is *A Warrior's Passion,* the ninth book in the medieval WARRIOR SERIES by the gifted Margaret Moore. Here, a young woman is forced into an unwanted betrothal before the man she truly loves—and whose child she carries—can claim her as his wife!

Whatever your tastes in reading, you'll be sure to find a romantic journey back to the past between the covers of a Harlequin Historical® novel.

Sincerely,

Tracy Farrell
Senior Editor

Please address questions and book requests to:
Harlequin Reader Service
U.S.: 3010 Walden Ave., P.O. Box 1325, Buffalo, NY 14269
Canadian: P.O. Box 609, Fort Erie, Ont. L2A 5X3

TERRITORIAL
BRIDE

LINDA CASTLE

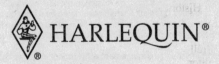

HARLEQUIN®

TORONTO • NEW YORK • LONDON
AMSTERDAM • PARIS • SYDNEY • HAMBURG
STOCKHOLM • ATHENS • TOKYO • MILAN • MADRID
PRAGUE • WARSAW • BUDAPEST • AUCKLAND

ISBN 0-373-29041-1

TERRITORIAL BRIDE

Books by Linda Castle

Harlequin Historicals

Fearless Hearts #261
Abbie's Child #321
The Return of Chase Cordell #348
Temple's Prize #394
Territorial Bride #441

LINDA CASTLE

Linda Castle is the pseudonym of Linda L. Crockett. Although she is a native New Mexican, Linda can trace her heritage to Comanche on one branch and all the way to Scotland at the time of the Spanish Armada on another. Perhaps this blending of blood and culture is what enables her to step back in time and capture tales from bygone eras. She is fascinated with both the American West and the British Isles. A recent trip to Scotland, England and Wales produced amazing links, such as finding an out-of-the-way kilt maker in Edinburgh who had plaids for the Crocketts and the Caudills.

Linda currently makes her home in New Mexico with her husband, Bill, two youngest children, Brandon and Logan, and their beloved Great Danes, Rebel and Destiny. You can reach Linda at the following address: Linda Castle, #18 County Road 5795, Farmington, NM 87401.

This book is lovingly and respectfully dedicated to Chris Reeves, Karin David and the Paralyzed Veterans of America, who valiantly face each day and teach us the meaning of courage.
May God bless you all.

Chapter One

New Mexico Territory, 1889

Missy sighed and watched Clell run his fingers around the inside of his high, stiffly starched white collar. His Adam's apple bobbed when he swallowed hard, and he gave her a why-am-I-being-tortured-like-this? grimace. It was plain as the nose on his face that he was as uncomfortable in his fancy duds as Missy was in her maid of honor dress. Still, they had all agreed to get gussied up for this occasion. And when she thought about it, she had to smile. All the fuss and wearing of stiff lace, starched petticoats and pinching corsets was worth it, because Trace and Bellami were getting married.

The surgeon had cautioned them to wait until Trace was fully recovered from his surgery. Then Donovan and Patricia James, Bellami's parents, had insisted the wedding wait until the winter weather cleared. They had arrived only a week past, with Bellami's eldest brother, Rod, her cousin Ellen and an assortment of distant relatives in tow. After so many obstacles, Bell and Trace were finally going to be wed.

The spinster who had played the organ for every wedding in the Territory for the last twenty years suddenly changed tempo. The ancient instrument droned and wheezed, announcing that the time was growing short and all should find a seat.

"Are you ready?" A resonant voice rippled over Missy like a warm summer breeze.

When she turned and looked up at the hardened visage of Brooks James, her middle tightened even more. Ranch life and the thick mustache he now sported had transformed his easy-on-the-eyes appearance into the lean, uncompromising visage of a true cowboy. His pale blue eyes gazed out at her from skin bronzed by more than a year in the Territorial sun and wind. Now he had the determined never-give-an-inch look of a work-hardened Western man and the elegant manners of an Eastern dude.

A deadly combination, Missy thought to herself.

She would be hard-pressed to pick him out of a crowd of Circle B ranch hands without taking a second look. He had learned to rope and ride with the best of them. When he walked, his body spoke of strength and economy of motion. He had succeeded in doing what she'd been sure he could not. But a funny thing had happened to her along the way: instead of becoming accustomed to Brooks over the long months, she had found herself growing awkward around him. At one time she had needled and picked at him, but as he settled in and learned to handle himself on the ranch, the situation between them had flip-flopped like a fish stranded out of water.

Brooks had slowly begun to get the upper hand at every confrontation. Now he openly teased her with a wicked twinkle in his eye. And every time it happened, she got all tongued-tied and fluttery. Her only defense was her sharp O'Bannion tongue, but even that weapon had failed her under the heat of that cool blue gaze.

"Missy?" he asked again. "Are you ready?"

"Yes—I am ready."

"You seem a little jumpy."

"Only like a tom turkey before Thanksgivin'," Missy admitted in a whisper. She tugged at the snug waist of her dress, trying to give herself enough room to take a deep breath. Bellami and Trace both had said she looked fine in the form-fitting, peacock blue sateen, but with Brooks's critical gaze skimming over her, Missy now doubted the truth of their words.

Damnation. She wished she could've worn chaps and boots. At least then she could be herself and would be able to inhale normally instead of taking panting little breaths.

This had been a dunderheaded notion. She wasn't a lady. Putting fancy duds on her skinny form wasn't going to change her. It was like putting a candelabra in an outhouse: it didn't change what was on the inside one little bit.

A deep, throaty chuckle drew her attention back to Brooks. He was staring at her, grinning like a fox who had found a way into the henhouse.

"It is customary for the bride to be nervous, not the maid of honor," he advised her in an easy tone. It could have been friendly teasing, or it could be that he was mocking her. "I didn't think the princess of the O'Bannion clan ever had a moment of fear about anything. Could it be you are only human like the rest of us, Missy?" His eyes glittered with the challenge of his words, while a devilish half smile peeked from under his cookie-duster mustache.

Now there was no doubt. He was poking fun at her—

again. Sure as God made little green apples, he'd keep on doing it until she flew off the handle and said or did something she'd regret, and she couldn't allow herself the luxury smack-dab in the middle of Trace's wedding.

Consarn him, she thought sourly.

What was it about this Easterner that got under her skin? She knew enough to walk away from a coiled rattler or a porcupine, so why couldn't she just turn her back on him? He was as prickly as a porky, and the way her belly knotted and her pulse was racing, he must be as deadly as any sidewinder—deadly to her, anyway.

She wondered for the twentieth time how he could just open his mouth and rile her up like an old range bull with a thorn in his rump. It didn't make a lick of sense. All she had to do was use the brains God gave her and ignore the grinning varmint, but somehow it never worked out that way.

"Well, Missy?" Brooks leaned a little nearer.

One thick brow rose over his crystalline eyes. She caught a whiff of bay rum clinging to hard-cut jaws that had been scraped bare less than an hour ago.

"Are you—*afraid?*" Brooks gazed at her with his seductive eyes. "Are you?"

"No, I am *not* afraid," she snapped. Several heads turned to stare in her direction because of the volume of her reply. "My—my dress is just tight as a narrow cinch, th-that's all." She lowered her voice to a respectable whisper. "And with all these folks squeezed in here there's barely a breath of air left." She forced herself to ignore the amusement etched in every line of his face. "So why don't you quit jawing so much and using up what little air there is left?"

He laughed.

Damn him to hell and back. He had the gall to stand

there and laugh. And then he raised a long-fingered, brown and roughened hand as if to touch her.

The thought sent her belly dropping to her feet like a stone.

"Rest easy, little lady. If you swoon, I promise I'll do my best to catch you before you hit the floor in front of all these people." Mercifully, his fingers stopped just short of touching her cheek.

Her face grew hotter and all the shallow little breaths she was taking seemed to be hanging at the back of her throat. It took all her control to keep from yelling at him, or slapping his face, but she managed to keep her voice low and controlled and her hands clenched at her thighs.

"I appreciate the offer, Brooks, but you'll never see the day when I can't stand on my own two feet around you." Her long, unbound hair tickled her backside through the silky material of her dress as she emphasized her speech with a little nod of her head.

Brooks did not laugh this time, but she felt his amusement sluice over her in a scalding wave. Her heart beat a tiny bit faster inside the sateen bodice of her dress.

Damn him. Double damn him!

He could affect her with just a look, or God forbid, the hint of a casual touch. And then, as if he had read her tortured thoughts, he reached out and took hold of her elbow with his bare fingertips. A myriad of peculiar and uncontrollable emotions ripped through her middle when his fingers tightened around her arm. She promised herself that she would not react, but she stiffened in spite of herself.

"Don't make a bigger fuss, Missy. Everyone is watching." His low warning rumbled over her while his gaze slid around the interior of the crowded Catholic mission, the closest house of God they could find.

Missy followed his line of vision. Just as he had said, the tiny adobe building was full to overflowing, and while not everyone was staring at her, more than enough curious eyes were looking her way.

She died a little inside, knowing that her confrontation with Brooks had been the object of their attention.

"Come on, Missy, I won't bite you—" he leaned close enough to whisper in her ear, tightening that possessive hold on her arm "—but I might nibble a bit around the edges." His breath fanned her earlobe. For one terrifying moment she was afraid he would nip her flesh.

Was she afraid he would—or that he wouldn't?

"It is time we took our places, Brooks," she managed to croak. "Stop all this foolishness."

Brooks grinned widely, flashing a glimpse of straight teeth, then he deftly maneuvered her and the wide ruffles of peacock blue sateen up through the narrow aisle. Missy marveled that he got them where they needed to be without tripping either one of them.

She shook herself and blinked. Without quite knowing how time was moving so fast and disjointedly, she realized she was now standing opposite Brooks in front of the slat-thin minister with the too-large Adam's apple.

Missy allowed herself one backward glance. Now every single person seated in the small chapel *was* watching her as she stood at the front of the church, twisting her fingers and plucking at the too-tight, unforgiving waist of her dress.

She whirled back around, staring at the shiny worn knees of the minister's trousers. She felt like a complete jackass—and she blamed Brooks for it and for making her feel things that confused and befuddled her.

A murmur of restrained voices, like a cooling breeze over dried leaves, moved through the chapel. Missy turned to see what had caused the stir, grateful that something, anything, had distracted the group's interest from her. Then she saw Trace, and all of her thoughts were for him alone.

He looked happy, healthy and more handsome than she'd ever imagined. His dark hair reflected the flames of the candles on the altar; his face was flushed with excitement.

The organ groaned and wheezed again. Then, with a reverberating sound that tickled the bottoms of her feet, the "Wedding March" began. Missy followed Trace's gaze to the side door.

Moving with all the grace of an angel fallen to earth, Bellami appeared in her flowing ivory gown. A heavy lace veil trailed behind her on the red, Spanish-tiled floor.

Throughout the long preparations for the wedding, Trace had made only one request: that Bellami wear nothing over her face. The operation had removed the bone sliver from his brain, but it had been Bellami's love that had truly restored his sight and his life. He had told Missy that he wanted to look upon the face of the woman he loved, now and forever.

Bellami shifted the bouquet of wild lavender and oxeye daisies to her empty hand while she stretched up to deposit an affectionate kiss on Brooks's lean cheek, then she offered a reassuring smile to Missy. The gesture made the hot dry lump in Missy's throat grow larger.

"Let us all bow our heads for a moment of prayer..." the minister intoned "...and ask God's blessing on this young couple as they embark on the road of life."

Brooks watched Missy's eyes flutter shut. He half listened to the prayer while he continued to observe her from the corner of his eye. Looking at her now, a feminine vision in sateen, it was hard to believe she was the same razor-tongued shrew that had pestered him for the last year—except that he had the emotional bruises to prove it. The little vixen had drawn blood, in a manner of speaking, a time or two. She was feisty and headstrong, the exact opposite of the women he'd formerly pursued.

A murmured amen brought Brooks's head up. He focused on his twin. Bellami was lovely, as all brides are, but even more so because she held her head up proudly and did not care who gazed upon her face. She no longer hid herself from the pity people might feel for her. Trace's love had been the spark needed for her to grow and change. For the first time in her life she seemed unaware of the scar.

The scar. It had altered her life and saddled Brooks with guilt for years. But then it had brought Bellami James to the Territory to find her destiny, and in a peculiar sort of way it had done the same thing for him. Bellami's scar and Violet Ashland's fickle heart had been the catalyst for Brooks to leave the city and the pointless pursuits he had once thought of as manly.

After Bellami left, Brooks had surrounded himself with a flock of beautiful ladies, but none had ever held his attention for more than a couple of weeks until he'd met Violet Ashland. The petite blonde had captured his interest in a way that no other woman had before....

A nervous cough pulled his attention to the raven-haired girl standing opposite him. Missy was a wildcat one minute and a siren the next. She could make him madder than any woman he knew, yet in the whole year he'd known her she had never shown the slightest interest in snaring him for his fortune—or any other reason, he thought with a smile.

Not like Violet.

He frowned and wondered where that thought had come

from. It was probably the magic of the candles and the organ music and the lethargy of a Territorial afternoon. A man would have to be made of iron not to be influenced by the romantic promise of this moment. The trappings of matrimony had resurrected memories that had long been buried, reminding him of his own proposal of marriage.

But that had been another man, in another life. Now his days were filled with work and with fending off Missy's verbal arrows. Yes, he thought idly, Missy O'Bannion could strip the hide off a man with one look, but under all that bluff and bluster she was honest and true.

The kind of woman to cross rivers and climb mountains with.

Brooks blinked in amusement at his thoughts. He was beginning to sound, or at least to think, like Clell. The idea that he had learned some wisdom from the irascible cowboy pleased him, and he caught himself grinning.

By accident he and Missy looked at each other in the same moment. Their gazes caught and held. Her dark eyes reflected the candlelight like a deep, shimmering stream in the first rays of morning.

Funny that he'd never noticed how wide and luminous her eyes were until now, Brooks mused.

"Dearly beloved…" the tall, lanky preacher's baritone voice filled the chapel. "In the sight of God and this company…"

Brooks adjusted the shoulders and front of his black broadcloth frock coat and tried to focus on the preacher's words. Missy fidgeted once more, and his attention became riveted upon her.

Was she nervous?

Naw. The answer came quickly into his head. Missy

O'Bannion was as steady a woman as ever walked God's earth. But if she wasn't nervous, then why was her softly rounded bosom rising and falling so rapidly inside the sateen bodice?

He frowned at her in speculation. Then, as if she felt his attention on her, she looked at him again. Her eyes were darker than bottomless pools, and for a moment he felt himself drowning in their depths. She wore an expression so poignant that he nearly reached out and touched her.

He shook himself and looked back toward the preacher. He shouldn't give a hoot in hell about how she felt. If she was frightened it was poetic justice. She had given him undiluted misery this past year. It would serve her right if she was stewing in her own juices.

No, he didn't care how she felt. He couldn't give a tinker's damn about Missy's feelings—or any woman's, for that matter. Life in the Territory had let him see that a lone wolf survived as well as one with a mate.

That was what he wanted now—to remain alone. A lone wolf, free, unattached and pleasantly sane. None of this madness called love for him, thank you. Brooks intended to remain a bachelor, like Clell. Clell was a man who knew what was what. He had helped Brooks learn to rope and ride and how to laugh at Missy's sharp barbs.

"Trace Liam O'Bannion..." The clergyman's deep voice gained volume. "Do you..."

The nearest group of candles flickered. Trace leaned over and gave Bellami a little peck on the cheek, quite improper when he was taking his vows, but the kind of thing that Brooks had grown to expect in this half-tamed place. Here men made their own rules to live by. Now that he had become accustomed to it, he liked it.

Missy shifted on her feet and Brooks glanced at her

again. She was smiling. It was an angel's smile, full of love and innocence. Something hot and liquid coursed through his veins while he watched her face.

"Bellami Irene James, do you take…"

The image of Violet Ashland flitted unbidden into Brooks's head. The memory of that cold, elegant woman filled his mind. Then he glanced at Missy. Where Violet had been cold, Missy ran red-hot.

"And her hot tongue will sear flesh, as well," he whispered to himself.

Brooks caught himself smiling at the memory of Missy's frequent outbursts and his determination to prove himself. If he was honest with himself, he'd have to admit that he had come to enjoy their verbal sparring. His taste in women had changed, or maybe he had changed in the rowdy environment of the Territory. One thing for certain, Brooks was not the same man he had been when he'd stepped off the train. Besides, if the time came that he wanted to settle down—and he wasn't thinking that it would—but if it did, then Missy would be here. He cast a furtive glance at her.

Yep, he could count on Missy O'Bannion to be constant and unchanging. She would always be Missy and she would always be tied to the Circle B Ranch.

It was a comforting thought, and one that Brooks tucked away in the corner of his mind for safekeeping.

"The ring, if you please…" The minister's voice snapped Brooks back to attention. He forced himself to quit woolgathering. He pulled the ring from the watch pocket of his brocade vest and gave it to Trace.

Bellami handed her spray of flowers to Missy and allowed Trace to claim her hand. Work-roughened fingers held hers within a protective grasp. In a few more years Brooks's hands would be as rough. He thought of his old life in New York—the champagne suppers, buggy rides through the park and trips to the athletic club. He glanced back at his parents, sitting side by side in the nearest pew.

Brooks grinned. He had withstood Miss Hell-for-leather O'Bannion. He turned back around in time to see Trace slip the ring on his sister's finger. A smile still curled Brooks's lips. He couldn't think of anything or anybody that would force him to return to New York City—not ever again.

Chapter Two

A side of prime Circle B beef sizzled on an iron spit over a glowing pile of coals several yards from the ranch house veranda. A coyote howled somewhere off in the twilight and a mournful answer echoed. The smell of burning mesquite wood filled the air. As Clell swabbed spicy chili sauce on the beef, some of the thick concoction dribbled onto the embers. Flames shot upward, as they would inside of everyone's bellies after a taste of Clell's secret sauce.

Missy's heart was beating hard with happiness and excitement. Clinging to the railing, she lingered on the veranda, content to observe the crowd. Firelight reflected off rows of silver conchas running down the legs of the black *calzoneras* worn by the mariachi singers as they got in position to serenade the newlyweds.

Bellami's cheeks flushed crimson as Trace softly translated their melodic Spanish. Then, as the fiddle players joined the mariachis, Bellami and Trace waltzed for the first time as man and wife.

It was almost painful for Missy to witness so much happiness. The persistent lump she had been choking on all day came again. She fought back tears of joy and laughed at Trace's mock awkwardness when the fiddles abruptly quickened and he was forced to dance a Highland jig.

Nobody could out-celebrate a cowboy, she thought. Fast-moving boot heels clicked on the wood in quick rhythm. Missy laughed out loud when Lupe joined in and lifted her skirt to reveal slender brown ankles and layers of snowy white petticoats. She executed a series of light-ning quick and intricate steps. Her movements flowed with such grace and speed that it was hard for Missy to believe the Circle B cook was nearing sixty years old. Her dark eyes flashed with Spanish fire as the mariachis played faster and faster to match her feet.

Without warning the tempo changed. Strains of two ad-ditional fiddles blended with the romantic Spanish guitar.

Another waltz for the married couple.

Trace kissed Bellami and pulled her close, and they began to float around the dance floor in a way that made Missy's heart catch. A part of her hungered to be in the middle of the swirling, twirling couples, but her awk-wardness kept her in the shadows at the edge of the ve-randa.

Bellami had shown Missy how to wear the complicated frippery of a lady, but she still did not *feel* like one. She clapped her hands to the brisk tempo while she watched other girls from nearby ranches being swept onto the dance floor by one handsome cowhand after another. Her one consolation was that she was in no danger of making a fool of herself while she was hidden alone in the shad-ows.

"Grab a partner," Hugh bellowed. "Everybody dance! I don't want to see anybody sitting this one out."

"Boo." Brooks's voice jarred Missy. "Penny for your thoughts, little lady."

She whirled to find him standing no more than six inches from her. His black string tie and long-tailed coat had been discarded. The white shirt was unbuttoned half-way down. An errant breeze ruffled the hair on his hard, muscled chest.

''And just when I was enjoyin' a private moment,'' she snapped, pulling her gaze from his torso.

He eyed her with cool detachment and picked a bud from the rose of Sharon that grew in abundance by the veranda. ''If I didn't know better, I'd swear you were hiding up here away from the dance floor, Miss O'Bannion.'' That mysterious half smile tickled his lips beneath the full mustache. His eyes twinkled mischievously in the firelight as he sniffed the blossom.

''I ain't doin' no such thing. What a fool notion.'' She turned back toward the dancers and started clapping again, but the toe-tapping music had changed. Now everyone was twirling in another slow, seductive waltz. She had been so caught up in her talk with Brooks that she hadn't even noticed. Her cheeks burned with inner heat and she brought her palms together awkwardly, not really sure what to do with her hands.

''Care to try?'' Brooks asked with an amused chuckle.

''Try what?'' Missy knew exactly what he was asking, but she'd sooner take a polecat for a walk than let Brooks James know she couldn't dance. She looked back at the dance floor, staring determinedly at the laughing couples, trying to ignore the knot that had taken up residence in her middle.

He stepped closer and leaned near her ear. His warm breath carried the faint trace of whiskey—and danger. ''Would you care to dance—with me?''

Missy whirled to face him once more. She summoned her voice, but the refusal that had been in her mind died in the back of her throat when she encountered his charming smile.

The night breeze lifted strands of his silky dark hair. Silvery moonlight and the amber glow from the bonfire made his eyes a most peculiar shade of blue.

Missy couldn't describe it, or what looking into his eyes was doing to her insides. It appeared, for one heart-lurching moment, that his eyes glowed with an inner fire like lightning playing on the horns of cattle in the midst of a storm.

Goll-dang, if he isn't a handsome cuss.

She swallowed hard. Her heart beat against her rib cage like a gloved fist. "I—uh, that is…"

"You can dance, can't you?" One winged brow rose in silent challenge. Then he raised his hand and deftly slipped the rose bloom behind her ear, tucking a thick lock of hair in place over it.

The heat of a blush raced up her cheeks. Her first inclination was to turn tail and run. She couldn't dance, but she had gotten to know Mr. Smart-jackass James well enough to know he would require her to prove it. That was a humiliation she would just as soon spare herself, if you please.

"I—I—" she stammered while visions of public indignity raced through her mind.

One side of his mustache lifted. "I believe I will take that as a yes, Miss O'Bannion." He slipped his arm around her waist and drew her close to his rock-hard body before she had a chance to flee.

Panic welled up inside her, but it was soon overwhelmed by the stunning impact of the way it felt to have his arm about her. A tiny voice in her head said *Dig in your heels and run while there is time,* but she didn't listen, she just let him clamp her against his body and pull her off the veranda.

"You know, Miss O'Bannion—" his grin widened "—back home I was considered to be quite a good dancer."

"Yeah, well, what do a bunch of Easterners know about anythin'?" she answered defensively, raising her chin a notch higher.

He laughed deep and low in his chest. He liked this easy, teasing banter; he liked Missy and the tug-of-war that went on between them. It was much more pleasant than getting all tangled up romantically. He looked at her face, sweetly flushed with lips that were soft and kissable, and he realized this was what he wanted. He wanted to stay in the Territory where he was safe from having to make any permanent commitments and decisions. He was content to stay where he could tease Missy and know that she was always there, day in and day out. She had no suitors hanging around, so he had a clear field. It was the best possible situation for a man who had no desire to settle down.

Missy blinked back her confusion while tingling heat meandered into her limbs from the spot on her back where Brooks's hand rested. She was afraid her knees would buckle, afraid she'd get all tangled up in the dress, fearful she would make a fool of herself, and sure Brooks would take an inordinate amount of pleasure in whatever indignity befell her. But to her surprise, he started talking to her in low soothing tones, as if she was a skittish filly he was determined to gentle. His voice was smoother than Clell's twelve-year-old whiskey and as hypnotic as a ripe summer moon.

"Put yourself in my hands, little lady. I promise I won't step on your toes." His deep voice vibrated through her rib cage, where he held her tightly against his body. "At least not too often." His rumbling laughter drew her eyes to his face.

"And what happens if I step on yours?" Missy managed to ask as her foot touched the first pine board. "You won't think your little joke is so funny then, will you, Brooks?"

The mocking grin faded from his face. "I hope I am tough enough and man enough to take whatever comes of this dance, Missy." He stared at her, unblinking, while her heart hammered in her chest. "Now and in the future."

His words hung before them like a spider's silken web. Then he laughed again and broke the enchantment. "Now wipe that frown off your pretty little face and act like you're having fun. Trace and Bellami will wonder what I'm doing to you if you keep scowling like that."

Missy swallowed hard.

Telling her that she was pretty was just about the nicest thing Brooks had ever said to her. How in tarnation could a man like him think a girl who wore chaps and boots was pretty?

He had been everywhere, seen everything.

For half a moment Brooks returned her serious gaze, then he tilted back his head and laughed. Rich, hearty tones of masculine mirth erupted from him. Her belly quivered in reaction to the sound of it.

"Oh, you were teasing. You are always sayin' the dangedest things to me—" She would've said more, but suddenly her feet had wings.

Brooks twirled her out onto the floor. With a sobering chill she realized the flames dancing beneath the side of beef and all the torches surrounding the dance floor had driven back the night. She might as well have been dancing beneath the noonday sun. Now everyone would see if she stumbled or fell or made an ass of herself.

She stared at her feet, trying to avoid stepping on Brooks's shiny black Justins.

''You needn't look so terrified, Missy. I promise I'll never let you come to harm—never.''

Brooks's words penetrated her gloom.

Her head slowly came up and she shifted her concentration from her feet to his face. Her breath lodged in the space beneath her heart.

I'll never let you come to harm—never.

All her fear flitted away into the night. She forgot about the crowd of people and the dance steps she didn't know. Her world compressed into the circle of space she occupied within Brooks's arms. He turned her in a tight circle that brought her bosom up against the wide, muscular expanse of his chest. Each time he executed a new step and expertly pulled her along with him, her heart beat a little faster.

Missy was put in mind of a midnight gallop on a half-broke mustang. Each time Brooks twirled her she had the sensation of jumping fences and swift-running washes. There was an excitement being in his grasp, a thrill and a danger. Nothing in her life had prepared her for this moment.

Brooks smiled at her and she realized she was good and truly at risk, but not of breaking a leg or even her foolish neck. As she stared into his silvery blue eyes and her heart thrummed inside her chest, she knew what she risked was her heart.

She could care about him if she let herself.

A slow, lazy smile teased the corners of his mouth. ''See, I was telling the truth when I said you were in good hands.'' As he bent a little nearer and drawled into her ear, his breath fanned out over her neck and left a trail of hot chills in its wake. "I spent a good many hours dancing before I left New York."

The spinning turns and his warm breath on her skin made her dizzy. She felt as if she had been at her father's bottle of whiskey right along with the menfolk. A thousand new and unfamiliar feelings sizzled through her. And even though she longed for something sharp and biting to say to diffuse the tension of the moment, nothing came to mind. She was trapped like a rabbit in a snare set by Brooks himself.

"May I have this next dance with my daughter?" Hugh smiled with fatherly affection as he tapped on Brooks's shoulder. An uncharacteristic flush crept up Missy's smooth cheeks. Putting on a dress had changed more than her outsides, it would seem. Wearing ruffles and petticoats gave her an aura of vulnerability, an attitude of shy unease.

Brooks released his hold on her tiny waist with some reluctance. He stepped back and allowed Hugh to sweep his daughter into the crowd of dancers. They made a striking contrast—the weathered rancher with steely gray at his temples, and his dewy fresh daughter whose hair was dark as a midnight sky.

Brooks shook his head.

All this silly sentiment was only the combination of moonlight and whiskey. He was about half-drunk and that was making him wax poetic, he assured himself. Tomorrow reason would return. In the light of day Missy would be herself. There would be no soft glow of fire, no waltzes, no strange tightening of his gut each time their eyes met unexpectedly. Tomorrow she would be herself and he would be fending off her hostility and her barbed words.

It was something to look forward to.

Chapter Three

Patricia might as well have been drinking muddy water for all the enjoyment the chilled punch gave her. Brooks had taken her aside and revealed his intentions to remain in the Territory. She sighed heavily and tried to wipe away the sadness in her heart. After all, Bellami was happily married to a man who saw beyond her scar to the beauty beneath, but Brooks...that was another matter altogether.

Patricia hadn't interfered when he'd decided to come west. Violet Ashland had deeply wounded Brooks, and he needed time to heal. Patricia had hoped that the time he had spent here had accomplished that, but now she was beginning to wonder. Was he really intent on burying himself here in this cultural wasteland?

"My dear?" Donovan appeared at her elbow. His snowy brows were pinched with concern. "Are you ill, Patricia? All the color has drained from your face."

Patricia glanced at Brooks, who was standing near the punch bowl. "No—no, I am perfectly fine."

"Truly? You look so...worried. Surely you are not still concerned about Bellami. Trace O'Bannion is as fine and steady a man as I have ever met."

Patricia tore her gaze away from Brooks. "No, it isn't that. I am worried about Brooks."

"Brooks?" Donovan said in surprise. "He is the picture of health!"

"On the outside, perhaps." She turned to Donovan and frowned. "But I am worried about him all the same."

"He is fine." Donovan rubbed the backs of his knuckles over his wife's cheek. "You worry too much. He is talking about buying some land to raise cattle here. That's all."

"Do you think it is really what he wants to do or is he still trying to get over Violet?"

At the mention of her name, Donovan's face became a mask of disapproval. "That is a subject best left alone, Patricia."

"But, Donovan…it would be a great mistake for him to stay here. Surely you can see that?"

"Patricia, what I see is a grown man. Whatever decision he makes and for whatever reasons, it is his business alone." Donovan turned her to face him and cupped her chin in his palm. "And I don't want you interfering."

"Oh, Donovan, surely I could just—"

"No, darling." He placed both hands on her shoulders and gently drew her closer to him. "Promise me, Patricia." His voice was soft but stern. "Promise me this time you will leave things alone. You mustn't say a word to the boy about this. And I think it is best if you don't mention the fact that Violet has returned to New York."

Patricia sighed and leaned into his hands. "Oh, all right. If you feel so strongly about it. I promise."

He smiled and kissed her on the forehead. "That's my girl. Now let's show these youngsters how to do a proper dance."

* * *

Ellen was breathless from all the dancing as she approached the punch bowl where Rod and Missy were chatting.

"You know, cousin, if Mother notices the glow in your cheeks she will have you staying in bed tomorrow," Rod warned Ellen as he nodded toward Patricia and Donovan on the dance floor.

"I suppose I should be sensible," Ellen replied, sighing wistfully. A cowboy with a thatch of unruly blond hair asked for the next dance. Ellen glanced at Rod like a child who wanted just one more stick of peppermint. Finally she turned to the eager cowboy. "I fear I must decline. I am a little out of breath." She smoothed the baby pink ruffles on her dress and sighed meaningfully.

The cowboy tipped his hat and backed away. "Maybe next time, ma'am."

"Yes, next time." Ellen's eyes followed him until he disappeared into the crowd.

"Very wise, cousin." Rod smiled. "You probably saved yourself a stern lecture and a full day in bed. "May I pour you and Miss O'Bannion a cup of punch?"

"Thank you." Missy took the cup he passed to her.

"You are quite welcome. I should be thanking you, Miss O'Bannion. I have enjoyed myself tonight." Rod poured a second cup of punch and passed it to his cousin.

"I'm glad you have had a good time, but I bet you have fancy parties all the time back in New York." Missy watched the couples swirling by in front of her and wished this night would never end.

"They are rarely this much fun, though," Ellen said softly. She fanned herself with a delicate, lily-colored hand. She smiled at Missy and batted brown lashes over eyes the shade of cornflowers. *How I wish I could wear my hair loose and flowing and have sun-kissed cheeks and be the picture of health like Miss O'Bannion,* she thought.

"That is a fact," Rod agreed. "New York parties are— stuffy."

"You're teasing me." Missy felt a blush working its way up her neck.

"No, I am not. I leave that to my younger brother." Rod placed his hand over his heart to emphasize his sincerity.

Ellen continued to study Missy's face while a wild idea popped into her head. "Why don't you come and visit? It would give me a perfect excuse to have lots of dances like this one."

"Leland might have something to say about that," Patricia told Ellen with a gentle smile as she and Donovan joined the group at the punch bowl. Patricia looked at the two girls standing side by side—near in age but as different as light is from darkness. Ellen looked frail and too pale, even by current fashionable dictates. And Missy…well, Missy was a little too wild, a little too exuberant, but the glowing picture of a woman in the bloom of youth. Clell had explained about her growing up without a mother. It did account for much of her behavior.

For a mad, impetuous moment Patricia wondered what it would be like to take the girl under her wing and help her become a proper lady…. The idea was silly, and Donovan would have a fit.

"I would still like for Missy to come and visit," Ellen said stubbornly. "Whether Papa would allow me to have a party or not. It would be fun to have someone my own age around." Ellen smiled at Patricia as she spoke. Leland had kept Ellen somewhat secluded. Her cousins had been her major source of companionship. With all the girls married and gone, Ellen had been extremely lonely the last few years. "And we could all go shopping together, Aunt Patricia. It would be fun, you know it would be fun!"

Patricia cast a sidelong look at her spouse. Ellen was right. It would be fun. Patricia had missed having Bellami to fuss over as much as Ellen missed their chats.

"I think it is a good idea, Ellen," Patricia said suddenly. "We must do our best to persuade Miss O'Bannion to come as soon as possible."

"Good idea, Mother," Rod agreed, in spite of Donovan's growing frown. He fussed too much over his wife and whether or not she was overdoing. "After all, Missy is family now."

"It would be nice to be in a place where I could dress like this every day," Missy said wistfully.

"You are charming no matter what you are wearing," Patricia assured Missy. "Isn't she, Donovan?"

"What? Oh, yes, charming." Donovan replied absently. Patricia had purposely avoided his suggestion about interfering.

"Oh, do say you will come soon. You would have a lovely time in the city." Ellen brightened with every word. "We could have some new gowns made. It would be great fun and I would love the company."

"Yes, my dear, we insist." Patricia smiled inwardly. The girl was always clomping around in men's trousers and boots—she would be a challenge. But she did have good bones, and with a little work…

Curiosity nipped at Brooks as he watched his family. He allowed himself one more pull from Clell's bottle before he started threading his way across the floor. He sidestepped to avoid dancing boots and whirling skirts and finally reached the other side of the room.

"That's awful nice of you, ma'am, but..." Missy began.

"What's going on?" Brooks whispered to Rod.

"Ellen has almost persuaded Miss O'Bannion to come to New York," Rod answered. "I think it would be a marvelous idea for Ellen to have some female company."

"What? You can't be serious!" The loudness of his voice brought Missy's head around with a snap.

"Is something wrong, Brooks?" She frowned at him. He swayed a little as she glared at him. It was obvious he had been sharing Clell's bottle.

"Nothing, nothing at all." Brooks shook his head.

"Good. For a moment I thought you might have been upset about the invite."

Brooks gave her a lopsided grin. "Nothing to be upset about. The whole idea is ridiculous. I know you are too sensible to even consider such a thing."

"And just why is the idea of me going to New York so comical?" Missy pressed.

"What?" Brooks tried to listen to what she was saying, but Clell's whiskey had brought a buzz to his head and a ringing to his ears. "Well, little lady, wearing boots and hats in New York drawing rooms is not the thing this year." Laughter bubbled up in the back of his throat as he imagined Missy sitting down to tea in her form-fitting chaps.

"So you think I ain't got sense enough to learn to act like a lady, is that it?" Missy's dark eyes narrowed with anger.

"Not exactly." Brooks blinked a couple of times and tried to clear the cobwebs from his brain.

"You learned to be a cowboy...."

"That's different." He blinked and steadied himself.

"What's different about it? If you could learn to be a

cowboy, why is it so hard to believe that I could become a lady?''

Even in his half-looped state, Brooks was intelligent enough to recognize a loaded question when he heard one. ''You just can't go. Now let's stop all this silly talk.''

''I *can't?* Did I hear you right?'' Missy shook her head in disbelief. ''Did you just tell me that I *can't* go to New York?''

Brooks sucked in a breath, tried to catalog his own thoughts into a proper order while he looked at Missy. Indignant fire burned in her brown eyes. She had lovely eyes when she was spitting mad. A part of him wanted to tell her that, but that kind of talk was the sort of thing that got men tangled up. He bit back the compliment, not wanting to do anything that would upset his plans of having no entanglements, no commitments. He had to keep a cool head. Then he could remain free as the wind. ''Now, Missy...''

''Don't you 'now Missy' me. And just when, oh-so-mighty Mr. James, did you start tellin' me what I can or can't do?'' She advanced on him, and to his utter astonishment, he retreated a step. She raised herself up on her slippered toes, but even then the top of her head barely reached his chin. She was narrow eyed with fury now.

He felt the current of excitement arc between them. This was what he wanted, what he liked—a hot channel of interest running between them like a river of fire.

''I know you have an overblown notion of your importance, but I didn't think it went so far as to include the whole of New York City!''

''That wasn't exactly what I meant,'' Brooks began, a smile tugging at the corners of his mouth. The whiskey was dulling his senses and slurring his words, but he was still acutely aware of *her*.

She would be bored in a brownstone instead of under a wide, azure sky. Patricia and Ellen, and especially women like Violet, would never—could never—understand the restless energy of Missy. He wanted to tell her that her spirit would wither without the wind in her face and a gallop each morning.

You would be unhappy.

"I should'a known you'd have something nasty to say." Missy inhaled a long breath. "Thank you for invitin' me, Mr. and Mrs. James. I'd love to come. Right now." She lowered herself back to the soles of her feet and glared at Brooks again.

"I was goin' to say no, but since you seem so all-fired determined that I *can't* go, I have changed my mind." She turned once again to face his parents. "I'll start packing and will be ready to leave with you at the end of the week."

Brooks frowned and tried to steady himself. Until this moment he had not realized how many toasts he had drunk to his sister's marriage. But the shock of Missy's words had begun to sober him up—real fast. This whole thing had gotten out of control.

"Now, Missy, calm down a minute." He reached out and put his hands on her shoulders. "I meant to tell you—"

"Don't you touch me, you sidewinder." She shrugged his fingers off, turned on her heel and stomped away in a flurry of peacock blue satin.

Brooks stared at the rigid set of her shoulders as she left. He made no attempt to go after her. The best thing he could do was wait until she cooled off before he tried to talk to her. Besides, she would be her old self in the morning. By noon they would back to their usual thrust and parry. There was nothing to worry about.

He had it all figured out. He had the perfect arrangement.

Missy tore at the tiny buttons running down the front of her dress. The touch of the beautiful fabric against her flesh was suddenly hateful to her, reminding her of the disdainful look in Brooks's crystal blue eyes.

Tonight when he had held her close she had allowed herself to think there was a feeling of tenderness between them. Now she realized it had been the whiskey, the sound of fiddles and the allure of the firelight.

Damn him.

The expression on his face when he'd heard she had been invited to New York had told her the truth. He considered her an embarrassment. It was obvious he thought his mother was setting herself up for humiliation by inviting a bumpkin from the Territory into her home.

Missy unlaced the hard-boned corset and flung it into a corner. The springs creaked and groaned as she flopped down on her bed.

Her pride had been badly bruised. She had tried to wear the clothes like a lady, and act like a lady, yet it had not been enough.

For him.

"Why do I let him get to me?" she asked aloud. "He's nothing but a greenhorn, a dude. His opinion isn't worth a hoot in hell. Not to me."

But in her heart she knew she lied.

He had become more than a greenhorn, more than a dude. He had set out to prove he could ride shoulder-to-shoulder with any man jack on the Circle B.

And he had succeeded.

That was the hell of it all, she realized with a ragged sigh. He had been able to do it.

Could she?

Could she do what he had done? Was Missy smart enough and determined enough to learn to be a proper lady?

She flopped over on her back and stared at the ceiling. He made her want to be soft and lovable like a kitten. Tonight when he'd taught her how to dance she had felt feminine. But then when she looked at his face and saw his true feelings etched in every sun-browned line, she'd wanted to rip him to shreds like a riled she-cat.

"Damn and double damn him." She tightened her fist into a tight ball and used it to pummel her pillow. "I'll show him. I can do it. I will learn to be a proper lady. I'll show Mr. High-and-mighty James I can stand on my own two feet. I won't quit until he has admitted that I have succeeded," she swore, then she buried her face in the down ticking and cried like a baby.

Chapter Four

The train car swayed and rocked like a green broke mustang. Mr. and Mrs. James lurched unsteadily up the aisle, doggedly making their way forward to the dining car, while Missy sat beside Ellen and tried not to notice Brooks sitting across the aisle from her.

He wasn't easy to ignore.

Soft worn denim and battered leather chaps hugged his long legs. Patricia James had been tight lipped with disapproval over his decision to travel in his ranch clothes, but that did not deter his outrageous behavior. In fact, he seemed to become more defiant as they traveled. Now a sooty stain of a two-day beard shadowed his cheeks.

Missy pulled her gaze from his face and once again focused on the worn Justins, hitched carelessly up on the back of the empty seat in front of him. He shifted, causing his arms to flex. Heavy muscle corded beneath the rolled-up sleeves of a sturdy gray-and-tan-striped work shirt.

He had filled out and turned rock hard in the past year, while he worked at the Circle B. She sighed and wished she could forget how much he had changed.

Rod, sitting in the window seat beside Brooks, gave his brother a sidelong look of amused curiosity. For his efforts he earned a flashy smile of cocky arrogance. Then Brooks pulled his Stetson low over his forehead and hunkered down in the seat.

His nonsense is enough to make a preacher cuss.

Why did he have to come along? Missy admitted a part of her was thrilled, for she wanted him there to see her triumph.

If I do triumph.

She shook the negative thought from her head. She would succeed, and she didn't give a hoot in hell what he thought, anyway.

Why did he have to be so goll-dang contrary about everything?

Why did she have to keep noticing?

There was no excuse for him to be dressing like that, and not shaving…unless it was just one more way to make her feel foolish. Each time she glanced at him she was painfully reminded of where she came from and how much she did not fit in.

That is why he is doing this—to shame me.

Anger and disappointment settled over her as she turned to look out the window. The landscape sped by at an amazing clip. At this rate they would be in New York in no time.

"Are you nervous?" Ellen's soft voice drew Missy's attention from the brown and green ribbons of landscape shooting by the window.

"Do I seem nervous to you?" Missy challenged.

"Maybe a little." Ellen gave her a sympathetic smile and nodded toward Missy's lap. Following the line of her gaze, Missy discovered her fingers were busy tying the strings of the borrowed reticule into tight little knots.

"Oh—oh, I am sorry." She stilled her hands. There was no use denying how she felt, not with the truth of it tangled in her fingers. "I hope I haven't ruined it," she moaned. Her entire outfit was borrowed, from the jaunty hat on her head, courtesy of Bellami before she'd left on her honeymoon, to the pale green skirt and traveling jacket from Ellen.

"Don't worry about it." Ellen waved her hand in a dismissive gesture. "I just hope you are not regretting your decision to take us up on this invitation since—since Brooks decided to come along."

Missy looked up and caught Brooks eyeing her from under the brim of his hat. The shadow turned his eyes a deep shade of evening blue. She drew herself up and stuck out her chin a little, determined not to let him see how much his scrutiny and his disapproval had unnerved her.

"No. I ain't. Not a bit nervous," she said, more loudly than necessary. "I am lookin' forward to it. It will be a great adventure. What do I care if he decided to go back home?"

Brooks's mustache twitched as he chuckled. He pulled the hat brim back down over his eyes, then he sank lower in the seat as if he was going to take a nap.

"Damn him," Missy cursed under her breath. "He would like nothin' better than to see me tuck my tail between my legs and run back home. He can't wait for me to get there and make a goll-darn fool of myself. That's why he changed his mind about coming and hopped on the train at the last minute."

Ellen smiled. "Cousin Brooks does seems to…affect you."

"I guess you could say that. He makes me so consarned mad I could just spit." Missy started to unknot the strings on the reticule.

"Is that all? He only makes you mad?" A skeptical smile tickled the corners of Ellen's Cupid's bow mouth.

"Yes. He makes me mad as a hornet." Missy nearly choked on the lie. Brooks did a lot more than make her angry, and had ever since she'd made the mistake of letting him wrap his arms around her and pull her out onto the dance floor. If only she had not been fool enough to think it meant something to him. "And I swear, if he gives me that superior look of his one more time, I'll...well, I'll think of somethin'."

She went back to untying knots, but she was still muttering under her breath. "How I wish..." Her voice trailed off.

"What, Missy? What do you wish?" Ellen turned pale blue eyes in her direction.

"Promise you won't laugh?" Missy lowered her voice so there would be no chance of Brooks or Rod overhearing.

"I promise."

"I wish I hadn't been stupid enough to accept this invitation." She swallowed hard. "But now I'm in it up to my hocks." She sighed and scooted lower in the seat, as if she could somehow disappear altogether.

Without conscious thought, her eyes slid over Brooks. Something about the way he looked, so relaxed and unconcerned, with the faded denim hugging muscular legs, his legs so casually propped up on the next seat, made her angry all over again.

She turned back to Ellen and the words came out in a rush. "But more than that, I wish I could be a lady. I want to learn to talk right and walk right and show..." her unwilling gaze slid back across the aisle to the manly form that so unnerved her "...*him.*"

Ellen smiled as if she understood, but Missy knew that she didn't. How could anyone understand that Brooks had wounded her deeply? For over a year he had endured her teasing while he went about proving himself. Then the sidewinder had made her think he had a feeling for her when he'd held her close in his arms, taught her to dance. How could Missy expect Ellen to understand these things when she didn't understand them herself?

"I'll teach you." Ellen's eyebrows rose toward her hairline.

"What?" Missy tore her thoughts away from Brooks.

"I'll teach you to be a lady," Ellen whispered. "We could make a bargain."

Missy's heart beat a little harder within the confines of her chest. "Now you are teasin' me, just like *he* does."

"No, I'm not." Ellen curled her index finger in a strand of wispy blond hair hanging beside her cheek. "I wouldn't tease about this." She looked up. "Trust me, Missy."

Missy swallowed hard. "I think you're funnin' me. I put on that dress for Trace's weddin' and I tried, I really did, but I saw the look on Brooks's face. He was shamed and embarrassed for me."

"He did look sort of stricken, but I am not sure you were the reason—at least not in the way you mean." Ellen regarded her cousin across the narrow aisle. "He has changed." She nodded in his direction. "Just look at him. If he can learn to be a cowboy, then why can't you learn to be a proper lady?"

Missy squinted her eyes and tilted her head as her gaze roamed over Brooks's long lean legs. He wore the clothes as if he were born to them.

"I'd find some way to repay you for your kindness." Missy allowed herself to consider the offer. "But it isn't possible, and what could you want that I have?"

"There is something." Ellen lowered her voice to a whisper. She raised her head slightly and glanced around as if she expected someone to be listening to their conversation.

"You name it." Missy leaned closer, inspired to whisper by Ellen's behavior.

"Teach me how to ride." Not a trace of humor could be found in her wide-eyed expression.

"You ain't serious." Ellen was obviously funning her. Missy's stomach dropped a little as the small glimmer of hope died.

"I am serious. I was a sickly child. My father insists I am still frail. It took weeks of begging my father just to be allowed to take this trip." A sheen of moisture sparkled in her eyes. "You can't imagine what it is like to be treated like a fragile china doll. I'd like to prove that I am strong and capable—like you."

Missy released the pent-up breath she had been holding. "But you...you're a real lady." Undisguised admiration rang in her voice.

"You can be refined, Missy. Though for the life of me I can't understand why it is so important to you." Ellen cheeks flushed and she ducked her head. "If you teach me what you know, then I'll do the same."

"I don't think it will be so easy for you to turn me into a lady—like makin' a silk purse from a sow's ear." Missy smiled. "But you've got yourself a deal."

"There is just one more thing, Missy." Ellen's pale blue eyes turned icy. "This has to be our secret. If my father finds out he will put a stop to our plan. He is a stubborn man, and he's afraid of losing me."

"It will be our secret," Missy swore solemnly as her defiant gaze raked over Brooks's form once more.

Brooks flopped over in his bunk. He was unable to sleep, even though the mattress was well padded and the sheets were fresh and sweet. As mile after mile slid by, he wondered why on earth he was going home. He told himself it was to keep an eye on Missy, to keep her from wreaking havoc over the whole of New York City.

Why had he hopped on the train?

He hadn't even had time to pack his clothes. But at least his mother was pleased by his impulsive decision.

If only I were.

As their journey was nearing the end he had finally come to accept that stubborn little Missy was going to see this thing through to the end.

It was a courtesy to his family and Trace that he was going along—just to keep her out of trouble.

It had to be that. What other reason could there be?

He had tried to speak to Missy, to let her know what a mistake she was making by leaving the Territory, but she always seemed to have her head bent in secretive conversation with Ellen.

"What on earth can they have to talk about?" he asked the night sky.

Brooks had tried to trap her somewhere and tease her into speaking to him. But so far he had not been able to steal a single moment alone with her. It was frustrating. And what was more puzzling was his unrelenting desire to speak to her.

Why did he care if she went to New York and made herself miserable? So what if she made a fool of herself by trying to be something she was not?

She had ridden rough and hard over him for a full year. He should be tickled to think of her going to New York, where she would be as out of place as a house tabby in a cougar's den.

He should've been, but he wasn't. And he knew why. There were men in New York—lots of young unattached men—who would find the unpolished Missy O'Bannion a novelty too tempting to pass up. She was innocent, had no experience with the jaded cads who would flock around her.

"Why should I give a good damn?" he muttered to himself. "She can go make a fool of herself, get her feelings hurt—hell, she can even get her heart broken. I don't care one damn bit."

But he did care.

"Only because she is Trace's sister. Hell, I owe it to Hugh to keep an eye out for her." Brooks mollified himself with that thought until sleep overtook him.

But he did not rest. Instead he dreamed of chasing Missy across the moonlit prairie. She was a fleet-footed sprite with flowing black hair, who remained forever just beyond his reach.

"Missy, you are still dropping your *g*," Ellen whispered in the darkness. The pair were curled up in their flannel gowns inside the snug sleeping berth as the train rocked and clicked rhythmically through the night. The only illumination was a weak shaft of moonlight peeking through the partially opened curtain, turning Ellen's pale hair to liquid silver. A late frost covered the early grass with a mantle of diamonds that sparkled as the train sped by.

"I never knew speakin'—I mean *speaking*—could be so goll-darn hard." Missy sighed.

"That's the other thing, Missy. You can't say things like 'goll-darn' and 'consarned.' And you'll have to quit damning Brooks in every other breath."

Missy giggled, fell back on her pillows and laced her fingers behind her head. "I may quit sayin'...*saying* it, but I won't promise to quit *thinking* it.'' She emphasized her *g* with precision.

''Just as long as you don't say it aloud.'' Ellen giggled in turn and pulled the carved bone brush through her hair. ''In your mind you may curse my dear cousin to whatever degree of perdition suits you, but a lady never lets such thoughts cross her lips.''

''That cousin of yours is going to be in for quite a shock. I can't hardly wait until he gets a gander at me.'' Missy closed her eyes and imagined it in her mind.

''A look at you,'' Ellen corrected softly. ''Not a gander.''

''A look at me,'' Missy repeated.

Ellen smiled at the enthusiasm of her pupil. ''We must spend some time working on your hair. It is so silky and thick, I am sure we can find a very flattering style for you. Perhaps something up off your neck… You have lovely features. We need to accentuate them.''

''Lovely features?'' Missy opened her eyes and sat up. She wasn't quite sure how to take the compliment. Nobody, not even Bellami, had ever talked to her the way Ellen did. Missy realized with a poignant tug on her heart that Ellen was her first real female friend. Missy had grown up talking to roadrunners, dogie calves and taciturn cowhands who spoke around chaws of tobacco. There was something sweet and satisfying about having a female friend for the first time. The bright blond girl was her exact opposite in every way, and yet they were already as close as sisters.

''At the next stop I want to send a wire home,'' Ellen continued. ''My dressmaker is a treasure. We must ask Aunt Patricia if you may come to my house straightaway. Miss Baldwin can get some dresses made for you and nobody will know what we are up to…not until we are ready.'' Ellen put the brush aside and clapped her smooth white hands together. ''It will be delicious. We can have a party and introduce you properly.''

''Do you really believe it will work?'' Missy crinkled her nose with doubt.

''Of course,'' Ellen said confidently. ''I can't wait to see the look on everyone's face when they see the transformation. And then you can teach me to ride and my papa will have to see that I am not a frail child anymore.'' Ellen cast a sly look at Missy when she spoke.

Chapter Five

Brooks tried to keep up with Missy and Ellen, but the crowd at Grand Central Station closed around him like a living wall. A sharp blow to his ribs sent the air rushing from his lungs in a painful hiss. He spun around on his boot heel, ready to do battle with his attacker, only to find a prune-faced woman over seventy wielding an umbrella like a cavalry saber.

"Excuse me, ma'am." Brooks reeled back half a step and touched his finger to his hat in apology. Evidently she was unimpressed by his show of good manners, because she harrumphed loudly and seared his flesh with a dour look before she moved on. By the time he turned back around, the feather on top of Missy's borrowed hat was disappearing into a hansom cab. Before he could utter a word of protest, the carriage departed, its yellow wheels winking in the bright spring sunlight as it rolled out of the station.

"Damnation." He dragged off his Stetson and slapped it against his thigh in exasperation. For three days he had been struggling to find an opportunity to talk privately to her, and now she had escaped him one more time.

"Are you talking to me, or to yourself?" Rod stood

beside Brooks, attempting to balance an array of boxes, bags and parcels. "If you are through accosting elderly matrons, I could use a hand."

Brooks stuck his hat back on his head. Then he took an octagon-shaped hatbox that had been awkwardly perched beneath Rod's bony chin. "Why did Ellen and Missy run off like a pair of scalded cats?"

"Scalded cats?" Rod repeated incredulously. "If a cat is scalded, does it run? And where on earth did you learn such a ridiculous expression?" Rod peered at his brother over the bulk of a string-tied bundle, only one of the purchases their mother had made at various stops on the way home.

Brooks rolled his eyes heavenward. "All right, I'll rephrase my question. Why do you suppose dear cousin Ellen and Miss O'Bannion fled the station as if it were on fire?" He tilted his head to see if his new query better suited Rod.

His brother shrugged and hailed a passing cab, obviously unimpressed by the question and its delivery. "No reason for them to wait for us." The hansom cab rolled by without stopping and Rod swore softly under his breath.

"They could've shared their carriage. That is a logical reason," Brooks snapped. "Why on earth hire two cabs?"

"I understand they are headed in the opposite direction. It would be silly to go to Ellen's house and then double back to the brownstone."

"Ellen's house?" The hair on the back of Brooks's neck prickled. "What do you mean, they are going to Ellen's house? I thought the whole idea of this little visit was so Missy could spend some time at the brownstone with Mother."

Rod stretched to peer over the crowd. "I heard Ellen

telling Mother that Missy is going to spend some time with her first." Rod smiled victoriously when a hansom cab responded to his hail. He hurried over and started handing bags to the driver. "Come on, Brooks, don't stand there with your mouth open like a carp that has been landed. Help us load this baggage."

Brooks stifled the sharp retort that bubbled up in his throat. How could he have been so thick as to allow Missy to come to New York? And on the heels of that thought, another more-sobering notion flitted through his brain. There wasn't a damn thing he could have done to stop her.

Missy tried not to gawk, but she had never seen so many people in one place in her entire life. A sound engulfed her, almost like a thousand spring peepers and katydids droning their tuneless songs. She leaned back against the padded leather seat and closed her eyes.

"Are you ill?" Ellen's voice broke through the fog in Missy's mind.

She opened her eyes.

Ellen was peering at her with concern etched in her pale face.

"I—I don't know what I expected, but it's awful big."

Relief flooded Ellen's face. "Oh, is that all? You had me worried. I thought you might be coming down with something. You'll get used to the city quickly, I promise." She smoothed her skirt and stared idly out the window, the very picture of serenity and confidence.

Missy couldn't help but wonder if she would ever possess that kind of poise or if she was chasing rainbows by even trying. But she had accepted the challenge, and now, for good or ill, she was set on her course.... There could be no turning back, not when Brooks was waiting for her to fail, like a hungry hawk waiting for a rabbit.

No. She could not fail—her pride would not allow it.

Missy and Ellen were lingering over a cup of creamed tea when the downstairs maid appeared at the parlor door. She carried a silver tray in her hand. A solitary piece of paper rested in the center.

"Pardon, miss." The maid bobbed a little curtsy.

Ellen leaned over and glanced at the envelope. "It is from Aunt Patricia."

"How can you tell?" Missy asked, frowning. The outside of the envelope was as blank as the expression on the maid's face.

"It's her stationery." Ellen scooped up the paper and nodded as the maid curtsied and left the room. "See the watermark?" Ellen held it up toward the light streaming in through the French windows. The outline of a fancy crest within the fibers of the paper became evident.

"Oh." Missy ducked her head in embarrassment. Another thing she didn't know, but if Ellen thought anything about her ignorance she did not show it as she busied herself opening the envelope.

"Well, this is unexpected." Ellen passed the paper to Missy, who read the neatly printed words and felt her stomach lurch.

"A party?" she gasped. "Mrs. James is throwing a party—for me?" Desperation rang in every word. "But I'm not ready." She stood up and started to pace. "I'll never be ready."

Ellen studied her face for half a minute, and then she brightened. "Nonsense. It will be fine. Aunt Patricia will only invite family and close friends. Actually, this will be good for you. We will ease you into New York society by degrees.''

''Do you think so?'' Missy stopped pacing and looked at Ellen.

''Absolutely.'' Ellen picked up a delicate china cup painted with yellow primroses and leaned back in the wicker chair. ''Now that I think of it, it's a wonderful idea.''

Ellen seemed completely confident, and if she wasn't worried, then Missy decided she wouldn't be, either.

The night of the party was hot and sultry from two days of uninterrupted rain. Then, as if the heavens knew that Patricia James would be displeased if her guests were inconvenienced, the sky cleared. A handful of bright stars twinkled overhead as Brooks stepped out the French doors with a glass of cognac in his hand.

''Well, well, well. Did you decide to grace us with your company tonight, or are you home for some other reason?'' Rod's deep, teasing voice brought Brooks around abruptly. His sibling was silhouetted against the gold and crystal glitter of his mother's dining room, dressed in a snowy white shirt, black coat and tie. Every candelabra in the house was blazing, in addition to the gaslights in the ballroom.

''What is that supposed to mean?'' Brooks sipped his drink and acted as if he were unaware of the pending festivities.

''You know perfectly well what I am talking about. You have not been home for dinner twice since we returned.'' Rod stepped outside. He was grinning. ''Interesting coincidence that you decided to come home on the first night that Missy O'Bannion is going to be here.''

''Don't be ridiculous,'' Brooks snapped. ''I just happen

to be home.'' He had made the same observation to himself earlier, but Rod was wrong, and so was he. He had simply tired of the giggling women who had begun to present themselves upon his return. He had grown bored listening to stories of how they all had been pining away in his absence. He had tired of telling the same stories of his life in the West—and the novelty of his unconventional mode of attire had worn so thin he was actually thinking of going upstairs to change.

''Perhaps you are telling the truth, since you are still dressed like you rode in from the range.'' Rod shrugged and glanced at Brooks's boots.

''I am thinking of changing—just to please Mother.'' Brooks took another sip of the liquid.

Rod chuckled. ''I am sure she will be pleased—but wear whatever you wish. As a matter of fact, those pants of Levi's suit you. I have almost grown used to the new you. Tell me, though, is your prickly attitude also part of the new you, brother?''

Brooks frowned. The front doorbell chimed. The pair watched the butler's back as he opened the door. Brooks caught himself rising on the toes of his Justins to see who it was.

''Anxious?'' Rod asked, a sly grin curving his lips.

''Not at all.'' Brooks shook his head and moved closer to the open doors.

The doorbell rang again.

Brooks drained his glass. ''I think I'll go up and change.''

''Better hurry, she will be here soon.''

''Who?'' Brooks asked innocently, but Rod only laughed and stepped inside.

By ten o'clock the Jameses' brownstone was a hive of social activity. Maids and butlers scurried about, making sure every glass was full, every plate picked up the moment the last morsel was consumed. Brooks had lingered in his room after he had changed. Now he stood with one foot hitched up on the top stair as he watched the activity below. He hated to admit it, but he felt out of place in his own home.

The sound of laughter drew his eye. There, surrounded by men, was a familiar head of lustrous dark hair.

A strange, tight coil of heat formed in his chest. While he watched, his grip on the banister tightened.

It was Missy, and half the unattached men in New York City were paying her court.

He was halfway down the stairs, focusing only on Missy, when he felt a hand on his arm. Brooks shrugged, intending to remove the unwanted restraint.

"It has been a long time, darling."

The words brought him to a halt and he turned, already knowing who he would see.

Violet Ashland lifted one brow and gave him her coolest smile. "I was coming up to find you." Her hand moved over the cloth of his coat in intimate fashion, and a hundred memories of stolen passion ripped through him. "I still remember the way to your room.... Shall we go catch up on lost time?"

It was at that very moment he looked down at Missy and she looked up. Their gazes caught and held, not going unnoticed by the men surrounding her or the woman who still possessively fingered his arm.

Violet followed Brooks's gaze. Her smile became cooler than ice. "Is this the little country girl I have heard so much about?"

Brooks frowned and looked at her. "What?"

"The sweet child your mother brought from the West.

The poor dear—how she must've suffered in that harsh environment.'' Violet scooted closer to Brooks and looped her arm through his. ''You must introduce me—I am just dying to meet her.''

Ghostly fingers traced a line down Missy's spine as Brooks descended the stairs and walked in her direction. She had never felt so trapped in her life as she did when he turned his blue eyes in her direction. Suddenly the velvet gown she was wearing felt about as attractive as a gunnysack. She tried to swallow the champagne one of the men had brought her, but it stuck in her throat and she choked.

''Miss O'Bannion, are you all right?'' a voice asked.

''What...? Yes. Yes, I am fine,'' she lied. Mercifully, a disembodied voice asked if she would like a glass of water. Within seconds her champagne glass was gone, replaced by a crystal goblet of water. She brought it to her lips, but the dryness remained.

''Oh, she is precious. Brooks, what a darling child.'' The blond woman clinging to Brooks surveyed Missy from head to toe. Without a word passing between them, Missy knew all she had to know.

This woman was her mortal adversary.

''Brooks, introduce me.'' Violet kept the smile pasted to her face while she inspected every inch of the dark-haired beauty before her. She had heard all the gossip about the lovely woman who had returned with Brooks. She had not believed it. But now that she was face-to-face with the little chit, she had no choice.

This woman was her adversary.

Missy felt her stomach knot up. In spite of the notion that the woman before her was everything she despised, there was a tiny part of her that was envious.

Violet Ashland was a lady, and she was holding Brooks's arm as if he belonged to her.

Brooks cleared his throat—and tried to clear his mind. Violet clung to him like a burr to a mustang's tail, as tenacious and as thorny. He wanted to peel her fingers from him and walk away, but he could not do what he wanted here.

This was his mother's drawing room, in New York. How he wished he were back in the Territory, where a man could be honest about his feelings.

"Violet Ashland, Missy O'Bannion." Brooks would not lie and say he was pleased to introduce them.

"I am so glad to finally get to see you, Miss O'Bannion. I have been hearing a lot about you." Violet turned slightly sideways and looked at Brooks. "Darling, she is a treasure. Such a charming child."

Missy stiffened. Images of Becky Kelly came unbidden to her mind. This woman was simply a more polished and older version of the woman who had jilted her brother, Trace. Anger and a desire to silence Violet Ashland spurred Missy on.

"It is very nice to meet you, but I am a long way from being a child. It probably just seems that I am young compared to you."

A silence so heavy it could be felt settled over the small crowd gathered around the two women. Brooks winked at Missy and his heart hammered inside his chest.

Damn if she isn't magnificent.

Brooks felt Violet's fingers dig into his arm, but, to give her credit, the smile never slipped.

"Oh, you are charming…in an untouched fashion." Violet inclined her head. The gaslight turned the strands of her hair to ribbons of gold. The crowd around them began to drift away. Evidently they had grown bored with the inane conversation. Now Brooks could drop his façade.

"When did you return, Violet?" he asked.

"Me? Oh, I have been back for ages now. I have been sitting at home pining away for you." She leaned close enough that he could smell her expensive French perfume. "You never even wrote."

Missy blinked back her surprise and tried not to feel what she was feeling. It was silly, but for some strange reason she felt...hurt to see the woman so *intimate* with Brooks.

"I saw no reason to write," Brooks said as he turned and looked at Violet. "When I left you were busy chasing a title."

"It was all a great misunderstanding, darling."

Darling. The word hung like a sword.

"A misunderstanding?" The tone of Brooks's voice was deadly. "It was a damn lot more than that."

"Nonsense." Violet removed her hand from his arm and tugged off her elegant, elbow-length glove. "It was nothing to me and I can prove it." She held up her left hand and wiggled her fingers. Gaslight and candlelight glinted off a huge stone. "I am still wearing your engagement ring. I think that says it all."

For the next few days Missy moped around Ellen's house, reading the latest Godey's magazine and practicing at solitaire, which Ellen taught her...trying to forget the scene at the brownstone. Then one day during breakfast Ellen surprised her.

"I think it is time we answered a few of these invitations."

Missy looked up and blinked. She was still numb all over, except for the unaccountable pain in her heart.

Why should I care if Brooks is engaged?

She had asked herself the question a hundred times and more, but she never came up with an answer that suited. It could be that she had harbored some silly girlish fantasy about him. Or it could be that it was just such a shock. After all, he had never mentioned the golden beauty who wore his ring. It might be all of those reasons...or none of them.

"Did you hear me, Missy?" Ellen frowned and pointed to a pile of calling cards and small white envelopes. "Gregory Whitemarten was here again this morning, and Charles Rutheford."

"I don't want to see anybody," Missy said glumly.

"No, you'd rather sit at home and let him win."

Missy's head snapped up. "What do you mean?"

"Cousin Brooks is having his cake and eating it, too, if you ask me." Ellen plunked two cubes of sugar into her tea and stirred it savagely. "He's got Violet Ashland hanging all over him, telling anyone who will listen that they will be married, and you are sitting at home pining away."

"I am not pining." Missy blinked at the harsh words. "What a silly notion."

"Prove it," Ellen challenged with a toss of her yellow curls. "If you aren't smitten with my cousin and you are not pining, then pick one of these invitations."

"I—"

"Right now. I won't believe another word you say unless you prove it."

Missy narrowed her eyes and leaned forward. She shoved the stack of cards and envelopes around on the table while she glared at Ellen. "I can't believe you would get such a dunderheaded idea, Ellen." When she could delay no more, she closed her eyes and picked up a slip of paper.

"Let me read it," Ellen said as Missy stared at it blankly.

After glancing at it, Ellen swallowed hard, but then she inhaled deeply and looked Missy straight in the eye. "It is from Cyril Dover."

"Which one was he?" Missy's irritation had momentarily banished her misery over Brooks.

"He was the tall slim man with the blue eyes—the one who brought the bouquet of roses the morning after Aunt Patricia's party."

"Oh, him." Missy sighed. "I guess he is as good as any of them to prove to you that I am not moping around because of Brooks. I don't care one little bit that your cousin is engaged."

Ellen's brows rose over cornflower blue eyes full of doubt.

"Well, I don't," Missy reaffirmed.

Chapter Six

For a few days Brooks went to his old haunts, including the theater and his favorite café, but everywhere he went he met with the memory of Missy's dark eyes and the unwanted presence of Violet Ashland.

She kept turning up, clinging to his arm. It was all he could do to bite down on the inside of his mouth and remember that he had been given a gentleman's upbringing. But it didn't take long to realize that he was a changed man—a man who found the simpering blond beauty of Violet more annoying than intoxicating.

One gloomy morning when the clouds were a great gray frown across the eastern horizon, Brooks was staring into the dark brew at the bottom of his china coffee cup. He largely ignored the conversation of his mother and brother, enjoying a hearty breakfast.

When the doorbell rang, Tilly answered it, then appeared carrying a flat silver dish containing a white envelope.

Brooks barely stifled his groan. He had been expecting a long overdue summons from his eldest sister, Clair. He knew the envelope was going to contain a family invitation that would be unavoidable. Her parties were boring affairs, attended by dozens of horse-faced girls of marriageable age and doubtful charms—and without a doubt Violet.

He drained the contents of his cup and stood up, ready to beat a hasty exit before Tilly reached him. But the bemused look on his mother's face as she read what was written on the creamy card stock she'd plucked from the silver tray stopped him in his tracks.

"Mother, what is it?" he asked. "Not bad news?"

She glanced up, as if only becoming aware of his presence. "No, not a bit. It is an invitation to a garden party." Her voice was soft and slightly bemused.

"Just as I thought," he grumbled under his breath. Clair *was* throwing another of her boring dinner parties and wanted him there. Well, he wasn't going to do it, not this time. He wasn't going to be there for Violet to use as a crutch to reenter the social set she had left when she was chasing a duke's title. She had scandalized herself, and he was not about to act as if it all never happened.

Brooks headed in the direction of the French doors and freedom. He was nearly there when Rod's hearty chuckle stopped him. Against his better judgment he turned and found Rod's face wreathed in a cunning smile.

"I haven't seen a smile that wide since the last stock report, Rod." Brooks crossed his arms at his chest and watched his brother. "What has made you so happy?"

"Read the invitation addressed to you." Rod returned his invitation to the dish Tilly continued to hold. "Perhaps it will bring a smile to your long face. Lord knows I am tired of seeing you scowl. I swear, you've had a frown since the night of Miss O'Bannion's introductory party."

"I have not." Brooks jerked the envelope from the tray and ripped it open. He was disgusted for allowing himself to be manipulated by family connections and social ties.

If his father wasn't such a good friend of Horace Ashland's, Brooks would simply call Violet a liar the next time she started all that nonsense about rings and engagement.

Hell, he just might do it anyway!

He scanned Ellen's flowing script and felt the pace of his heart increase as he read. "A garden party..." His voice trailed off as he quickly read the entire invitation. "At Uncle Leland's house. That might be nice." He looked up to find Rod studying him, undisguised amusement twinkling in his brown eyes.

"Nice? Missy and Ellen are throwing a party and you think it is *nice?*"

"Yes."

Rod grinned. "And what a happy coincidence, brother, that you'll finally get to see Missy O'Bannion again." He rose from the chair and pulled on his coat.

"Why in blue blazes would I want to see Missy? I have rather enjoyed not having my hide flayed off." Brooks cleared his throat and wondered why his pulse was racing like a runaway mustang.

The image of her dark eyes as she'd turned and left him standing with Violet had kept him awake more than one night. He just wanted to explain that he had no intentions of settling down with *any* woman. That was all.

Wasn't it?

Rod shrugged. "It was just a joke, little brother. Take it easy." Rod walked to his mother's chair and dutifully bent to deliver a kiss to the top of her silver curls. "I never dreamed you'd return from the Territory so serious, Brooks. Perhaps a garden party is what you need."

"Where are you going, Rod?" Patricia looked up, still holding the invitation in her hand, with a happy smile on her face. Parties did that to her, Brooks mused.

"It is my morning at the gentlemen's club."

"Oh yes." Patricia frowned at Brooks. "Why don't you go too, Brooks? You have been a bit grumpy lately."

"I have been grumpy?" Brooks repeated in astonishment. "I don't know why you all keep saying that."

"Well, you have, dear, and I can't for the life of me imagine why, especially when things seem to be working out for you and Violet Ashland."

Brooks rolled his eyes to the ceiling and counted to ten. "Mother, there is nothing between me and Violet. I've told you this before."

Patricia smiled. "All right, dear." She held both her hands up. "If you want everything to be a surprise, then fine, I will act as if I haven't heard a word." She beamed at him. "Just as you say, there is nothing between you and Violet."

"Mother—" Brooks started to explain, but Rod snagged his arm and tugged him toward the door as if he were a shavetail.

"Come along, little brother, or I'll box your ears. It will do you good to work up a sweat instead of just getting hot under the collar." Rod laughed aloud when Brooks flashed him another dark gaze, but he continued to tug his sibling toward the door.

The carriage lurched through a light drizzle of rain. Brooks had been silent on the way to the club, trying to figure out why on earth his mother could be so convinced that he and Violet were still romantically involved. But before he had found a scenario that seemed to fit, Rod was opening the carriage door.

Moisture accumulated on Brooks's face and his mustache as his eyes traveled up the craggy facade of the club. Vermont granite, the color of the storm clouds scudding overhead, soared upward without a break for seven stories. Stark, unadorned rock, solid and unyielding, met his eye.

"It never changes, does it?" he muttered.

"Not on the outside, at any rate." Rod tilted his head, endeavoring to see what held his brother's attention. "We have had one or two minor alterations on the inside."

Brooks's eyes scanned each floor while memories of his former life flooded through him. He'd had his first liaison here with Violet after a boxing match. "What? Have they installed new leather sofas?"

The carriage clattered away as the pair took the polished steps two at a time, side by side. "Not exactly."

"I know—new humidors," Brooks teased, suddenly glad that Rod had insisted he come along.

Rod smiled thinly at his brother's attempt at humor. "A group of forward-thinking young women came to attend one of the weekly sparring matches." He chuckled.

Brooks raised both brows, a little doubtful of the story. "I'll bet that caused some of the older members to need three fingers of brandy and a short rest."

"You would think—but that wasn't the way it turned out at all. After the hoopla settled down, everyone noticed the pugilists actually seemed to be putting forth a little more effort." Rod shook his head and laughed. "Because of the record amount of wagers won and lost on that day, a new tradition was started. Now, once a week, ladies are invited—actually welcomed—to observe the exercises. It has caused some raising of brows from other gentlemen's associations, but we are standing firm."

"Remarkable." Brooks found himself chuckling along with Rod. The staid and conservative founders of the club were probably turning over in their graves while the present members won wagers of staggering amounts on each bout. The women were allowed in, so long as it profited the stodgy members.

"You should understand, brother, a man will endure all kinds of pain to impress a woman." Rod kept a straight face, but his eyes twinkled.

"Perhaps, if she is the *right* woman," Brooks acknowledged, while his thoughts vacillated from Violet to Missy. He found himself lost in a world of his own while Rod went to change his clothing. It seemed like only moments had gone by before he returned.

"Last chance to come and take a shot at your older brother. Those hands of yours are tough and callused as shoe leather from the work you did out West. Now is the time," Rod taunted as he danced around in his high-topped boots, feigning punches and rotating his broad shoulders as he warmed up.

"No need to break a sweat to see who the winner is. I concede defeat from right here." Brooks leaned back in a heavily padded chair and laid his coat over the arm. He stretched his long legs out in front of him and crossed them at the ankles. "I have no desire to get up there and have my face pummeled. You carry on without me." He intended to remain seated; there was nothing Rod could say, no inducement he could offer, to get him into the ring.

"Suit yourself." Rod turned and focused his attention on a young man who entered the ring bare chested, wearing similar knitted wool tights and high-topped, laced boots of black leather. They met in the middle, shook hands and then, during the next few minutes, proceeded to pound each other's face.

Brooks unconsciously grimaced each time Rod took a punch. Brooks had eaten enough dirt and tasted his own blood more than enough in the Territory. The sport of bare-knuckle pugilism no longer interested him.

Sweat covered Rod's exposed upper body in a glossy sheen, but he danced on his toes, obviously still fresh. A young man who stood outside the ring rang a small bell and both men stepped away, going to opposite corners.

"He's got a nice punch," Brooks offered. "Who is he?"

Rod spat a mouthful of water into a bucket and grinned at his sibling. "I believe that is Cyril Dover—you remember him."

"No, don't think I do." Brooks looked at the man.

"Rumor has it he has been squiring Missy O'Bannion around town."

Brooks's head snapped up. Something hot and liquid coursed through his veins.

Jealousy.

Brooks stood up and started unbuttoning his shirt. "I think I'd like to—" *be the man who escorts Missy* "—have a go at him," he said.

Rod raised his brows, but he didn't laugh. "Suit yourself. Go change and I'll ask Cyril if he's up to a fresh comer."

Brooks planted a solid fist on the young man's chin. Blood smeared his knuckles. Brooks advanced, driving Cyril back. Surprise—or was it knowledge?—gleamed in Cyril's eyes as they stood facing each other.

Blood, or a knockdown, marked the official end of a contest between gentlemen at the club. Brooks knew he had to break off his assault.

"Well done, brother," Rod said to Brooks, who was breathing heavily. Cyril joined them, not nearly as defeated looking as Brooks had hoped he would be.

"Anytime you want a go with me, just be here before seven in the morning," he said cheerfully. "I am always looking for a man to give me a good workout."

Rod picked up a towel and offered it to Brooks. He took the towel and dabbed at his face.

"How's business going?" Rod asked.

Cyril shrugged. "My father makes the money, I consider it my sacred duty to spend it." Straight white teeth flashed when he smiled. "By the way, I wanted to thank you, Brooks."

"For what?" Brooks held both ends of the towel, looped over his neck, and gave Cyril an undisguised scowl.

"For bringing home such a lovely guest to stay with your cousin." Cyril smiled again, and Brooks found himself actually counting all those white teeth, thinking how he would like to forcefully remove a quantity of them.

"Yes, Bellami's new sister-in-law is visiting," Rod said with a sidelong glance at Brooks.

"She is quite lovely," Cyril continued.

Rod's face was unreadable. "You have met her?" he asked innocently.

"Yes." Cyril grinned wider. "I would stay and have another go in the ring, but I have an engagement with her this morning. Would you like a ride? I have a carriage waiting." He paused with one leg through the ropes.

"No thanks, Brooks and I are making a morning of it. He has been a little gloomy since his return from the West."

Brooks flashed his brother a dark look.

"No? Well then, I'd better go and change." Cyril slipped to the floor and disappeared.

"You know, Brooks, according to the gossip Cyril has been spending quite a bit of time with Missy."

Brooks didn't answer.

"I got it from the Mulligans' cook, who heard it from the Bentons' upstairs maid, that Cyril has seen her nearly every day." Rod waggled his brows.

"Then it is practically gospel," Brooks snapped.

Rod chuckled at his brother's terse answer. "Cyril has also been asking a lot of questions about the O'Bannion family."

Brooks refused to encourage him to continue.

Rod shrugged and continued as if Brooks had done so. "A lovely woman, new to town—"

"I thought Cyril had an understanding with Carol McLain," Brooks interrupted. "After two scandals in the past, and that breach of promise suit, I am amazed good ol' Cyril would show more than a passing interest in any new woman."

"Ah, but I have it on good authority that his father has laid down the law. The rumor is that Cyril must find a bride or be cut off."

"Isn't Carol suitable?" Brooks's brows lifted.

"I dunno. But if he is seeing Missy every day, then I would think it is safe to assume his attentions have turned in a new direction." Rod slapped his brother on the shoulder. "It sounds as if Cyril has set his sights on your Miss O'Bannion."

Brooks whirled on him, only to find an annoying smile curling Rod's lips. "She is not *my* Miss O'Bannion," he snapped.

"Perhaps not…" Rod frowned again. "But if Cyril Dover's intentions are what I think they might be, she may not be anybody's Miss O'Bannion for very much longer."

Chapter Seven

Brooks shrugged on his dove gray suit coat, worn over a charcoal silk vest. He indulged in an uncharacteristic moment of masculine vanity as he paused in front of the cheval mirror.

The carefully tailored coat hugged his shoulders, now heavy with muscle from months of hard riding and roping half-grown steers on the Circle B.

Will Missy notice?

Where had that thought come from? Surely he had learned from his experience in the Territory that Missy was never impressed by the cut of a man's clothes—at least not his. Brooks scowled and let his dark thoughts continue. Missy had shown a modicum of curiosity in the way he sat a horse, but absolutely none in the way he dressed.

Perhaps that was because she was waiting for you to be thrown on your ass.

A knock at the door brought his melancholy musing to a halt. He crossed the room in four long strides and opened the door. Rod was leaning against the jamb, his expression a study in annoyed forbearance.

"If this invitation had come from anybody but Ellen, I

swear I'd take off this damn coat and go to the office to get some work done,'' he threatened.

''So don't go. I am not looking forward to your chuckles and smirks, anyway. I am sure she will understand.''

''Oh no. You can't get rid of me so easily, brother dear. I have a feeling there is more to this little party than meets the eye. Mother has been positively closemouthed…and I have not heard from Clair since we returned from Bellami's wedding. Silence among the James women is never a good sign, and then, of course, there was that conversation with good ol' Cyril. The pot is simmering.''

Brooks opened his mouth to deny Rod's suspicions, but snapped it shut again. Something *was* going on, and he had the uneasy feeling that Missy O'Bannion would end up right in the middle of it. Missy and debonair Cyril Dover.

Across town at Leland James's mansion, Missy sat worrying her bottom lip with her front teeth.

''Stop that.'' Ellen's reprimand brought immediate composure to her face. ''Now come sit down so I can finish your hair.''

''I'm so consarn—'' Missy quickly amended her speech. ''I mean, I am terribly nervous, Ellen.'' She sat down in front of the French-style vanity and watched Ellen's reflection in the mirror.

''You'll do fine.'' Ellen sighed heavily. ''You have learned a great deal these past few weeks.''

''Thanks to you and Cyril. Are you feeling all right?'' Missy frowned. There seemed to be even less color in Ellen's already porcelain complexion.

''Don't fuss—you sound like Papa. Of course I am all right. Cyril has been a dear, hasn't he?'' Missy tried to turn around and look at Ellen directly, but a sharp tug on her hair kept her in place. ''Be still,'' Ellen said as she fastened and looped long strands. "And remember, Missy is gone…you are a different woman with a different name." Ellen braided a tiny length of pearls and a spray of small white flowers into the side of her hair to frame her face.

"I do feel like a different person. If I can just remember to answer when I'm called." Her laughter was brittle with tension.

Ellen stepped back and assessed her handiwork. "Now you are all ready. Go to the gazebo in the backyard, but don't let anyone see you until I introduce Miss Marisa O'Bannion to my guests. Cyril knows what to do once he arrives."

Missy's mouth went dry as a sun-baked arroyo. "Do you really think Br—everyone will notice the change in me?"

Ellen paused at the bedroom door. "*Everyone* would have to be stone-cold dead not to notice the change in you. Missy is gone. Don't even think of yourself as Missy anymore. You are Marisa O'Bannion and you are every inch a proper lady."

Three downstairs maids efficiently directed the new arrivals to the back garden, creating a steady stream of traffic through the house. The fragrance of roses wafted through the open French doors on a rain-freshened spring breeze.

Small tables set with crisp white linen and a crystal vase holding a single pink rosebud had been strategically placed among the flowering shrubs and sweet-smelling vines.

From her perch within the gazebo, Marisa took in the magnificent, romantic garden. She peered out from among the blooms surrounding the gazebo and studied each new

arrival with excitement and dread. "Marisa O'Bannion—
my name is Marisa O'Bannion," she chanted over and
over under her breath.

A new group of arrivals spilled through the French
doors and out onto the lawn. Ellen stood ready to greet
them. She smiled widely, but Marisa was concerned by
the pale blue smudges beneath her eyes. While preparing
for this party, Ellen had not been getting enough rest, she
thought guiltily. But then Marisa's gaze fell on a cluster
of people, and her heart lodged like a stone beneath her
breast.

"Welcome, cousins." Ellen stood on her tiptoes to give
first Rod, then Brooks, a peck on the cheek.

Brooks scanned the garden with squinted eyes. Marisa
felt like a rabbit, cringing in the brush while a hawk
sought her out. She drew back into the gazebo and flat-
tened herself against a pillar.

"Have some refreshments, please," Ellen suggested.

Brooks picked up a crystal cup of punch and brought
it to his lips. He was oddly disappointed not to find Missy
among the fresh-faced debutantes and their escorts.

Rod nodded toward the door. "Just as I suspected..."
he said cheerfully.

Brooks turned, expecting to see the elusive Miss
O'Bannion. Instead he saw his mother and eldest sister,
Clair, and Cyril Dover. A tiny shiver worked its way
down his back as the trio stepped into the mottled patterns
of sunlight filtering through the russet leaves of the copper
beeches.

"Rod, Brooks..." Clair released Cyril's right arm to
make her way to the pair. Her gown of pale blue lace and
darker gray silk ruffles caught the light. "My favorite little brothers. I have missed you. Wasn't it a lucky thing
that Ellen decided to have a garden party?"

Clair obviously did not expect an answer, since she never halted her prattle long enough to receive one.

"Where is your husband?" Rod asked, peering over her head at the door behind her.

"Australia. Sailed off two days ago. He is helping Father with some business involving Ashland Shipping." Clair's brows arched as if to emphasize her complete shock that he had left her. "Very inconvenient timing considering…but no matter. I have a little announcement to make later." A smile replaced the frown as she turned her attention to her youngest sibling. "Brooks, let me look at you. You have filled out and, my goodness, you are as brown as a native! Oh my lands, there are calluses on your hands!" She grasped one hand and turned his palm up to examine it, as if she had never before beheld the results of physical labor.

Brooks accepted her sisterly attention in good humor. She was, after all, his oldest sibling, and accustomed to hovering over him and Bellami. Finally Clair drew in a breath, and Brooks seized the rare opportunity to speak to his mother.

"Mother?" He frowned. "Rod and I would've been happy to escort you and Clair."

Patricia still had her slender hand draped through Cyril's arm, a gesture of familiarity that puzzled Brooks. He had not been aware of any friendship between them or their families.

"How very sweet of you, darling, but Cyril was happy to bring us in his carriage."

"Cyril? You and Cyril traveled over in his carriage?"

Brooks saw Rod nod once as if to say "I told you so."

"Yes. He dropped by and was a dear to offer to drive me and Clair. There was no reason for you and Rod to trouble yourselves."

Brooks had never known his mother to tell an outright lie, but she had been known to bend the truth fifty different ways. He wondered if she was doing so right now. Brooks studied her face, trying to guess what she was up to, and if Rod's dour prediction of trouble was correct. A ripple of distrust and suspicion twined its way through Brooks's belly when he scanned Cyril's unreadable face. The two men stared at each other while the silence grew strained. Then Ellen appeared, all blond bouncing curls and happy smiles, and the tension of the moment evaporated.

"It is so good to see you, Aunt Patricia." She turned and looked at Cyril. Brooks wasn't sure why, but two small circles of high color appeared on her cheeks as she spoke. "And you, Cyril. Thank you so much for coming." She leaned closer and lowered her voice. "We are in your debt and could never have done it without you."

Brooks frowned, wondering what her remark meant, but he had little time to speculate because Ellen turned toward the gazebo and extended one milk white hand. "Allow me to introduce Marisa O'Bannion."

Telling herself she was indeed Marisa O'Bannion, Missy lifted her chin and stood straight. She silently recited every instruction Ellen had given her about deportment as she made her way down the three shallow steps of the gazebo. She felt like a fairy princess when she stepped into a shaft of sunlight and her satin-slippered toes touched the verdant turf. She inhaled a breath of air refreshed and sweetened by yesterday's rain, and brought her chin up a notch.

There was no turning back now, not with *him* watching.

Brooks knew he was staring, bug-eyed and ill-mannered, but he could not seem to help himself. A diffused heat spread from his belly to his limbs. He devoured the woman with his eyes, while a little voice in his head reminded him that this confection was only opinionated, bullheaded Missy—nothing to get all hot and bothered about.

Yet his eyes and senses questioned what he saw as a new woman smiled shyly and glanced his way.

Marisa?

Where had she gotten the name? Had she made it up? Had Ellen? Where did Cyril Dover figure in this transformation?

Sunlight peeking through the thick canopy of coppery leaves cast alluring shadows on her face.

Marisa O'Bannion. The name ran through Brooks's head like a crystalline waterfall. Wherever it came from, it suited her.

Patricia smiled widely and stepped forward. "Cyril, is this what you were telling me about? My stars, you did not exaggerate. How she has blossomed...." Her voice trailed off as she and Cyril walked past Brooks toward Marisa.

"You look lovely, my dear, simply lovely." Patricia's gaze swept from the dark shimmering hair to her satin-clad toes. "Do I call you...Marisa?"

"Thank you, ma'am. And yes, my given name is Marisa...I decided to begin using it." Marisa's knees were shaking, but she managed to keep her hands still within the folds of her pale yellow dress. She forced herself to be calm, all the while telling herself that if Brooks could break a horse, then she could certainly survive a garden party.

"Your frock is stunning," Patricia exclaimed. "The soft pastel color is so becoming to you, with all that dark hair. I never would've been so creative."

"Ellen has been kind enough to allow me to use her

dressmaker,'' Marisa replied, carefully pronouncing each word. "The two of them advised me on the most becoming shades of fabric."

Patricia shook her head, sunlight glinting along the waves in her silvery curls. "If this is the result of a cleverly sewn frock in the proper hue, then I must change dressmakers at once." She laughed and touched Marisa's arm affectionately.

"Nonsense, Patricia, you are the most handsome woman in New York." Cyril quickly and gallantly denied any need for her to change her modiste. "And you well know it," he added with a playful wink.

Brooks felt his gut lurch. Cyril was flirting with Marisa and flattering his mother. It was too much. The knot in his middle tightened. He told himself that it was foolish. Missy would never be interested in a slick-haired dandy like Cyril.

Would she?

Marisa smiled at Cyril and allowed her lashes to sweep down modestly.

"Cyril, you are shameless." Patricia smiled again at Marisa. "But then, of course, Marisa, you would already know that about the most charming bachelor New York has to offer."

Brooks scowled. How would she know?

He took a deep breath, determined to get his rebellious pulse under control.

I don't care. If Missy has fallen under the spell of that slick-haired, macassar-oiled lothario, then fine. It means nothing to me.

"Better be quick, brother, the bees are at the flower," Rod whispered behind Brooks.

While Brooks searched his mind for something scathing to say, the air became alive with the sound of formal introductions, as every unattached young man in the garden stepped up to meet Marisa O'Bannion.

"Miss O'Bannion, I would be honored if you would let me take you to see the statue in our harbor. It is called Liberty Enlightening the World," one tall, lean fellow with thin brown hair exclaimed.

"If you are not otherwise occupied, please say you will accompany me to the theater on Saturday next," another fresh-faced swain pleaded as he elbowed his way closer to Marisa.

I don't care. My plans do not include romance or marriage or standing court with all these fawning young men.

Brooks's feet began moving before his brain fully registered the thought. He nudged his way through the circle of new admirers, and by sheer brute strength finally found himself standing directly behind Marisa. He stared at her smooth elegant shoulders, revealed by the clever bodice of her pale yellow gown. Her hair was piled on her head, twined with tiny white flowers and pearls in an elaborate style that made her look older and more sophisticated than he had ever imagined possible.

Brooks had always thought her thick hair was straight as a string. But now, in the spring humidity of New York, he could see it wasn't true. Several damp curls were forming at the nape of her neck.

Her smooth alluring neck.

It was charming, feminine and utterly enchanting the way the ebony tresses caressed the delicate column.

The way I would like to rest my fingers against her flesh.

For one mad instant he thought about pressing his lips to the sweet depression on her nape, then reality overtook him.

He shook himself, but the mental image of tasting her

skin remained at the edge of his mind like a sleeping predator. He had to speak to her, had to hear her fling insults at him so this magical snare would be broken.

"Marisa?" His voice was deep and husky. The sound of his own undeniable interest surprised and embarrassed him.

There was no mistaking the teasing male voice that sent shivers down Marisa's spine. Every nerve in her body prickled and danced. She drew in a breath and waited, hoping the butterflies would leave her middle.

"Well, is it Missy or Marisa?" Brooks taunted. He leaned so close that his mustache actually tickled her earlobe. "What shall I call you?"

She turned slowly, determined not to fall into the trap he baited. In the past she had always obliged him by re-acting before she thought. *Not today.*

"I was christened Marisa Shelagh O'Bannion."

For a moment his smile slipped and something—she was not sure what—clouded his eyes. Then he lifted one brow and gave her a sensual, teasing smile that made her breath catch. "Now that has a ring of the old country to it."

Brooks stared into her shimmering eyes. He was im-patiently waiting for her to flay the hide off him with her sharp tongue. When the cool Marisa revealed the fire that simmered inside the stylish yellow dress, these young bucks would fall away like dried leaves. Any minute now she would start to cuss and bluster.... But to his shock and dismay, she only smiled and allowed those remark-ably thick, dark lashes to sweep over her chestnut eyes once again.

"As you say, Brooks," she agreed demurely. "I do stick out like a sore thumb here in New York, part Irish and part Indian—a cat's whisker from being a barbarian, wouldn't you say?''

Missy—brave, blunt, wonderful Missy—was still beneath the lovely veneer.

''No, I wouldn't call you a barbarian, and neither would anyone else within my hearing, I assure you, *Marisa*.'' A sudden burst of possessiveness flared inside him. All he wanted to do was take her away, enjoy her company alone and keep these men from looking at her with hungry eyes.

Brooks's gaze locked with hers. Heat rose between them like fog on a warm April morning.

Breathe, you idiot, a voice inside his head screamed.

''Tell me how you ended up being Missy all these years.'' Cyril's voice broke the enchantment, and the young man smoothly insinuated himself between them. Brooks felt something—*not jealousy*—burn inside him.

Marisa's lips curled up a little at the corners. It wasn't really a smile, but seeing her look at Cyril that way grated against Brooks's sensitive nerves.

''My youngest brother, Logan, could never quite get his tongue around Marisa Shelagh. It always came out 'Missy.' Soon everyone was calling me that. Back home there would be no chance at all of changing it, but here in New York... Well, I decided to put little Missy aside.'' Marisa glanced at Brooks from under the fringe of her lashes. ''I am a grown woman now and it is high time everyone realized it.''

''It is a lovely name, if you don't mind me commenting.'' Cyril moved closer yet.

If Cyril gets any closer to her he will be touching the edge of her skirt.

Brooks told himself he was being a fool, but he also took a step nearer. She tilted her head and glanced at him again.

"The name suits you, Marisa," Cyril said.

"I am glad you approve, Mr. Dover." She lowered her lashes.

"Please, call me Cyril."

"I am not sure that would be proper. Do you think so, Brooks?" She looked directly at him. It was as if he had been poked by the hot end of a branding iron. "You are so much more knowledgeable about the way things are done in the city. Would it be proper?"

"Absolutely not," he snapped.

Marisa shrugged and sighed. "Then I suppose I can't call you Cyril—yet. Of course it is fine for Brooks and me to use each other's first names." She slanted another look at Brooks. "Did you know, Mr. Dover, that he and I are practically related?"

The impact of her beauty hit Brooks like a closed fist.

"Practically cousins now, I guess." She laughed.

His loins tightened.

"Cousins?" Cyril seemed to be weighing that information. "Then I won't waste any time being jealous of you, Brooks. It is good to know that there is no, uh, arrangement between you two. Leaves the way clear for the rest of us." Cyril grasped her hand. "I am giving you fair warning, Miss O'Bannion, I intend for us to become much better acquainted."

Brooks's mind began to spin like a dust devil sweeping across the prairie. For some unaccountable reason he had to stop himself from dragging Marisa through the French doors, on through the house and into the nearest carriage. His heart beat against the inside of his rib cage like a rejected suitor's fist on a locked bedroom door. Each time Marisa smiled at Cyril something hot and liquid poured through his chest.

What is wrong with me? Is this jealousy? It sure as hell can't be love.

"Now, Marisa—pardon. I mean, Miss O'Bannion, let's you and I find a quiet, private corner so you can tell me more about yourself." Cyril moved close enough for his thigh to crush her full skirt in a way that was almost intimate. "We never finished our conversation the other evening."

The other evening?

Brooks's eyes widened. Damn it all to hell, this had gone on long enough. Marisa had some explaining to do. After all, she was Trace's sister. Brooks was responsible—at least that was what he told himself to justify the hot tide of possessive jealousy sweeping through him.

He took a step forward, prepared to bodily remove Cyril Dover. But Patricia suddenly appeared and looped her hand through his arm. "Brooks, you have totally ignored your sister all afternoon." His mother gently tugged him away, leaving Cyril standing at Marisa's side. "Come and have a cup of punch with us and let Cyril get to know Marisa better. Clair has some surprise she wants to share with the family."

Brooks's head remained fixed, looking back over his shoulder at Cyril and Marisa, until the muscles in his neck pinched and cramped in protest. He wanted to stalk back and keep an eye on Cyril. But even more he wanted to toss Marisa over his shoulder and take her to the brownstone.

To ravish.

The gentle pressure his mother exerted on his arm was all that kept him in check.

But there is always later, a lecherous voice inside his head promised.

Patricia smiled inwardly. She had seen Missy's possibilities back in the Territory, but thanks to Ellen, everyone else now did as well. It made Patricia happy to think that she could help Marisa by finding her a suitable young man. Ellen had performed magic upon her, and some young swain would sweep her off her feet in quick fashion, offering her a life of culture and comfort in the city.

"Brooks, Rod, Mother—I have a surprise for you." Clair smiled widely. "Rossmore and I discussed it before he left. We were going to wait to tell you, but..."

"Tell us what?" Patricia's forehead crinkled. "What have you been keeping from us? Are you ill?"

"No. I'm not in need of medical attention, at least not in the way you mean, Mother." Clair smiled at Brooks and then looked back at Patricia as she took a seat in a nearby chair. "In about six months you will become a grandmother and you two will be uncles."

Patricia's jaw gaped open. For a full minute she held her stunned pose, then she knelt beside Clair, unmindful of what the position on the lawn was doing to the fragile fabric of her gown. "A grandchild? My very first grandchild. Oh, Clair, this is wonderful. It is more than wonderful."

"Ross and I were not sure how you and Daddy would take it. I hope you don't mind—I mean, does it make you feel old?"

"It makes me feel splendid. Donovan will be as delighted as I am. I cannot tell you how he has yearned for a tyke to bounce on his knee." Patricia's bottom lip quivered. "But dear, how do you feel? Are you all right?"

"Actually, I feel good." Clair smiled wider.

"Rod, call for the carriage at once." Patricia stood up, unaware of the grass stain on her gown. "I want to go home with Clair right away."

Rod smiled. "Do you mind if I ride along with you as far as the office?"

"Not at all, but don't dawdle." Patricia smiled and dabbed at her moist eyes.

Brooks heard laughter, and his interest was immediately transferred from Clair to Marisa. Cyril was leaning close, whispering something in her ear. "That is wonderful news, Clair, congratulations," Brooks said distractedly. He wanted to stalk to Cyril and ask him what he thought he was doing. But as much as he wanted to, he could not do anything but stand there with a smile pasted on his face.

Two hours later the party was progressing well. The news of Clair's pregnancy had added another dash of festivity to the crowd. Ellen took a moment from her duties as hostess and found Marisa. "See, I told you it would be fine."

"Yes, you did." Marisa studied Ellen's face. There was almost no color to her cheeks. "I think you should sit down for a moment." Worry for her friend, and guilt over all the party preparations, nudged at the corners of her mind. "Are you feeling all right?"

"Stop worrying over me. You are supposed to mingle and meet new people, be adored by young bachelors and let *some people* see that you can be a lady." Ellen smiled, but the expression seemed tired. "Besides, when I have kept my part of the bargain you have to begin teaching me to sit a horse."

"You know I will." Marisa caught Cyril's eye across the lawn. Within a moment he approached with a chair in hand.

"Listen to Marisa, Ellen—you need to rest a bit."

Ellen smiled up at Cyril. "Thank you. I believe I will,

since you both won't be satisfied until I do." She slid into the chair. "I never realized you were so gallant, Cyril."

"Then it's high time you started appreciating me. I am far more than meets the eye." Cyril waggled his brows. "You know, Ellen, there are some new animals being brought into the zoological exhibit at Prospect Park in Brooklyn. Allow me to take you there tomorrow morning."

"Well..." Ellen looked at Marisa. "Only if you will go with us. I wouldn't feel right going without you, Marisa. Besides, Papa would have a fit if I was not chaperoned."

"I have been tagging along with you too much," Marisa said. "But if you insist."

"I am glad that is settled." Cyril grinned. "I have an engagement at my club at seven, but as soon as I am finished I'll bring a carriage around." His smile widened. "Why don't I bring a picnic lunch? We can make a day of it."

"That sounds absolutely wonderful." Ellen glanced adoringly at Cyril for half a minute, then she lowered her eyes. "If you will excuse me, I must see to my guests." She placed her palms on the arms of the chair and started to rise, but swayed unsteadily and sagged back into the chair as a wave of dizziness folded over her.

"My goodness, Ellen, you are not well." Marisa watched the remaining color drain from her friend's face. "You stay put. I'll get your father."

"Nonsense." Ellen shrugged off Cyril's gently restraining hand. "Don't get Papa. I am just fine—a little light-headed is all." She struggled to her feet, then suddenly crumpled like a broken china doll on the turf beside the table.

"Oh no!" Marisa cried.

Brooks paused long enough to see Marisa kneel beside Ellen and tenderly lift her head into her lap. He turned and hurried toward the house, yelling for his uncle Leland as he went.

"Fetch the physician!" Leland barked at a maid when he had been informed. He plunged out of the house to the garden and burst through the circle of guests that surrounded Marisa and Ellen.

"Ellen…Ellen?" Marisa gently cradled her friend in the folds of her full skirt. Her fingers stroked the silky blond hair.

Ellen's eyes fluttered open and she smiled weakly. "No, I am not hurt. Please don't worry about me."

Leland dropped down beside Marisa and gathered his daughter into his arms. "Brooks, if you don't mind, would you see that our guests make their way to their carriages?" He stared coldly at Marisa. "I knew this would happen. I told her she was doing too much."

"Papa, stop it." Ellen reached out a slender hand to take Marisa's fingers. "I have enjoyed myself more than I can tell you." She smiled at her weakly.

"That is no excuse for your *friend* to take advantage of you."

"I will be fine." Ellen looked at Marisa, who had unshed tears in her eyes. "But I think we shall have to postpone your half of our agreement for a little while."

Chapter Eight

"Mrs. James, how long do you think it will be until Ellen is up and around?" Marisa looked down the long dining table at her hostess. After Ellen's collapse, Brooks had insisted that Marisa come home to the Jameses' spacious brownstone. Considering Leland's reaction to his daughter's condition, Marisa was very grateful for the offer.

"Oh, dear, it is difficult to say." Patricia rubbed the furrow between her brows. "Donovan, will you speak to Leland tomorrow? Perhaps you can get some information about Ellen's condition."

Donovan James nodded at his wife. He had been silent and his face was drawn with what Marisa judged to be worry over his niece, but then perhaps he, too, held her responsible for Ellen's illness.

Marisa nervously ran her finger over the edge of one delicate blue-and-white china plate. Everyone was so somber. It was nothing like her dinners at home in the Territory.

She thought of all the hours she had practiced her table manners on a card table in Ellen's room. Guilt and worry over her friend enveloped her. Marisa closed her eyes and prayed that Ellen would recover. The doctor had assured them all that she was not in mortal danger, but Marisa could not forget the image of her friend's pale face. She opened her eyes, but kept them focused on her plate and the silver-plated charger beneath it. If she dared look up, she would be forced to see Brooks, who was positioned directly opposite her. She did not want to find disapproval in his eyes, as she had in Leland James's.

She shifted uncomfortably on the soft padded chair, occupying herself by plucking at a row of tiny ribbons on the bottom of her burgundy sateen bodice.

"It troubles me to see you so worried, Marisa. Ellen will recover." Patricia's voice drew her attention. The maid, Tilly, was serving fillets of whitefish covered in a thick cream sauce. "There is no need to be so concerned."

"I feel so responsible."

"The physician said it was nothing serious," Rod interjected.

"Do you hear that, Marisa?" Patricia continued. "You must try to put it out of your mind. If you don't eat you will become ill yourself, and that will not do Ellen any good."

"Yes, ma'am, I'll try." Marisa watched Patricia lay her napkin in her lap. Mechanically she mimicked her graceful movements.

"Uncle Leland will call in a battery of specialists," Rod stated solemnly. "Ellen will have the very best of care. Our uncle is a bit overprotective, Marisa," he explained with a gentle smile, "but I am sure she will have roses in her cheeks soon."

Brooks tried not to notice the deep furrow between the dark wings of Marisa's brows. She was upset, but she would force herself to be strong, because she was the most stubborn O'Bannion of them all.

He wished he could think of some way to make Marisa feel better. But on the heels of that thought he wondered why he yearned to comfort her.

He was being ridiculous. Still, a gnawing ache materialized in his belly each time he looked at her pinched face. How could his uncle have been so insensitive as to imply she had in any way caused Ellen's collapse? With Ellen's medical history it was foolish to try and lay blame at Marisa's feet.

"Uncle Leland didn't mean what he said, Marisa," Brooks heard himself say. "He is just worried about Ellen and picked you as the easiest target for his anger."

Marisa looked up and swallowed hard. In her mind she knew that Brooks was right, but in her heart a kernel of guilt remained. She ducked her head and went back to her silent prayers for Ellen's quick recovery.

As Tilly served, Brooks allowed his eyes to skim over the slender column of Marisa's neck, lingering on the hollow of her throat. He watched her pulse flutter beneath her silken skin. He shifted position in his chair and willed himself to ignore her.

"Well, at least some wonderful news came at the party," Patricia reminded everyone in the silence. "Isn't it wonderful? Donovan and I are going to be grandparents."

Marisa looked up, and she could swear that Donovan's chest puffed out a little.

"It is great, but Ross picked a helluva time to leave his wife," Brooks said with a frown.

"It couldn't be helped," Donovan said, shooting daggers at his youngest son. "James Shipping is in the thick of a business merger with Ashland Lines. Rossmore was needed in Australia to oversee negotiations. The whole situation is very delicate—the slightest little thing could blow the whole deal.''

''Are things that serious?'' Brooks asked. He had his own investments, separate from the rest of the family, and rarely got involved with the business.

''Serious is too mild a word,'' Rod answered. ''Horace Ashland has been prickly about the whole thing.''

''Now don't say anything against Horace,'' Donovan said defensively. ''He is just being cautious because of…well, because of the past.'' Donovan's gaze locked with Brooks's, who understood only too well what his father was saying. Violet was the apple of her father's eye, and if Violet wasn't happy, then Horace would make sure nobody else was, either. And Horace had never heard the real version of what had happened.

Brooks focused on his plate, but suddenly his appetite was gone. Violet Ashland was becoming a thorn in his side. He had thought he was free of her machinations when he went to the Territory, but now it seemed she was binding him in a web once again.

Marisa looked up and found Brooks studying her face intently. His mustache twitched. She wondered if he had been about to speak…. She wasn't sure she could stand his teasing tonight, not with the thought of Ellen's illness hanging over her shoulders like a shroud. If only she had not allowed Ellen to plan the garden party.

''Let's not speak of things in the past. Clair is expecting a baby and Ellen will recover.'' Rod picked up his glass by the stem. ''I propose a toast. To the future!''

Everyone, including Marisa, followed his lead. ''To the future,'' they said in unison. But while Brooks swallowed a mouthful of wine, he asked himself if he was so sure of the future that he had planned. Marisa drank and looked at Brooks from beneath her lashes. His wide hand was brown and work roughened from his time in the Territory. For a moment his expression softened, but then he frowned and looked back down at his glass.

He was dressed in a plain white shirt, without a tie. A dark russet coat hugged his shoulders. His hair was swept back from his face, the marks of his fingers still evident in the thick waves. He looked as if he had dressed quickly and somewhat carelessly. It gave him an air of ease. He looked more like her brothers did at dinner than how she imagined he would look when living his life as a New York gentleman.

While she studied him an almost overwhelming wave of homesickness folded over her. She drew in a deep breath and fought back the sting of tears.

What is the matter with me? she wondered.

Abruptly he looked up, and their eyes locked in a compelling gaze. Her breath lodged in the back of her throat. Beneath the thick mustache she saw his lips curve up slightly. Her face began to heat from the base of her neck to the roots of her hair.

The meal progressed from soup to dessert in silence. After coffee was poured Rod leaned back in his chair.

"I suppose Ellen will be in an invalid's chair again," Rod said softly, shaking his head sadly.

Marisa gasped, pulled from her own thoughts. "An invalid's chair? Is she so ill that she needs an *invalid's chair?*" Her voice cracked. She inhaled deeply, determined to steady herself. "I can't imagine anything worse than having to be dependant—not being able to walk, or to do for yourself." A painful lump lodged in her throat. The image of being trapped in a body that would no longer do her bidding was more frightening than anything she could think of. Hot tears stung the back of her eyes.

"Rod, sometimes you are absolutely thick," Brooks snapped. "You did nothing, Marisa. Ellen is simply delicate. She will be all right."

Marisa managed to draw herself up and place both her palms on the table. She held her chin steady and blinked back the hot sting in her eyes. Suddenly Brooks reached out. He laid his hand on top of hers. It was rough, heavy and warm. He stared at her, and the hold of his gaze was almost hypnotic.

"And she would not be so frail if Uncle Leland would stop treating her like a hothouse flower," he said to everyone, but his eyes never left her face.

Patricia clucked in disapproval. "How can you say such a thing, Brooks? What an unkind sentiment."

"Yes, brother, when did you find the time to attend medical school?" Rod's brows rose in mock curiosity.

"I may not be a sawbones, but I learned a few things while I was gone." A strand of dark hair fell down across his wide brow as he spoke, still staring at Marisa as if he were speaking to her alone. "Look at what Bellami accomplished when she left the doting care of this family. There are no frail women in the Territory, only strong women of grit and determination."

Marisa felt heat climb to her earlobes. It was obvious he was directing his comments to her. But instead of being comforted, it made her feel rough and unfeminine. She forced herself to meet his gaze, even though her heart was breaking.

"If you don't mind, I think I will go up to my room." Marisa pulled her hand from beneath his and pushed her chair back, moving carefully so as not to tread on the edge of her skirt.

"Yes, get some rest." Donovan smiled, but his thick graying brows were still pinched together. "Things will look better tomorrow. They always do." He gave her a little wink.

"Thank you, and please accept my gratitude for inviting me into your home." She took one step, then paused and turned. "Oh, I forgot, Mrs. James, Mr. Dover had planned to take me and Ellen to the zoological exhibit tomorrow." Marisa worried her lip with her teeth. "I hope you had not made plans."

"You agreed to go to the park with Cyril Dover?" Brooks blurted out.

"Yes." Marisa saw his expression grow even more grim. Her chin came up a notch as she prepared to defend herself and her decision. For a moment she almost explained that she was only going to accompany Ellen, but then her temper flared. "Is there some reason why Mr. Dover should not take me—and Ellen—to the park?" Her words were clipped and defensive.

"Yes—no...." Brooks bumped his saucer, spilling coffee on the linen, turning it a dirty dull brown. He dabbed at it for a moment, then flung his napkin down in frustration and glared at Marisa. "Oh, damn it all, that wasn't exactly what I meant."

"Brooks, are you trying to tell me what I can and cannot do again?" Marisa carefully enunciated each syllable.

Brooks stood up and leaned forward, coming as near to her face as he could with the table between them. He placed his palms on either side of the coffee cup and narrowed his eyes. "Don't start putting words in my mouth, *Missy*. What I meant to say is that this is New York, not the Territory. You cannot go about in carriages with men who are practically strangers to you."

She glared at him and leaned closer. "Oh, you are impossible. Mr. Dover is hardly a stranger to me or your family. And I will go with whomever I wish."

His mind raced, searching for a sound reason to contradict the truth. "Not without a chaperon," he blurted. He tilted a brow, infinitely pleased that he had been able to grasp a plausible explanation for his behavior and objection to Cyril. No one could twist his meaning or his intentions, and nobody could accuse him of not looking out for Marisa's best interests. He assured himself that he was acting out of respect for her family and Bellami. He was going to take steps to see Marisa did not ruin her reputation. It was the least he could do to repay Hugh and Trace for their hospitality.

Patricia made a clucking sound. Brooks turned to look at her. She was staring at him with a puzzled expression. "Cyril is a perfect gentleman, as you well know. Now I think it is time for Marisa to get some rest." Patricia turned concerned eyes on Marisa. "And don't worry about any of this, dear."

Marisa nodded. "Yes, ma'am." She turned to Brooks and gave him a stare that could have frozen water. "I am flattered by your concern, Brooks, but as your mother says, there is no cause for you to worry about me. You are *not* my keeper." She turned on her heel and walked to the curving staircase. Brooks could only stare at her with his mouth agape.

Brooks lay in his bed and listened to the ticking of the clock below. He had not slept—could not sleep with the thought of Marisa only a few yards away.

He'd heard his parents go to bed hours ago, and even the soft sounds of Rod moving around in his room had long since subsided.

And yet I cannot sleep.

He rose from his bed and shoved his window up. The sultry night air washed over him. He wanted to speak to

Marisa, to get this silly misunderstanding cleared up, to explain.

Explain what? That you are driving yourself mad with jealousy? Or that you can think of nothing but kissing her? Or that you were a stupid dolt to think you wanted to be a bachelor forever?

He silently cursed himself and dragged his hands through his hair. He had shed his shirt and boots, but was still wearing his trousers. A night bird called and he shivered.

"This has gone on long enough. I have to talk to Marisa."

Brooks eased open his door and tiptoed down the hall to Bellami's old bedroom. He stood there, with his hand poised to knock, while he tried to imagine what he would say. Finally, when nothing came to mind, he turned and started back to his room, but the pull of Marisa would not let him go.

Taking every care to be quiet, Brooks put his hand on the knob. He turned it slowly, expecting it to be locked.

It wasn't.

He pushed the door open and stepped inside, telling himself that he had lost his mind.

He didn't care.

The soft sound of breathing could be heard coming from the canopied bed. He crept closer, intent on getting a glimpse of Marisa, determined to satisfy his craving for her with one innocent look. The glow of gaslights from the street beyond illuminated half of the room. Brooks tiptoed nearer the bed.

Marisa had woken the moment the door closed softly. Growing up in the Territory meant sleeping with one eye open. She had nearly called out, but then something— some instinct—told her the intruder was Brooks.

Her pulse escalated as the dark form crept toward the bed. She could hear the echo of her heartbeat against the feather pillow, and strangely, the thud of her heart seemed to mirror a dull throbbing between her legs.

He moved into the slender shaft of light and she saw his chest, so wide and muscled, then his neck and finally the lower half of his face. She longed to touch his mustache and see if it would tickle the way she thought.

Lord Almighty, she wanted him in her bed.

The realization made her breath catch in the back of her throat. Marisa could no longer hide from the truth or her feelings.

She wanted Brooks to love her.

Brooks stopped only inches from the bed. He touched the curtains at the nearest poster, telling himself to turn around and leave before he woke her up and she screamed like a catamount.

"I am not asleep, Brooks," she whispered.

And with that admission, Brooks knew he was not leaving.

With a husky moan of submission and lust, he was beside her. His hands were on her before he even knew that was his intention.

"Oh, Marisa." He inhaled the scent of her hair, touched the soft fleshy mounds of her breasts.

"Why did you come?" she asked.

"How could I not?" He kissed her then. It was a kiss full of savagery and hunger. A kiss that he had denied wanting—a kiss he would never forget.

Her hands were curious and seemed to have a mind of their own. She found the width of his shoulders. His muscles flinched as she explored the feel of him. He was as hard and lean as she had imagined he would be. As she touched him a wave of heat enveloped her.

"God, Marisa—Missy—I have wanted…" His voice trailed off as he nuzzled her neck, nibbled on the ear that had been fascinating him for weeks.

She had never been with a man, but growing up on a ranch left little to the imagination about how they would couple. The persistent throbbing between her legs urged her to explore more of his body, even while a voice in her head warned that she was playing with fire.

"I want you." Brooks climbed into bed beside her. A part of him knew that what he was doing was wrong. "I should've come sooner."

"What made you come now?" She twisted her fingers in a whorl of his hair, feeling the soft tickle of the hair upon his chest against her body as he moved nearer.

"Tomorrow I'll get our tickets," he said while he kissed her throat, feeling her pulse beneath his lips.

"Tickets? For what?"

"So we can go back—to the Territory—just you and me."

She became still as death. Her body seemed to grow cold as his hands came to rest on her tiny waist.

"Missy? What is it?" He raised himself on one elbow and looked at her shadowy face.

"You just naturally assume that you can come in here, climb in my bed and start making decisions for me." There was anger in her voice.

"We don't belong here, neither one of us. Let's go back where we belong."

"What about Violet Ashland?" She sat up.

Moonlight accentuated her full round breasts.

"What about your fiancée, Brooks? What will you do about her if we tuck our tails between our legs and run back to the Circle B like a couple of thieves in the night?"

Now it was Brooks's turn to grow cold. He felt his

desire wither. For some foolish reason he had thought—hoped—that Marisa did not know about Violet.

He was wrong.

His voice was as brittle as his control. "Where have you heard about Violet?"

"The lady herself says you are going to be married." The throbbing longing she had felt for him chilled in her veins. "And I don't hear you telling me that she was wrong. I saw the ring."

Silence hung between them for half a heartbeat. Brooks was torn. Should he tell Marisa that he had once loved Violet—had given her a ring and his heart, and had been crushed when she threw him over for bigger game? How could he explain that he had been entranced by her cool beauty, by what he had thought was a *lady?*

"I think you had better leave," Marisa said softly as she drew the sheet up to cover herself. "I may not be a lady but I won't be any man's fancy woman."

Brooks glared at her in the half-light for a few minutes, and then he turned and left. He had to do something about Violet Ashland's lies, and then, by God, he was going to set Miss Marisa O'Bannion straight on a number of home truths.

The next two weeks passed slowly for Brooks. He had tried to quell the rumors of marriage to Violet that were spreading like wildfire through his mother's social circle, but it was not easy—not when Violet flitted around, showing off that damn ring. Why hadn't he taken it back when she ended it?

Violet Ashland had done her work well.

But why?

Surely she did not believe he would forgive her and want her back?

Of course she would.

Violet Ashland was just that spoiled and just that simple. It would never occur to the beautiful, cold-hearted bitch that any man, much less Brooks James, who had been so besotted with her, could or would ever turn down the offer of her company. And even though she knew he no longer had any regard for her, she would not be above using his family's business interests and partnerships as blackmail to accomplish what she wanted. His mother would be mortified by such a scandal. And Violet knew it.

Bitch!

He took a drink of whiskey and then threw the glass as hard as he could. It hit his mother's favorite wallpaper, staining one pink rose a dirty brown with the last of the whiskey. Shards of glass peppered the tile floor. Within seconds he heard the rapid staccato of Tilly's feet.

"Oh, sir. What has happened?" Tilly's eyes were wide.

"Sorry, Tilly," Brooks muttered.

"No problem, sir. I'll get a pan and broom."

"Just bring them to me, Tilly. I made the mess—I'll clean it up."

She stared at him for a protracted minute, then she bobbed her head and hurried off.

I made the mess—I'll clean it up.

His words echoed in his head. He was the only person who could get Violet and her lies under control. He flopped down on the settee and dragged his fingers through his hair. It would be a damn sight easier if he didn't see Missy everywhere he went.

Missy at the park with Cyril. Missy at DelMonico's with Cyril. Missy and Cyril or Missy and any number of young swains that now squired her around the city. It galled him every time he saw her but it galled him even more because he had not ever managed to speak to her, and as far as he knew she had never even known he was there.

He was miserable. And he was getting mad.

Chapter Nine

Brooks tiptoed down the stairs, careful to avoid the third rung, which had squeaked since before he started to shave. He breathed a sigh of relief when his boots touched the parquet floor in the foyer. The first pink-and-gray fingers of dawn showed through the transom, the light tracing a jagged line across the toe of his boot.

"Sneaking out, brother?" Rod's voice caused the hair on Brooks's nape to prickle.

Brooks turned to find Rod, fully clothed, watching him over the rim of a steaming cup of coffee. Brooks wondered why he had not smelled the aroma. In the back of his mind he could almost hear Clell's derisive comment about his lack of awareness—how if Rod had been an 'unfriendly,' Brooks would be in a world of hurt.

Brooks shook his head at the thought and glared at his brother, but Rod only sipped at the hot brew.

"You know, Brooks, you used to do this the other way around—sneaking in before dawn, instead of out." Rod's voice was spiced with dry amusement.

"Shh…" Brooks crept toward his annoying brother, his irritation growing with every step. "Keep quiet, you'll wake the entire house." His voice was a husky rasp, accompanied by a vicious slice of his hand through the air.

"Hmm… I wonder which one of this household you do not want to wake, and why?" Rod leaned against the doorjamb of the dining room.

Brooks would liked to have had a cup of the coffee that now seemed to fill the whole house with its aroma, but he didn't have time. "I am on my way out," he whispered harshly.

"That, I think, is rather obvious. The mystery is where are you going at this early hour? And who are you going to see?" Rod's brows arched over his brown eyes. Rod could be as tenacious as a terrier with a soup bone when he wanted to be. "An assignation, perhaps? A clandestine meeting with a woman?"

Brooks yanked his watch from his vest pocket and looked at the face. He had no time to spar verbally right now.

"Just out," he snapped. "Do I need your approval?"

"How about a cup of coffee? I can rouse Tilly. She'd be glad to fix some eggs and we could talk over breakfast—"

"Enough of this!" Brooks cut him off. "I can see I'll have no peace until you know my business. I am on my way to the gentlemen's club."

Rod nearly choked on a mouthful of coffee. "Indeed? The club? But the only pursuit that starts this early in those hallowed halls is boxing.…" He grinned. "Wait a minute, I'll throw on a coat and come with you."

"I don't have time for this inquisition," Brooks snapped. "And I don't have time to wait for you to finish your coffee and grab a coat." The last thing he wanted was Rod coming along. He glanced back over his shoulder. "And don't you dare mention this—to anyone."

Rod held one palm up as if taking a solemn oath. "I assure you, brother, I will be the very soul of discretion." An expression of feigned innocence swept across Rod's face and left Brooks feeling as if someone had just walked on his grave.

Tilly opened the shades, allowing brilliant morning light to flood the bedroom. Patricia yawned and stretched.

"Is Miss O'Bannion still asleep?" Patricia rose and pulled on her yellow silk wrapper.

"Yes, ma'am, I peeked in and she was sleeping sound as a babe," Tilly answered.

"Good, she needed it. Poor dear. What time is it, Tilly?" Patricia yawned again as she pulled the silver-backed brush through her long white hair.

"It is just now eight, ma'am. Will you be wanting your tray up here?"

"No, not today. I'll be down directly. Please wake Miss O'Bannion, then tell Cook I am ready for breakfast."

Tilly quietly shut the door behind her.

Patricia washed her face at the basin, then patted it dry. She had not slept well. Memories of her conversation with Brooks had kept her awake. She stared at her features in the looking glass and tried to make sense of what he had said.

Mother, I want you to ignore everything you hear about me and Violet Ashland. I can't explain now, but I promise that I will—soon.

She sighed and forced herself to focus on her ablutions. When she opened her door she heard the long clock downstairs chime the half hour. She was on the second-floor landing when Marisa appeared, dressed in a mint green print frock. There were dark circles beneath her eyes, as if she had not slept. Her hair was pulled back with a simple ribbon, and wisps curled about her neckline.

"Morning, ma'am," Marisa said.

"Good morning. Did you rest?"

"Yes—no. I must've been more tired than I thought."

Patricia studied Marisa's face in silence. She decided that Marisa must have slept badly because she was worried about Ellen. "Would you join me for breakfast in the dining room?" Now that Patricia had spent some time with Marisa, she was growing very attached. Marisa was a breath of fresh air, guileless and unaffected, and amazingly good company. For the first time Patricia realized how much she missed having her daughters at home.

She slipped her arm around Marisa's waist and went into the dining room where she took a seat. The sound of the front door being opened caught her attention shortly afterward, and she swiveled in her chair.

Marisa found her curious gaze following Patricia's line of vision. She nearly choked on her coffee when Brooks appeared.

"Brooks?" Patricia smiled. "What a surprise. I thought you were still in your room. Come have coffee with us."

Brooks glanced at Marisa and she felt his anger—or was it disapproval? "No, I..."

"Brooks." Patricia used a motherly tone that made Marisa sit up a little straighter.

"All right, Mother. One cup." Brooks walked into the dining room and sat down at the table. He kept his eyes averted, as if he couldn't bring himself to look at Marisa.

A cold finger traced a line down her back and she fidgeted in her chair.

"What have you been up to so early?" Patricia poured coffee from the silver pot and cast a speculative gaze at her son. She put the pot back and turned her full attention on him.

"Nothing much." Brooks reached for the cup and Patricia grabbed his hand.

"What on earth have you done to your knuckles?"

Marisa found herself looking up against her will. The raw flesh of Brooks's barked and skinned knuckles met her eye.

Patricia fastened a tight-lipped gaze on her son, but he gently tugged his hand free and picked up his cup.

The room became oppressive with the silence that hung over the trio. Just when Marisa thought she would scream from the unspoken strain in the room, Tilly entered.

"Mr. Cyril Dover has come to see Miss Marisa."

"Cyril is here? He came here?" Brooks practically choked on the words. "The man has more damn brass than I gave him credit for," he muttered. "I never would've thought he'd show his face—especially not *this* morning."

"What?" Patricia frowned at her son. "Whatever are you talking about? I think Cyril is smitten with Marisa and I applaud his good sense."

Brooks stared at his mother with his jaw slack. He clanked his cup into the delicate saucer with so much force, Marisa was sure it would crack. Then, he turned to the maid. "Tell him to wait," he snapped.

"Yes, sir." Tilly's eyes were wide.

"Thank you, Tilly, that will be all," Patricia said evenly. When the maid was gone she turned to her son. "Brooks, I don't know what's gotten into you but I will not tolerate you abusing my staff."

"Abusing?" He shoved back his chair and stood up. "I didn't say an abusive word!"

"You didn't have to, with a face as dark as a thundercloud. Now I am going upstairs to change for my meeting with the hospital charity committee. I want you to apologize to poor Tilly.'' Patricia rose from her chair with all the dignity of a duchess. ''I'll see you later, Marisa.''

As soon as Patricia stepped into the foyer, where she could be heard speaking to Cyril, Brooks turned to glare at Marisa.

''What in the hell is *he* doing here?''

''Don't use that *tone* with me!'' Marisa hissed.

''Oh, so now I am using a *tone.*'' Brooks inhaled two long breaths, then began again in a low, controlled voice. ''Please tell me why Cyril Dover is here?''

''No.'' Marisa tilted her chin upward in a gesture of open defiance. ''I don't have to answer you.''

''Well, you are damn well going to.'' In the blink of an eye he was out of his chair and around the table. He hauled Marisa to her feet and glared into her face. ''What are you doing?''

''I am keeping company with a *gentleman.* One who is not engaged to another woman.''

Brooks flinched as if she had slapped him. The tight grip he had on her shoulders eased and he stared into her eyes. She thought he was going to walk away, but without warning he captured her mouth with his.

Every bone in her body turned to hot butter. She sagged against his chest while the heady power of his kiss took her will. The world disappeared. Marisa could no longer hear Patricia and Cyril in conversation. She could no longer smell the coffee, or hear the birds singing in the garden.

Her entire being was centered on Brooks's hot, possessive mouth as he invaded her, claimed and branded her with that kiss.

Then suddenly he released her and took one step away,

while she sank into the chair. "Take that with you while you are out with Cyril Dover." And then he stalked out the French doors and disappeared into the garden.

Brooks paced the grounds while he tried to get his temper under control. He didn't know what had gotten into him. Sneaking into Marisa's bedroom was bad enough, but kissing her in his mother's dining room—good God, he was going to pieces.

He raked his hand through his still-damp hair. He heard Marisa's clear, sweet laughter and his gut twisted like a sidewinder.

He sat down on the stone bench near the flowery arbor. He looked at his knuckles with a certain amount of satisfaction. Marisa clearly wondered how he had barked his hand—he could see it in her eyes as she had stared at him.

What would she say if he told her that he had done it on Cyril's too-handsome face?

He swallowed hard. In the back of his mind he could hear Clell's laughter. Yep, he had it bad. As much as he wanted to deny it, he was in love.

He was in love with Missy O'Bannion.

An hour later Marisa bent her knees and dipped low enough to see her reflection in the gilt mirror in the foyer. Ellen and Miss Baldwin, the dressmaker, had instructed her on which frock to wear with each bonnet and set of gloves, but she was never sure the jaunty angle where the bow rested against her jaw was quite right. She untied it and retied it once again in a different position.

"You look lovely," Cyril said from his position against the wall of the foyer. "I will be the envy of all the men in the park."

"Yes, Miss O'Bannion, you do look especially

lovely." Brooks's voice made her start. She turned to find him watching her from the dining room. His eyes were like blue fire and the expression she saw in them made her shiver.

Marisa tilted her head to look at her escort. Light spilled through the arched transom and onto the parquet floor where Cyril stood. Tiny dust motes floated around the starched crease of his navy trousers and onto the white leather gaiters above his shoes. He was impeccably dressed, as usual, but there was something different about him. Marisa studied him carefully from under her bonnet. There was a certain familiar sootiness to the skin around his left eye....

"Cyril, you've got a shiner!" Marisa blurted out. Then she clamped her gloved hand over her mouth, but it was too late.

Brooks sauntered into the foyer and smiled at Cyril. "Why Cyril, you do have a mouse beneath your eye. What have you been up to?"

Cyril stared at Brooks with an arched brow. When it was evident he had no intention of answering, Marisa turned and walked out to the waiting carriage.

The carriage rolled along a lane canopied by horse chestnut trees. The beautiful pinkish blossoms hung like ripe grapes overhead. Marisa sat on Cyril's left side, while Brooks sat alone in the opposite seat. She had her hands folded in her lap, trying to ignore his constant scrutiny.

"I don't know why *you* had to come along," Marisa said to Brooks. She glanced at Cyril from under the brim of her bonnet. His swollen eye was beginning to take on rainbow hues. She was not fooled by his lie about running into a door. *They* had been up to something together—Brooks's knuckles and Cyril's eye were somehow connected, and she wondered if it had been literally.

"I feel responsible for you, for your reputation," Brooks replied. "Cyril, I hope your, uh, accident running into that door does not give you too much discomfort."

Cyril smiled broadly. "Not a bit of it. And this eye was not enough to keep me from visiting Marisa."

A look passed between them, and if Marisa had been betting, she would have laid even odds that it was a silent challenge. She wondered what in blazes was going on.

"What would it take to keep you away, I wonder?" Brooks flexed his fingers, drawing Marisa's attention to his skinned knuckles.

"It might be interesting for us to find out," Cyril said happily.

Marisa frowned at both of them. As she sat there watching them she suddenly felt like a tattered old piece of leather being stretched between a couple of squabbling coyotes.

"Marisa?" Cyril's voice interrupted her woolgathering.

"I'm sorry, I didn't hear you," she murmured.

Cyril grasped her hand. Even through her thin lace gloves she could feel the smooth flesh of his palm. A man should have wide rough hands, callused hands. Strong hands a woman could trust to keep her safe. The kind of hands that had pulled her out of her chair this morning.

She found her gaze going beyond Cyril to Brooks. His expression was darker than Hades and his eyes blazed with...*jealousy?*

The word popped into her head, but she discounted it. No, Brooks was not jealous. He liked to tease and belittle her and he liked to play with her emotions by kissing her until she lost all her good sense, but he didn't care enough about her to be jealous.

She forced her attention back to Cyril. "Yes, Cyril?" She tried to dispel the thought of Brooks's hands and the feel of his kiss, but she couldn't. A hot band tightened around her heart.

Marisa studied Cyril's handsome, unlined profile. His features were smooth and even, but they lacked strength. He would never be able to withstand hardship, she thought to herself. And he would never know the kind of satisfaction she had seen written across Brooks's lean jaw at the end of each tiring day on the Circle B.

"I paid Ellen a visit before I came to pick you up," Cyril said.

Marisa swiveled in the seat as far as she could without knocking her knees against Brooks's. "How is she? How soon can I go and visit her?" A burst of excitement rippled through her.

"She is much improved. She specifically told the maid to send her regards, and it was she who suggested I come and take you for an outing." He slid a glance at Brooks and swallowed hard. "But seeing her may be difficult." Cyril patted Marisa's hand.

"Difficult? Why?" she asked. Brooks shifted in the opposite seat. His knee brushed against her leg. He gazed out the window as if he were interested in the scenery rolling by, but she could tell he was listening intently.

"I hope this doesn't upset you too much, Miss O'Bannion, but Leland has forbidden Ellen to see you."

"What?" Marisa recoiled as if she had been struck. "Is Ellen that ill? Did you see her?"

"No. I had a long chat with the downstairs maid. She assures me that Ellen is chipper and wants company, but Leland won't be budged."

Brooks glanced up. "You seem to spend a lot of time gossiping, Dover." There was ice in his voice.

Marisa seared him with a look. "Please, I want to know about Ellen."

Cyril nodded solemnly. "The maid swears she is regaining her strength, but…"

"But?"

"Oh, dash it all. Everybody knows Leland is just looking for somebody to blame, but he has it in his head that you caused her collapse. I am sure he will come round, but for now you can't see her. Ellen is very upset by his stubbornness."

"I see," Marisa said softly. Tears burned the back of her eyes, but she wasn't sure if it was from being falsely accused or if she was indeed responsible.

"I'll talk to him if you want," Brooks offered softly.

Marisa wished she hadn't noticed how the flesh around his blue eyes crinkled handsomely or how wide and rough his hands were.

Damn his no-good polecat's hide. She cursed him silently, as Ellen had taught her. She didn't want him to be nice to her. That was the hardest thing to handle, but even as she mentally denied his help she found herself nodding her assent. "I'd appreciate that, Brooks."

"Do you want to come with us for tea, Brooks?" Cyril asked.

"I don't know what I want anymore," Brooks mumbled. He turned and raked his fingers through his hair. He was all tied up in knots. One minute he wanted to turn her over his knee and spank her, the next he wanted to fold her in his arms and kiss her obvious hurt away.

Marisa was driving him crazy with her new grace and manners, but if he was honest, he'd have to admit he missed their daily battles and the simmering emotions that used to flare between them. A mixture of anger, excitement and melancholy twined through him.

An hour later the carriage drew up in front of the Jameses' brownstone. Brooks immediately slipped out his door. He stalked up the wide stone steps without glancing back at either Cyril or Marisa.

He wished he had not insisted on going along. What had he been thinking?

He opened the door and disappeared inside the house before Marisa had even stepped out of the carriage.

"How about dinner tonight?" Cyril pressed as they strolled up the walk. "I promise I will have nothing but good news of Ellen." He smiled. "She doesn't want you moping around, you know."

Marisa wasn't sure she wanted to spend an evening with Cyril. Brooks's kiss still burned on her lips and she was confused. Then she saw him standing just inside the doorway, watching her with disapproval in his eyes.

"What time will you be picking me up?" she blurted out.

"Seven o'clock." Cyril's happy smile grew broader.

"Then I'll make sure we are ready and waiting for you, Cyril ol' boy." Brooks's deep voice erupted behind Marisa as he stepped from the shadows and insinuated himself into the conversation. He was close enough for her to feel his breath on the nape of her neck.

Hot chills flowed through her. "*We? We* will be ready?" she said with arched brows.

"Of course. I can't let you run around town unchaperoned. Remember? I feel responsible to keep your good name intact." He held her gaze for a moment. Images of his moonlight-kissed skin and the hot, stolen kisses flooded her mind, and she knew he was thinking of them, too.

"Yes, I remember—only too well."

Cyril glanced from Brooks to Marisa. "Fine. I'll be here at seven." He leaned forward as if to give Marisa a kiss, but Brooks placed his hand on her forearm and cleared his throat in an exaggerated manner.

"Well—yes, uh, until seven then," Cyril mumbled as he turned and walked toward the waiting carriage.

Chapter Ten

Marisa sat in front of the vanity and stared at her reflection. The image in the glass was almost a stranger. Dark hair was carefully piled on her head. The navy gown she wore was elegant but not gaudy. Smooth shoulders were exposed in a way that Ellen had assured her would be demure and yet alluring.

"So why do I feel like a bagful of barn cats are tied up inside my belly?" she asked her reflection.

She rose from the padded stool and straightened the folds of the white sash draped over the front of the blue velvet skirt. It was drawn up at each hip with a small rosette. To emphasize her small waist, Ellen had said, in contrast to the moderate-size bustle.

The thought of Ellen and her friendly advice made Marisa blink back fresh tears. She tried to swallow, but there was an obstruction at the back of her throat. Her nerves were raw and she was edgy as a longhorn in a thunderstorm.

"I am just lonely for Ellen's company," she muttered as she paced the length of her room. "That must be why I am so high-strung."

It couldn't be because of that consarned, goll-danged Brooks.

Marisa tried to think of some way to appease Leland so she could see her friend. Maybe she could just apologize.

No.

Perhaps she should bake a cake?

No. He would accuse her of feeding Ellen a poor diet.

A forceful knock on her door stopped her in mid-thought.

"Yes?"

"It's me. Are you ready?" The deep rumble of Brooks's voice sent a shiver up her spine. "Cyril is at the door and evidently panting for your company, since he is a full twenty minutes early." There was a sharp edge to Brooks's voice and it made her all the more irritable.

"I'll be right down." Marisa took a deep breath and turned to look at herself one last time. The image was one she had not yet grown accustomed to. Nobody would ever doubt that she was a lady, except perhaps Brooks James. And for some strange reason that brought an even larger lump to her throat because of the note she had received earlier in the afternoon. She picked it up and re-opened the envelope, unable to ignore the strong floral scent on the elegant stationery. The handwriting was precise and neat, the message short and to the point:

"Don't get too comfortable with my fiancé or you and all the James family will be sorry."

It had been signed V.A.

Marisa folded it and returned it to the envelope. A raw ache had settled beneath her heart. For what woman would dare write such a note unless she was very sure of herself?

* * *

Brooks tiptoed down the back stairs and out the servants' entrance. He had no intention of running into Rod this morning. He had endured Cyril's moon-eyed glances toward Marisa and had listened to the mewling chatter until his digestion had been ruined. She had barely acknowledged his presence. The last thing he needed was to run into Rod now.

What he needed was to get a little satisfaction.

He opened the doors to the gentlemen's club and stalked inside with all the finesse and manners of a horny grizzly.

"Somehow I knew you would be here early." Cyril grinned at Brooks as he unfolded himself from the leather side chair.

"Let's get to it," Brooks practically snarled as they fell into step with each other. Within moments they were climbing into opposite sides of the padded ring.

"What made you think I'd come in early?" Brooks asked as he stretched his tendons and warmed up his shoulders.

"I don't believe I'll tell you, not just yet." Cyril cheerfully positioned his fists and jogged on the balls of his feet. "I'll make you a deal, James ol' boy. If you land one punch this morning, I'll tell you how I knew you'd be early."

"You've got yourself a deal, young pup."

They met in the middle of the ring like dueling knights. Brooks danced on his toes, determined to turn Cyril's handsome face into a bloody mess. That little voice, the one that sounded oddly like Clell, asked why Brooks was so determined to mess up Cyril's face. But like a lot of things, he managed to ignore it.

Cyril threw a lightning-quick punch. Brooks was preoccupied with his own demons, which made his reflexes slow. He ducked, and only a portion of Cyril's fist connected. The stinging blow made his eye water and his ear ring.

"Now we are nearly even," Cyril said with a happy grin. "I had to tell that lie about running into a door far too many times."

"We are nowhere near even, to my way of looking at things. Not by a long shot." Brooks rushed in, throwing punches at Cyril's lean middle.

Cyril backed up a step.

Brooks rammed his fist upward, catching Cyril's square chin. The bones in Brooks's hand tingled and stung.

"Pax! Pax, Brooks!" Cyril chuckled and wiped his hand across the smear of blood on his chin. "You win. You landed a punch." His eyes twinkled with amusement, and that only made Brooks want to hit him again.

Brooks lowered his fists, but for some reason he wasn't all that happy about winning. A part of him was hungry to keep on hitting Cyril. "How did you know I'd be here early?"

Cyril picked up a towel and rubbed it along his chin. A crimson stain marred the thick white toweling. "It is obvious to everyone but you. I knew you would be here because of Marisa O'Bannion."

"What's she got to do with this?"

When did any thought in your head not revolve around Marisa? the Clell voice challenged.

Cyril shook his head from side to side and laughed. "You are crazy in love with her. Though, as contrary as you are, you will probably deny it just as you keep denying a wedding between you and Violet is in the wind." Cyril climbed through the ropes. "I always thought you Jameses were an intelligent lot, but I have never seen a man as thick as you."

"Come back in here. I'll show you how thick I am."

Cyril held up his hand and kept on walking.

"I am not in love—and if I were it certainly would not be with Marisa O'Bannion," Brooks growled.

Cyril paused. "Does that mean you're marrying Violet?" Before Brooks could answer, Cyril disappeared into the changing area.

"I am not in love!" Brooks yelled at Cyril's retreating back. He turned and there, dressed in tights, grinning from ear to ear, was Rod. "Nor am I marrying Violet!"

"Who are you trying to convince, brother—Cyril Dover or yourself?" Rod asked blandly.

"I am not trying to convince anyone. I am not in love with Marisa O'Bannion," Brooks said stubbornly. "And I am getting damned tired of having Violet's name linked with mine."

"Fine. Would you care to take a punch at me, or is that honor reserved only for men who dare to court Miss O'Bannion—the lovely young woman you are not in love with?"

Brooks narrowed his eyes and walked to the center of the ring. He raised his fists. "Funny, Rod, very funny. You know, it has been awhile. I would enjoying taking you down a peg."

"Not likely, little brother, but perhaps the effort will cheer you up." Rod snorted. "Hey, that's a nice-looking scar. Did you get that in the Territory?" he said, pointing at Brooks's bicep.

Saving Missy from certain death.

Rod stretched and threw a few mock punches. "Tell me, little brother, did you duel with knives when you weren't chasing cattle?" He laughed.

"No. It was a disagreement with an angry longhorn."

"Really? I am impressed." Rod danced a little closer.

"I hate to bring it up—I mean, since you made it clear that you're not interested—but Miss O'Bannion left the house this morning."

"So?" Brooks didn't want to listen, didn't want to care.

"Oh, yes, I forgot. She means nothing to you."

Silence stretched between them as they threw punches that never quite landed. Finally Brooks could stand it no longer.

"Well?"

"What? Oh, you *are* interested." Rod grinned. "She left this morning carrying a traveling bag."

Brooks looked up into his brother's eyes and felt the knot in his gut twist harder. "A bag?"

"You know, a container for one's clothes...when one travels. You don't suppose she is leaving without saying goodbye, do you?" Rod asked before he landed a solid punch to Brooks's cheek and sent him reeling backward into the ropes. "But then again, you wouldn't care because you are not in love," he taunted with entirely no mercy.

Damn, but his older brother could be irritating at times.

Marisa yanked her skirts and petticoats up between her legs and stuffed as much of the full ruffled edge as she could into her belt. The result she achieved by altering her yellow plaid frock wasn't trousers, but it would have to do.

She looked up at Ellen's window, craning her neck backward so far that for a moment she became dizzy. The sound of a horse and buggy clattering by drew her attention, but luckily Ellen's bedroom faced the flower-bordered alley. Marisa could not be seen from the street.

She squinted her eyes against the sun while she tried to judge the distance she would have to climb. Including the thick stone foundation, she guessed it to be about twenty-five feet up to the wrought-iron balcony railing that surrounded Ellen's French windows.

"No higher than the lightning-struck cottonwood in the arroyo back of the ranch house," she assured herself.

Hell, she had shinned up that old tree since she was big enough to run away from—or after—her brothers.

Of course, it did grow at a crooked angle because of the scars on its weathered gray trunk, and that slope made it more like a ramp than a tree…but that shouldn't make much difference.

Besides, there was no other way to visit Ellen.

With a sigh of resignation Marisa looped the straps of the carpetbag over her arm, grabbed hold of the ornate black iron trellis and started to climb.

The rosebush tangled within the trellis was old and gnarled. The greenish brown stems, loaded with thorns, were thick as her fingers. By the time she reached the first-floor roof cornice her palms were stinging from pricks.

Her skirt was tangled in the grip of the briar rose. She tugged on the stubborn cloth and finally it jerked loose with a ripping sound. A scrap of her petticoat was left dangling from a long scimitar-shaped thorn.

"Damnation," she muttered.

A few more tense minutes of picking her way through the maze and she was finally able to hoist herself and the bag over the second-story balcony railing.

Brooks finished buttoning his shirt during the carriage ride to the brownstone. He silently carried on a running argument with himself about why he had rushed from the athletic club and why he allowed Rod to needle him about Marisa.

She is not leaving. She can't be.

But his thoughts gave him no reassurance. Maybe she *was* leaving. He wouldn't be a bit surprised. After all, he had known she would be like a fish out of water. Still, it wasn't like Missy to just turn tail and run back to the Territory—not like her at all.

But she isn't Missy anymore. She is Marisa—mysterious, sensuous, unpredictable Marisa. And it was just possible that Violet's nonsense had her on the run.

He argued silently back and forth, and by the time the carriage rolled to a stop in front of his family's brownstone he was in a fine fit of temper. He strode up the steps and flung open the door.

"Tilly!" His voice echoed through the oppressively quiet house. He had never noticed how silent the stately brownstone was until he had stayed at the Circle B ranch. That house hummed with laughter and arguments. It vibrated with life.

As he was comparing the two places, Tilly appeared, round eyed with surprise. "Yes, sir?" Shock and perhaps fear were written across her features.

Brooks tried to wipe the scowl from his face. It wasn't the maid's fault that Marisa O'Bannion had once again riled him, so why take it out on her. The memory of how her lips had trembled when he apologized for his beastly behavior at breakfast stung his conscience. "Is my mother in?"

"No, sir, she went to Miss Clair's," Tilly replied quickly. "They were going shoppin'."

Brooks raked his hand through his hair and sighed in frustration. "Was Miss O'Bannion with her?"

"Oh, no, sir."

Hope died in his chest. When the James women went shopping, they planned their strategy like conquering generals and did not come home until the campaign was over. He looked up at the staircase, willing Marisa to appear.

"Has Miss O'Bannion returned then?" He couldn't entertain the thought that she had left him. *Had left New York,* he mentally corrected.

"Returned, sir?" Tilly replied evasively, twisting and mangling her apron between her fingers.

Brooks turned his full attention to the maid. "Rod told me Miss O'Bannion went out carrying a traveling bag." His voice was stern and too loud.

Tilly wrung her hands in the white apron. "Sir?"

"This is important, damn it. Is Miss O'Bannion here?" Brooks pressed.

Tilly ducked her head and made the sign of the cross. Brooks was sure this was the first time she had heard him swear.

If I don't find Marisa it won't be the last profanity I say in this house.

"No, sir."

"Do you know where she is?" His patience was shredding like the bit of lace at the edge of Tilly's apron.

"She did not say what time she would return, sir."

A prickly kind of relief washed over him. Tilly's reply indicated that Marisa planned to return. The maid continued to avoid his eyes like a disobedient spaniel that has chewed a slipper, and Brooks's instincts told him that she knew what he needed to hear.

"You know where she is, don't you, Tilly?"

Her head snapped up. "I can't say. That is, I don't know, sir." She backed up and drew in a breath. There was a flicker of fear in her eyes.

"For pity's sake, Tilly, I am not going to hurt you, or Miss O'Bannion, but I need to speak to her. Now tell me where she has gone."

Tilly's cheeks reddened. She sighed, and her stiff uniform seemed to lose all of its starch and crispness. "I ain't supposed to say, sir. I promised."

"You promised what?" Apprehension crept up his spine. What could Marisa be doing that she wanted to be kept secret? And who was she doing it with?

"I promised not to tell who she is seeing." Tilly slapped her hand over her mouth and her eyes grew round as gourds.

Brooks tried to calm his runaway heartbeat. The feeling he refused to acknowledge as jealousy washed over him.

Who was she seeing?

Something hot and bitter rose in the back of his throat. He drew in a breath, willed himself to school his features and did his best to smile at the maid.

"Miss O'Bannion is our guest." His voice was low and taut with false control. "We are responsible for her welfare while she is visiting. Surely you can understand that?" He rationalized this for his own as much as for the stubborn maid's benefit.

"Ye-yes, sir."

"Now, tell me, Tilly. *Where has she gone?*" He measured each word, matching the cadence to his thudding heart.

"But I promised, sir." Her tone was pleading.

"Damn it all to hell! *Tell me.*" He fastened what he hoped was a stern gaze on her face. "I only want to make sure she is all right," he added as an afterthought, when Tilly's face grew as pale as snow.

"She went to see Miss Ellen," Tilly whispered.

Once more relief flooded through Brooks's constricted chest. He released the breath he had not been aware of holding. "Ellen's house?"

"Yes, sir. Please don't tell her I told you, sir. She

trusted me," Tilly said, sniffing. "I wouldn't want the young miss to think she can't trust me no more."

"I won't say a word about where I got the information, Tilly. You have my word on it." Brooks smiled in relief. "You can go now."

"Yes, sir." Tilly bobbed her head and scurried toward the kitchen, making no effort to hide her relief.

Marisa was not leaving. She was visiting Ellen.

A strange joy settled over him like summer sunshine, and then a new question popped into his head.

Why was Marisa swearing Tilly to secrecy about visiting Ellen?

A premonition of doom swept over him. Past experience had taught him that Marisa was not likely to take Uncle Leland's exile in good grace. There was going to be trouble, Brooks was sure of it.

Brooks leaned against a black oak tree across the street from Leland James's house. Indecision ran hot and cold inside him. Should he just go knock on the door and stop all this ridiculous cloak-and-dagger business?

"No," he answered himself. Cyril swore that Leland had forbidden Marisa to see Ellen, and there was no reason to believe he had softened his stance.

Brooks frowned at the imposing mansion while he lurked beneath the sheltering old tree across the lane. It irked him to be spying on his own uncle.

His gaze swept over the solid brickwork. The ornate facade of plaster and stone on the first-story roof hip needed repair in several places.

Leland had probably not noticed the grout and mortar were crumbling and falling away. Vines grew abundantly, finding niches and cracks in which to cling, and causing crevices to grow between the bricks. Virginia creepers hung in green profusion and the heady scent of Leland's prize roses filled the spring air.

It was quiet, the only noise the droning of yellow-and-black bumblebees tasting the nectar of Leland's flowers. Then suddenly the silence was shattered by a series of excited yips. The black-and-white bull terrier in the yard next door barked furiously. The agitated canine bounced on his stiff front legs while his hoarse, raspy yelps echoed through the neighborhood. He shoved his nose through the iron fence that separated his domain from Leland's, and the hackles rose along his muscled back as he focused intently on something—something in Leland's yard.

A fire? A burglar?

Brooks roused himself from his sentry duty. He crossed the street and cautiously crept toward the side of the house. Fear that Ellen and Marisa needed help spurred him on.

The little dog barked louder.

A carpetbag narrowly missed Brooks's head and landed at his feet. He looked up, scanning the trellis with his eyes. About midway up a small bit of white cloth and lace caught his attention.

A scrap of a woman's petticoat.

He tilted his head and looked higher. Brooks had to stifle a moan of lust when a familiar feminine backside appeared over the railing.

The voluminous, yellow-plaid skirt billowed around her legs like the pennant on a sailing vessel each time the wind caught it. From his vantage point beneath her, Brooks had a clear view of her legs, petticoats, lace-trimmed drawers and sweet round bottom.

It was a tantalizing sight.

Each time she moved, the fine lawn pulled tight across her fanny in a most seductive way. He folded his arms across his chest and stared while a pleased and lecherous smile broke out beneath his mustache. Images of what he would like to do with that firm derriere burned in his mind.

Marisa cursed silently as her skirt caught on one of the iron crossbars. She did not wish to wake Ellen, who had finally dozed off with a smile on her face. Marisa did not want to erase what had taken an hour to put there.

She looped her arm through the trellis, allowing her weight to hang on her bent elbow while she tugged the fabric free. When she was released and able to move again, a thorn poked her hand. She looked at her palm and discovered the thorn had broken off inside. It stung like liquid fire, and blood began to pool in her palm. While she was looking at the spot the trellis seemed to shiver beneath her weight.

"Silly, it's only your imagination," she chided herself. The strange shudder came again, and even though she assured herself that she was not frightened, she ignored the thorn and started to climb down as fast as she could manage.

Brooks grinned at the view above his head. A warm breeze caught the plaid skirt again. It fluttered out and filled with air like a sail. He was not a green youth who had never seen a woman's body before, but the sight of Marisa's firm bottom, encased in those fine white drawers, made him feel like a virgin glimpsing the female form for the first time.

She was coming closer.

In fact, she was near enough for him to make out the details of embroidery on the edge of her petticoat ruffles. He thought about letting her know he was there.

But he didn't.

He just stood and stared up her dress like a Peeping

Tom, while a sensation like warmed honey poured over him and moved through his veins.

Her toe snagged on a cluster of heavy blossoms. She jiggled her leg to free herself, causing her backside to flex and quiver in a most provocative and enchanting way.

Damn, I would like to make her quiver like that.

His appreciative grin widened beneath his mustache. She had a finely shaped backside. Of course, he already knew that about Missy O'Bannion. He had watched it encased in trousers, emphasized by leather chaps on more than one occasion on the Circle B. But this was different.

He was different.

Until now he had never allowed himself to really comprehend the sheer perfection of her form as a woman. Perhaps it was simply the novelty of seeing her in women's clothing that made all the difference. Or perhaps it was the absurdity of seeing that most feminine body climbing a trellis like a tomboy.

Or maybe Cyril was right.

Whatever it was, the impact of watching her now was akin to being punched in the belly by a strong right hook. A sense of wonder swept over Brooks as he inventoried each and every asset she possessed. Her legs were incredibly long for someone so delicate. Each time she placed her foot on another rung and lowered herself downward, the supple muscles of her thighs moved in a way that made his own body quicken. Yes, a rock-hard fist had been planted in the middle of his gut while he watched, and other parts of him were growing rock hard, too.

Cyril's words came drifting through his consciousness. *Anybody can see you are in love with Marisa O'Bannion.* Brooks shook his head at the notion.

He wasn't in love. Damn it, he couldn't be. He wanted to remain footloose and free to enjoy himself. He would

know when he fell in love. It would take his breath away
and rob him of sleep, and he wouldn't know which end
of the world was up.

No, he would know when love struck him, and he
wouldn't need a dandy like Cyril-the-smooth-talker to tell
him so.

Brooks might not be in love, but he sure as hell was
enjoying the sight of Marisa O'Bannion's womanly form
above him. She was a beautiful work of art on display,
and he fully appreciated the exhibition she was inadver-
tently giving him.

The harsh sound of grating metal intruded on his plea-
surable thoughts. He watched as the trellis suddenly
started to lurch and jerk.

She tightened her grip on the bar. Then one metal
bracket squealed as a thing alive. Brooks watched in horror as it pulled loose from the ancient and crumbling ma-
sonry around the window frame.

Marisa was only halfway down the trellis. It was too
far to jump and too far for him to be able to reach her.

The one rusty bracket that remained in place cracked
with a snap. With a kind of disjointed slowness the top
part of the heavy iron trellis broke free. Fragrant blossoms
rained down on Brooks's head while the old iron buckled
under the strain. The hot flow of lust ebbed and was replaced by the cold reality of fear. The bush and its support
swayed away from the solid security of the house, pro-
pelled by the weight of Marisa's delicate body.

She was going to fall.

Chapter Eleven

Brooks allowed himself one second to scan Leland's flower bed and size up her chances. The drop was not extreme, but when the mansion was built Leland had hired skilled masons to install thick paving stones around it, with borders of jagged rocks to protect his prized rose beds. The serrated edges of Vermont granite would rip and tear Marisa's tender flesh.

She'll be killed or maimed.

Her smooth-bottomed shoes slipped off the crossbars that supported her and she gave a muffled cry. As he watched, feeling more helpless than he could imagine, she lost her grip on the iron crossbar.

As if in a hellish nightmare she fell like a wounded sparrow that could no longer fly. Her yellow-plaid skirt fluttered and flapped like broken wings.

His heart lurched to his throat and he was consumed by utter desperation.

Marisa landed against a chest so strong and hard the impact drove the air from her lungs in one mighty swoosh. Black stars danced before her eyes as she struggled to remain conscious. She sagged weakly against the muscular chest of her rescuer, trying to drag air into her lungs, while relief folded over her like cotton batting.

"Dear Lord, Marisa, are you hurt?" Brooks's voice roused her from her stunned lethargy.

She drew several ragged breaths into her body and forced herself to focus. Sure enough, it was Brooks who cradled her in his arms.

"What—what are…you doin' here? I mean *doing* here?" She corrected her faulty speech, feeling a mixture of gratitude, amazement and stubborn disbelief.

One dark brow rose over his cerulean eyes. "Saving your life?" His mustache twitched above the cocky grin, and she couldn't decide if she wanted to slap him, or kiss him until she was senseless.

Her breathing had returned to normal, but strange prickling sensations of heat danced along the backs of her thighs and spine, where his arms supported her. He held her close enough for her to count the auburn hairs scattered throughout his black mustache.

Too close. Not close enough.

"No. I mean what are you doing here, at Ellen's?" She willed herself to stop studying his face, noticing the craggy strength of each line and angle.

"The question is what are *you* doing climbing the trellis like a second-story burglar?" His voice held a trace of teasing mockery, but his gaze roamed over her face in an intimate way that made the air catch in the back of her throat. She fancied she could actually feel the touch of his probing gaze.

It was hot and strong and she wanted more of it.

"Well, Marisa?" Brooks's arms contracted and her body shivered in response. "What in God's good name were you doing up there?"

"I came to visit Ellen."

A muscle beside his eye flinched. "Most guests use the front door."

"I probably would've done the same, except I wasn't exactly invited," she admitted. "You know that Leland has forbidden me to see Ellen." Her voice cracked and her bottom lip quivered.

"And we have told you that he will come around. He is only worried about Ellen and looking for someone to blame."

"I didn't want to wait any longer to see if he changed his mind."

"So you decided to climb the trellis and break your pretty little neck in Leland's rose garden. That seems like an extreme form of revenge, even for you, Marisa." He gave her a lopsided smile.

"I didn't plan to fall," she snapped, but the realization that he had called her pretty took some of the sting from his words. "Don't tease me, Brooks, not now." She squirmed, thinking he would release her, spare her further humiliation. "I can't take your teasing today. Now let me down."

He didn't.

"I apologize for teasing you." He gave her a wide, warm smile.

Her heart missed a beat.

"It is just that you scared the hell out of me, honey."

Honey?

The word battered her defenses. Her thoughts scattered and blew away like dried leaves in a strong wind. She fought to master her reaction. "I got in just fine." She looked away from his face, hoping that would clear the heat from her veins. "I didn't know the old trellis was going to break."

"I should speak to Leland about it. Lord knows it is

almost criminal the way he has let the trellis into his daughter's balcony fall into disrepair." Brooks grinned. "What if some gallant young suitor should want to climb into her bedroom? Downright neglectful. I will speak to him immediately."

"You're teasing me again," she noted as her gaze returned to his too-handsome face.

"I am just relieved that you are not hurt." His eyes flicked over her face once more, and a sensation like a silken ribbon being trailed along her skin remained. "I don't know what I would've done if you'd been hurt."

"You almost sound as if you care." She squirmed again, but regretted it immediately. As she moved, her breast nudged against his chest. Marisa did not move again.

"What on earth am I going to do about you?" Brooks sighed, and she felt the edge of desperation in his question.

"What do you want to do about me?" she whispered.

He glanced at her with a hard, assessing expression on his face, but then smiled tenderly.

"Stop being nice to me or you will make me cry," she warned.

"You are reckless beyond belief, Missy."

"I am not." She knew he was telling the truth, but for some reason she had to disagree—had to keep fighting him.

"Yes, you are." He inhaled deeply and looked at her for a moment. "And you are driving me to distraction. I can't sleep, I can't think straight. I believe I will have to marry you to keep you out of trouble."

Then he lowered his head and kissed her.

The last thing Marisa expected was for Brooks to kiss her. But the surprise didn't stop there. She had wantonly wrapped one hand around his strong shoulder, while the other palm kneaded the column of his neck. It felt so natural to be locked in his embrace. She opened her lips to draw in a tiny sigh of satisfaction. Yes, this kiss was the last thing she'd expected, but it was wonderful and exciting. A flock of butterflies winged their way through her middle, and she managed to keep the nagging question of his fiancée pushed to the back of her mind.

Brooks couldn't stop kissing her—or maybe he was afraid if he did they would go back to the same old silly bickering. Whatever the reason, he held her tight as if to reassure himself that she was solid and not some nymph he had conjured from thin air. He nibbled her bottom lip and told himself to let her go, but he was no more able to do it now than he had been able to let her fall.

Her firm breasts nudged against him as she nuzzled his jaw and returned his ardor. That warm contact sent his temperature soaring two degrees. He grew bolder, pushing his tongue between her teeth. She stiffened and drew back a wee bit at the invasion, but it was more an act of astonishment than protest. Slowly, deliberately, he traced the inside of her mouth, committing every delicate impression to memory.

Sugar cookies and lemon tea.

He inhaled deeply, struggling to stop his pulse from racing.

She smells like summer sunshine.

Her flavor and scent made a heady combination, innocent and sensual, demure and yet wild as the territory that had spawned her.

His heart was beating inside his chest like a marching band's drum at the Founder's Day parade. He had understood that breathless, heart-pounding reaction when he thought she was falling. But now she was safe in his arms.

Yes, sweet Marisa was safe, but his heart was in great jeopardy. Desire thundered through every fiber of his being like a locomotive gaining momentum on a steep, downhill grade. His body warmed and tightened in an age-old way as she responded to him.

She moaned softly.

He could no longer ignore the truth. He wanted her so badly he hurt.

Wanting is not loving. He recalled Clell's words.

He pulled away and looked into her dark eyes. They were cloudy, like coal smoke filtered through thin winter clouds. Her soft lips were moist and becomingly pink.

Her body had answered him in a way that confused him. How could they want each other when they didn't even get along? Hell, most of the time they didn't even like each other.

"Put me down now, Brooks." She blinked several times, as if waking from a dream.

He obeyed her order, placed her on her feet and told himself it had been a momentary lapse of control but nothing more. It had been the passion of saving her life. He had just been swept away in the excitement and urgency of the moment. But the more he tried to convince himself of it, the more a nagging fear that something momentous had happened nudged at his consciousness. It was not an emotion he could easily explain.

"I'll take you home." He put his palm at the small of her back. A hot sensation sizzled through him. He jerked his hand away and stared at it, but it looked unchanged. Whatever had made his knees go weak and had clouded his judgment was not going to be found in his rough and callused palm, but perhaps within the dark, smoky eyes of Marisa O'Bannion.

Marisa squeezed herself back against the leather squabs of the carriage seat. Each turn and sway brought her knees brushing against Brooks's legs as he sat in the seat across from her. The innocent contact made her middle twist.

He is engaged.

What could she have been thinking of? She wasn't thinking, that was the problem. She had simply responded to his kiss. But that kind of behavior was unforgivable here in the city—Ellen had said so.

She sighed and promised herself that it wouldn't happen again. Just when she was learning to ward off his taunts and silent disapproval, he had found a new way to baffle her.

Like save your life and then kiss you? a voice inside her head quizzed.

All right, so he had saved her from harm, but why did he have to go and kiss her?

She watched him from under the protective fringe of her lashes and thought about her talk with Ellen. For the first time she had openly broached the subject of Violet Ashland, but Ellen had been little help. All she could tell Marisa was that yes, Brooks had given Violet a ring shortly before he'd left for the Territory. And that scandal could taint the family name.

His kiss had curled up her toes. The simple touching of lips had made her heart beat so hard that for a moment she'd thought she might die from the sheer physical pleasure. It had been more potent than the night he'd come into her room. He kissed her in a way that made her soft and vulnerable.

And then he had simply stopped kissing her and had

turned cold. She lowered her head and sneaked another glance at him. Had he suddenly remembered Violet? Had he recalled his promise?

Marisa was careful not to look straight at him, but she needn't have worried about him noticing her scrutiny: his eyes were fixed unblinkingly on something outside the carriage window.

She doubted he was even aware she was there. A cold chill swept over body. That kiss had addled her brain and turned her blood to liquid fire, but it hadn't done the same thing to him.

Because he loves Violet.

Damn him, she thought with entirely too much zeal. *Damn, damn, damn him.*

Why did he do it? Why had he given her that bone-melting kiss if it meant nothing? He had a goll-darn lot of nerve to kiss her like *that* and then sit and stare out the window!

She didn't mean a thing to him.

He was as unpredictable as a rattler shedding its skin. She turned to stare out her own window, refusing to give him any more notice at all, determined to make that damn kiss as insignificant to herself as it was to him—determined to make it the last.

Brooks knew the moment Marisa turned away and quit watching him. No, that wasn't actually right; he *felt* her stop looking at him. It was like the caress of spring sunshine being replaced by a bitterly cold winter wind when her sly gaze left him.

What in hell have I done? he asked himself for the twentieth time. How could he have allowed his control to slip like that? This was *Missy,* for God's sake. No matter what her real name was, no matter how she had altered

her appearance, she was Bellami's sister-in-law. Trace's
baby sister.

Had he lost his mind? Probably. Certainly while he held
her in his arms he was beyond rational thought.

The memory of Cyril's voice drifted through his head.
A muscle in his jaw twitched in response.

He couldn't allow himself to be in love with Marisa
until the sordid situation was resolved with Violet.

And he could not do that until the negotiations were
complete. Only then would he be prepared to bring scandal crashing down on his family.

As soon as the carriage arrived at the brownstone, Marisa pleaded a headache and escaped to the privacy of her
room. She could not look at Brooks and she could not
face his family with the guilt of what she had done burning in her mind.

But the afternoon wore on slowly as the memory of the
kiss lingered. Then later, as the moon rose and made its
arc across the sky, she still tossed and turned in the lovely
canopied bed.

She told herself that kisses didn't mean a thing—not to
him—and therefore she couldn't allow them to mean anything to her. But if that was true why did she tingle from
head to foot each time she thought about him? And why
did her eyes burn with unshed tears?

Marisa was awake to see the first gray streaks of dawn.
She forced herself to remain in her room until she heard
the sounds of Tilly moving about downstairs, preparing
breakfast and opening the house for the day.

Marisa dressed in a simple green twill sprinkled with
tiny bouquets of white flowers bound with lavender ribbons. Then she spent extra time coiling her hair and twist-

ing it into a chignon, which she covered with a finely woven white net.

By the time she opened her door and stepped out into the hallway, she was in control, determined to act and feel the same as she had before. But when she neared Brooks's room a combination of dread and hope surged through her. She paused, fingers frozen on the banister, staring at his closed door.

"Oh damnation, what do I care if I see him?" she asked herself sharply. "I don't. I don't care one whit."

With more confidence and indifference than she really felt, she lifted her chin a notch and marched downstairs.

"Marisa? Is that you, child? Come in here, dear, and have breakfast with me." Patricia greeted her from the dining room table as soon as Marisa appeared at the foot of the stairs.

Marisa refused to allow herself to be in a bad mood when the glory of spring was beaming through the windows. Patricia was in her customary morning attire of a colorful silk wrapper, with her ribbon-tied hair trailing down her back. Watermarked stationery lay near a half-full cup of coffee.

"You are up early," Marisa remarked.

"A message came this morning. I am surprised you didn't hear all the commotion. Donovan and Rod have been summoned to Chicago." She sighed and sipped her coffee.

"Not bad news, I hope." Marisa frowned as she laced her coffee with cream and sugar.

Had Brooks gone to Chicago also? Was he still upstairs? Would he walk through the door and join them? Questions filled her head until Patricia's voice drew her attention.

"It is a small problem with the shipping business. Donovan has been working on some sort of merger. He never tells me anything, but I think there has been some sort of crisis. He rarely discusses these things with me because he thinks I will worry too much.'' She smiled indulgently. ''I do miss him, but I know how much he enjoys the world of business. The only thing I regret is that they will both miss the party tonight.''

''Party?'' Marisa gulped down a swallow of hot coffee. She searched her mind while Patricia continued talking.

''The fund-raiser for St. Michael's Hospital is this evening.''

How could I have forgotten? Marisa chided herself, knowing that this fund-raiser was the social event of the season, according to Ellen.

''Oh, yes, Ellen insisted that my dress for tonight be very special,'' she said, but the idea that she would go without her friend made her sad once more. ''Since Ellen is ill, I don't know if I will go....''

Patricia's head snapped up. ''What? Of course you will go. We both will attend. I refuse to let a little thing like Donovan's absence prevent it. And put your mind to rest. I have it on good authority Ellen was so much improved yesterday afternoon that Leland has finally relented and will let her go. He was very puzzled by the abrupt change in her health, but he has agreed to let her resume a normal social schedule as long as she is careful.''

The memory of falling from Ellen's balcony made Marisa shiver.

''Are you feeling all right, my dear? Are you cold?'' Patricia reached out and softly touched the back of Marisa's hand. ''You are not coming down the with the ague, are you?''

''I'm fine,'' Marisa assured her. ''Just a little chill.''

"Good, I am glad to hear it, because I have a special favor to ask of you."

"Of course, anything." Marisa took another sip of her coffee, then replaced the cup in its saucer. She was grateful for anything that would keep her busy and her thoughts away from Brooks.

Patricia wrote as she spoke. "I need you to take a message to Brooks."

Marisa's stomach lurched. The coffee threatened to come back up. "Brooks?" His name was a strangled sound on her lips.

"He evidently left the house before Donovan got the message and could speak to him. Rod was very reluctant to tell me where he was, but I managed to pry it out of him before he and Donovan left." Her grin was quite triumphant. "I don't know why he made such an issue over Brooks taking his exercise at the gentlemen's club." She looked at Marisa and frowned. "Sometimes my sons are very odd." Then she smiled as if she had dismissed the thought. "I need you to take a message to him for me." Patricia scrawled something more on the piece of stationery, then folded it and slipped it inside an envelope.

"I'll have the carriage brought round when you're ready." She handed the envelope to Marisa and smiled. "And if you can, dear, persuade him to come back with you. I really must speak to him."

Marisa stared at the envelope as if it were alive. Her stomach had balled up.

"I know you two haven't been getting along all that well, Marisa, but this is rather important to me."

"I'd be happy to do it," Marisa lied with a smile on her face. And it was, after all, only half a lie, because some deep, hungry part of her longed to see Brooks, to recapture the tumultuous sensation of that kiss, even though it was madness. Strange hidden longings had bubbled to the surface.

She pushed herself up from the table. Each time she thought of seeing Brooks her middle did a series of flip-flops like a catfish in shallow water.

Marisa felt like she must be some sort of polecat by the way men stared at her when she walked through the main lobby of the gentlemen's club. The scents of bay rum, brandy and tobacco smoke hung in the air as several sets of eyes followed her progress. One elderly man, bald as an egg, looked up from his paper. She nodded and gave him what she hoped was a proper smile while she felt eyes scrutinizing her from the top of her hat to the curve of her bustle.

"Excuse me, I am looking—" she began.

"Yes, I know what you are looking for," he said knowingly. He laid the paper in his lap and graced her with a grin that showed a set of gleaming gold teeth.

"You do?" Marisa frowned.

"You are not the first one to come *looking* this morning." He cackled.

"Not the first one?" she repeated dumbly. Were other women looking for Brooks?

Violet Ashland.

An unexpected jolt of possessiveness ripped through Marisa. She had to stop this, had to get a rein on her emotions. Damn it, he was *engaged*.

"Just go straight down the corridor and turn left. There are chairs set up." He chuckled again. "And enjoy yourself." He lifted his paper and went back to reading.

Marisa stood there for a moment, puzzled over his bizarre statement until she felt her flesh crawling under the steady stares of the other men. The old gentleman had said he knew who she was looking for. Perhaps Patricia had sent word that she was coming to find Brooks. Yes, that had to be it. Marisa put the matter out of her mind and turned away, leaving the man to his reading while she felt eyes watch her bustle sway down the corridor.

Her heels clicked on the diamond-shaped patterns of lustrous gray-and-white marble, the sound echoing sharply off the polished stone walls. A bright shaft of light from a set of double doors on the left bisected the hallway. She turned and went through them, surprised to find herself in a room of enormous proportions.

A square platform constructed of padded canvas had been roped off in the center of the room. Rows of chairs were positioned around it, and young women of every size and shape were observing the pair of men standing inside the roped-off space. Marisa scanned the group until she was sure that Violet Ashland wasn't there.

Something like relief washed over her. But she shook off the silly notion and tilted her head to watch what the other women were watching.

The men in the ring shook hands. But from that moment on things seemed to get stranger and stranger. The men started bouncing around like Mexican jumping beans on a hot August morning while they punched each other in the face.

Marisa had never seen anything like it. She had witnessed plenty of fistfights, both the sober, serious kind and the drunken, foolish kind, but she had never watched anything like these two galoots.

They just stood there toe-to-toe and traded punches. Having four brothers in the family had insured at least two donnybrooks a month, but never in Marisa's born days had men pranced around in their long underwear like a couple of banty roosters while women oohed and aahed.

New York City was a mighty odd place.

One of the men landed a haymaker that made her unconsciously wince. His adversary staggered backward until the rope halted his momentum. The hemp rope hummed with the impact of his hard, muscled body.

The dark-haired man who had been hit in the face sagged against the ropes. "I suppose you think that makes us even?"

Brooks.

His voice sent shivers skipping over her arms and down her spine.

"Hardly even, but it is a start."

Cyril.

Marisa mentally cursed and turned away from the spectacle. The two fools had lost their damned minds!

Chapter Twelve

A flash of movement caught Brooks's eye as he laughed and pushed himself off the rope.

Marisa.

She disappeared out the door in a blur of green fabric and a flash of white petticoats. He felt a tug on his heart that shocked him.

"Uh-oh, it looks as if we have been caught in the act," Cyril said cheerfully. "Of course, I am not the one in love with the dark-haired vixen, so…"

"Oh, shut up, Cyril." Brooks vaulted out of the ring and grabbed a towel. "And for God's sake, stop saying that." He rushed past the surprised female spectators, their murmurs of embarrassment and appreciation humming in his ears. By the time he reached the hallway Marisa had covered a considerable distance.

Luckily for him, she had lost her direction. She was practically running toward the wrong end of the corridor. He knew the moment she realized her mistake. She abruptly halted and drew her shoulders taut. Her bustle jiggled as she pulled herself up and inhaled.

Brooks could almost hear the string of epithets bubbling in the back of her throat.

"Did you lose your way?" he asked in a voice that was too sweet to be sincere.

She turned and glared at him with all the fury of an Atlantic squall. There was no other way to exit the building than for her to pass him, and it was evident that was the last thing she wanted to do.

He grinned, waiting for her to admit that fact to herself. As he watched, she lifted her chin a notch and stiffened like a captured hare, but she did not move toward him.

All right, my stubborn, little spitfire. I will come to you. This time.

She held her ground while he strode toward her. Each step narrowed the distance and intensified the tension between them. He looped the towel around his neck, trying his damnedest to ignore the lovely contour of her jaw and smooth column of her graceful neck where her pulse beat under skin softer than the finest French silk.

He stopped two feet away from her just to get his own pulse under control. The nearness of her delectable body was like iron striking stone. Sparks of emotion flew off in all directions, burning him as they slid by. He fought two impulses—one to turn tail and run, the other to take her in his arms.

"Why are you here? Did Rod tell you where I went?" He was going to wring his big brother's neck—

"No."

Now his curiosity was really pricked. That tempestuous look in her eyes did something nearly fatal to his insides. He started to grow hot and rock hard. He felt like a warrior preparing to take his deathblow, his veins pumping with blood lust. Well, lust anyway.

He took another step closer, feeling as if he was stalking his quarry.

But what will you do if you catch her?

"Alone? You came here alone? Are you looking for me?" Out of his vanity he secretly wished that were true, but he suspected something different. "Or Cyril?"

The urge to kiss her crept into his mind. He fought the desire by digging his fingers deeply into the thick ends of the towel looped around his neck, all the while praying she would not drop her eyes to his crotch and see the evidence of his arousal beneath the thin fabric.

"I was looking for you." The admission seemed to cause her physical pain.

"Oh." Something hot and liquid filled his middle. "Why?"

He moved closer.

"I came to deliver a message."

She backed up tight against the stone wall.

Trapped.

Her eyes flicked over his chest and left a trail of goose-flesh in their wake. He wished she would stop looking at him like that.

No. He wished she would never stop looking at him like that. Hell, he didn't know what he wished anymore, he realized as he gazed into her hypnotic dark eyes.

"Brooks?" Her voice drew his gaze to her outstretched hand. There, within the grip of her very ladylike gloves, was a small white envelope.

He tried to subdue the impulse to grab her hand and pull her to his chest.

He finally snatched the envelope.

"Who recruited you to be a messenger?" He wished he could diffuse the electrically charged mood surrounding him.

"Your mother." Marisa took a certain amount of pleasure when his brows arched in surprise. His blue eyes were alive with energy and...

Desire?

She could not help but notice the sweat-dampened ten-drils of dark hair curling at his temples.

"A message from Mother?" He unfolded the flap and read the card. One side of his mouth tilted upward. "This sounds ominous. What does she want to talk to me about?"

"I have no idea." Marisa's gaze meandered over the breadth of his shoulders, lingering on the pale jagged scar he had earned by saving her life the first time.

"It healed pretty well, don't you think?" he asked abruptly.

Her eyes snapped up to his face. "What?" Her voice was too breathy, too *interested.*

"The scar. Hugh did a fine job of stitching me up."

She realized with a start he had seen her staring at the scar...

And the deep corded muscles of his upper arms...

And his bare torso...

And every inch of his exposed flesh.

Dear Lord.

Heat flooded her cheeks and she fought for some sem-blance of control. "Yes, Pa has a real nice hand with a needle." Her voice cracked; her throat burned. She wished her jaunty bonnet had a veil so she might draw it over her face and prevent people from seeing her, as Bel-lami had done.

"Your eye is beginning to swell." Her fingers came up automatically, and before she had time to stop herself, her gloved fingers gingerly touched him.

The flesh above his cheekbone could have been branded, the sensation was so searing.

He flinched.

She drew her hand back as if she had been struck.

She wanted to stop the fluttering inside her belly. She didn't like the strange tension that lay between them.

"Why have you and Cyril been fighting?" She hoped his answer would relieve the awful, hungry ache she felt each time she looked at his body.

Brooks's mustache twitched, while his eyes narrowed slightly.

"I am not stupid, Brooks. This is not the first time," she challenged. "First Cyril had a shiner and you had barked knuckles…" She pinned him with a smug gaze.

"Boxing, exercise. Nothing more," he lied.

What would her lips taste like today? Would they be flavored with sugar cookies and lemon tea?

"I see," she murmured.

He studied her face and wished her hair were free of the white netting. He could almost feel the weight of the dark locks between his fingers as he imagined unpinning her chignon.

His belly began to tie itself into a tight knot. "What if I told you that we had been fighting over you? Tell me, Marisa." He stared down at her. "What would you say if I told you we were doing battle to see which one of us would propose marriage to you?" His voice was a husky purr of sensuality.

Her eyes widened. Brooks took a step closer. She wanted to retreat farther, but her back was against the cold wall of polished stone.

She could not run away.

He closed the last tiny space between them and placed his hands on either side of her shoulders, trapping her within the circle of his bare arms. He inhaled deeply, drinking in the light floral scent she was wearing. Heat emanated from her body and warmed his arms, his chest, his heart.

She was so lovely, so feminine.

"What would you say?" He pressed his body against hers and saw her eyes grow wide when she felt the heat and bulk of his arousal.

"I would say that one of you had better remember that he already has a fiancée." She tried to return Brooks's gaze, but the sultry expression in his eyes was too much for her to withstand. To her mortification, she found her glance sliding away from his.

He wanted her to look at him again so he could study the gold flecks around her dark irises. "What if I told you all that nonsense about Violet Ashland being my fiancée is a lie?"

Marisa's eyes snapped back to his face and held. "I would...I would have to hear it said in her presence."

Was it a lie?

"Can't you trust me? If I say it is a lie, can't you believe me?"

"No." In a lightning-quick movement, she ducked beneath his arm. He was left holding nothing but air.

He turned to her while the delicious warmth of her body faded away. "Why, Marisa? Why can't you trust me?" He stared at her rigid back. She was breathing heavily, even more raggedly than he was.

"Because I want to believe it too much to trust you, or myself." She spoke without ever turning around. Then she started walking as fast as she could toward the exit.

Chapter Thirteen

He stood there watching her. Missy, Marisa…he knew her in many guises, but somehow this woman who fled from him was a tantalizing stranger. She was a delicious mystery he yearned to solve. At that moment he laughed aloud at the irony.

He was in love with Marisa O'Bannion. The Territorial wildcat had come all the way to New York before he admitted it.

He could deny it until Judgment Day and it wouldn't change a thing. Cyril had been right; Rod had been right.

So Brooks needed to settle things with Violet Ashland so he could start convincing Marisa.

The ride to the telegraph office seemed to take forever, but once Brooks sent the message to Rod a strange sort of calm settled over him.

Now that he had finally decided on a course of action, the whole world looked different. He was going to court Marisa O'Bannion—court her, woo her and win her. And he was going to start as soon as he had taken care of the rumors Violet had so artfully kept circulating through New York society.

He still had not figured out what her game was, but tonight at the charity drive he intended to find out.

Marisa fumbled with the ribbons on her chemise, trying for the third time to make a bow. She didn't want to admit the episode with Brooks at the gentlemen's club had affected her, but she felt so odd, she couldn't quite put the disturbing incident out of her mind.

There had been a moment when he had trapped her against that wall that her heart had leaped at just being near him. She had smelled the manly musk of his body and something akin to lightning had seared the innermost parts of her soul. She had noticed the color of his eyes, the tilt of his brow, all the things that made Brooks James.

At that moment she would've given him anything—her body, her soul...her love.

"I am a silly fool," she told her reflection. Marisa had become a moonstruck fool since she came to New York. After all, Brooks James was a charmer. He had broken more hearts than could be counted, if half of what Ellen told her was true. And he had never actually said that he was not engaged to Violet Ashland.

She stared into her own eyes.

He had asked her to trust him, but what did that mean?

How could she trust him when she couldn't even trust herself to do the right thing? When he was near her she felt like a drunken idiot, incapable of rational thought, unable to keep her own code of honor.

"Damn it," she swore. "Damn him."

It rubbed against her O'Bannion grain to admit that he had gotten to her. "I won't let it happen again. I won't become a simpering fool and be a party to him betraying another woman's heart."

She picked up the emerald green, taffeta moiré gown

and shook out the wrinkles in the underskirt. It weighed nearly ten pounds. Ten pounds of glistening elegance that Ellen promised would win her every man's attention.

With a sigh, Marisa started at the bottom, gathering yards of material and lace into her hands until she had cleared an opening for her head. It took some squirming, but finally the gown settled over her shoulders. The weight of the full skirt pulled the rest of it down around her hips with a heavy swish.

At least, she reasoned, by attending the party with Patricia, she would be spared any further teasing from Brooks tonight. He would not dare to take liberties in front of his mother.

With that thought to comfort her she brushed her hair and waited for Tilly to arrive and help her with the hundred other details of her grooming that were still a partial mystery. Marisa tried to clear her mind of Brooks and think only of the party. She was determined to look her best and act the part, even if she had never felt less like doing so.

An hour later Tilly was still fussing over each ruffle and bit of lace at the bottom of the full skirt.

"Oh, dear, it is almost time to go," Marisa whispered breathlessly. She had managed to subdue thoughts of Brooks and replace them with the happy prospect of seeing Ellen. In fact, she had silently vowed to steer clear of all men this evening—Brooks, Cyril and anybody else in trousers. She resolved to find a quiet corner where she and Ellen could spend the evening talking about something besides men.

Maybe if Leland saw her keeping Ellen quiet he would soften his attitude toward her and lift his ban on her visiting.

It was something to look forward to.

"Yes?" Marisa called, when she heard a knock on her door.

"Are you ready, dear?" Patricia peeked inside. The gaslight reflected off her snowy curls and the diamonds at her throat and ears. She looked cool and richly elegant in her plum-colored satin gown.

"Patricia, you are just beautiful," Marisa exclaimed sincerely.

"Thank you, dear. And you—there is a certain glow about you…" she said as she stepped inside. "You have been seeing a lot of young Cyril." Patricia's brows rose. "Could it be that love has brought a maidenly flush to your cheeks?"

"I don't think so, Patricia," Marisa murmured. She turned away and busied herself in front of the mirror.

Did she look different? Was she in…love?

Marisa banished the notion from her mind and focused on her gown. "My Pa would have a fit of apoplexy if he saw me in a dress this low," she mumbled. The green taffeta moiré shimmered like the head of a mallard drake in the morning light, just barely covering enough of her chest for modesty and to keep the top from falling down.

Patricia laughed. "Well, fortunately your father will be spared apoplexy." She smoothed one wayward curl at Marisa's temple. "We'd better go or we will be too late to be considered fashionable."

Marisa gathered her pale green, elbow-length gloves and followed Patricia downstairs. She stopped and looked in the downstairs mirror, still wondering if there was something different about the way she looked. An errant curl required her attention and she was busy with it when Brooks appeared behind her.

Marisa's heart leaped to her throat.

He was dressed in a black tuxedo. The shiny points of

jet studs dotted the front of the ermine white shirt. The sharp, clean lines of his form-fitting coat emphasized the width of his shoulders. In his hand he carried a cane and a tall black hat. A cape was draped over one arm.

She whirled around to face him.

He stared at her, unblinking, while she studied his face. His left eye was a little swollen and discolored from the morning with Cyril, but he still wore the ruddy glow of the Territory. Rather than detracting from his looks, the black eye only made him look more manly, more dangerous and more irresistible than ever.

He was every inch the dashing New York gentleman Marisa had always imagined him to be. And as she stared at him she began to feel as attractive as a mud hen and as restless as the wind that blew over the Circle B. How could she ignore him? How could she not?

"You look magnificent," Brooks said.

Patricia appeared and Brooks turned to her, but Marisa continued to feel his attention focus on her from time to time. After compliments all round they were finally ready to go.

But abruptly Brooks halted at the door and turned once more to his mother. His face was pinched into a frown. "Marisa certainly cannot go out in that condition."

"Brooks!" Patricia's eyes widened in shock. "How can you say such a thing?"

Marisa's heart fell to her feet. She lifted her chin to hide her pain as she stared into his cool blue eyes. If he started teasing her now she wasn't certain she could hold back the hot tears.

"I am surprised you did not see the difficulty." His eyes roamed over Marisa's body, savoring each curve, each valley and plane of her form as he played out the silly charade. For a moment he nearly lost courage, but he knew she would never accept anything from him if he gave it to her in the usual fashion.

Patricia turned and allowed her eyes to skim over Marisa. "I cannot for the life of me see what you mean...." She looked at Brooks, obviously puzzled and flustered.

"She is practically *naked*." His eyes focused on her cleavage and he felt his loins tighten in that familiar way.

"Brooks!" Patricia gasped.

Marisa's bottom lip quivered.

He kept a straight face while he pulled a long, slender, navy blue box from the folds of his cape. "But I have the remedy right here." He opened the box with a pop and drew out a string of lightning.

"Turn around, Marisa." The sound of his husky demand made her stomach fall.

How could she refuse him anything?

His bare fingers grazed her collarbone, leaving a trail of molten heat that was immediately replaced by the chill of metal and cool glittering stones.

She stared into the mirror, unable to speak, unable to do more than swallow a hard lump.

The mirror revealed a delicate row of emeralds and diamonds resting against her flesh. Brooks leaned close enough for her to feel the whisper of his breath across her earlobe as he fastened the clasp. "Trust me," he murmured so only she could hear.

"Now she is ready to go out, Mother," he said to Patricia when he stood up straight.

"Brooks, that is absolutely stunning!" Patricia gasped. "And what a nice gesture." She gave her son a kiss on the cheek. "You can be so nice—when you want to be."

Marisa's gloved fingers skimmed along the shining stones. "I—I can't accept it. I can't take something like this from a man who isn't—" *free* "—isn't family."

"Nonsense. Weren't you the one who pointed out to Cyril that we were practically related?" One brow rose, and Brooks smiled. "I believe you compared us to cousins."

"Well, yes. But I—"

He held up his hand to silence her. "No buts. It looks lovely on you."

Marisa gazed at herself and Brooks behind her in the sheet of glass. "I don't know what to say."

"Don't say anything, not yet."

Patricia glanced at them in confusion, but then she shrugged. "We'd better go. It is getting late."

Brooks stifled his smile of satisfaction. He had once again terrified poor Tilly into telling him what color Marisa's gown was, then he had rushed to the jeweler in search of the necklace.

Now if fate was on his side, this would be the night when all the misunderstandings between them would be cleared away.

The trio traveled in relative silence. Patricia seemed preoccupied with her own thoughts and Marisa had been tongue-tied ever since Brooks had whispered in her ear.

Trust me.

Just the memory sent chills trailing over her neck and shoulders.

Within a quarter hour the carriage turned up a long torch-lit driveway. Brooks roused himself and gestured toward the sweeping lawn, which glowed from the moon, as well as from dozens of gaslights.

"John Preston must've spent half his fortune on this," Brooks remarked dryly.

Marisa swallowed hard. This was the biggest party she had attended since coming to New York. Her old fears about being a lady nipped at the corners of her mind, but she pushed them aside, determined to conquer her fear of inadequacy once and for all.

As the carriage rolled along the paving stones of the driveway she got a better look at the house beyond. Torches burned along the walk, bordering the edge of the spacious lawn all the way to imposing steps that were flanked by a pair of carved lions.

"I hope he has not squandered all his fortune." Patricia smiled. "I would like a bit of it for the hospital. And I intend to spend the evening persuading Mr. Preston to endow St. Michael's."

Brooks chuckled and shook his head. "I should've known there was a reason you insisted I come along. Do you think you will need reinforcements?"

Marisa's eyes darted to Patricia's face. The older woman lowered her lashes as if she might be a little embarrassed. "No, I do not. I want you to spend the evening with Marisa. It is rude for her to be unescorted." She turned her gaze upon Marisa. "I hope you don't mind, dear, but it is very important that the hospital receive some money."

Marisa would not allow herself to look at Brooks. But even as she thought it, her eyes met his.

A river of molten passion seemed to pass from one to the other in that gaze.

"I promise I won't leave her side for a single moment," Brooks said as his eyes raked over her hotly.

"I am so pleased you two are getting along better," Patricia said.

The moment her back was turned Brooks leaned across the carriage. "Do you hear that? I have my own mother's blessing."

* * *

True to his word, Brooks stayed at Marisa's side through the ritual of being received by the host and hostess. Ellen was escorted in by a stern-faced Leland, who made sure she went to the most comfortable-looking couch. He cast one dark gaze Marisa's way, and she knew her hope of talking all evening with Ellen was a hollow one. Leland had not softened his opinion of her, and now she was saddled with Brooks.

"Shall we dance?" Brooks whispered into her ear. He grasped her arm, just as he had at Trace's wedding, and then maneuvered her through a maze of couples. Before she knew what was happening his unyielding arm was at the small of her back, drawing her close to him. Then he tilted up her chin and looked deep into her eyes.

"Remember, I am good—put yourself in my hands."

As they started to spin out onto the floor, she wondered if he was talking about his dancing or some other ability....

During dance after dance Marisa stared at Brooks's face and tried to deny her feelings. A sensation, as if she were falling from a great height, much higher than Ellen's balcony, engulfed her. Just when she felt so dizzy she was unsure of her legs, he stopped and pulled her through a series of halls and doorways. Soon the noise and the crowd were far behind.

They stood in a quiet alcove where a fountain bubbled water from an urn held by a winged cherub. Plants of every variety surrounded them. Tall trees created a green canopy overhead. It was a magical place, peaceful and secluded.

Marisa let out a sigh of relief while calm settled over her. She looked up and found him watching her with a serious expression of speculation on his face.

"It is time we had a talk, Marisa," he said.

Her fingers kept straying to the necklace, while doubt and suspicion about why he had given it to her flitted in and out of her mind.

"It suits you," Brooks said in a voice that was smoother and more potent than Clell's aged whiskey.

Marisa stared at him, mesmerized by the liquid blue of his eyes. "Why did you do it?"

"Do what?" He cocked his head and squinted one eye. She wondered if his vision was impaired by the swelling of his other one.

"Agree to be my escort?" She cleared her throat, but the lump remained. "And give me this necklace?"

He took her hand and led her to a stone bench. It was secreted in a nook, surrounded by leafy plants and almost invisible. He pulled her down beside him, shoving the fullness of her skirt away so he could sit very, very close. She found herself staring at the strong muscles of his thigh as it nudged against her.

"Don't you understand, little spitfire, I would give you much more than that." He drew her near and covered her mouth with his lips, and suddenly Marisa knew with a sharp wrenching in her chest exactly what she wanted from Brooks James.

She wanted his heart. A heart that was pledged to another.

Chapter Fourteen

She smelled of gardenias and she tasted like...

Sugar cookies.

The thought made Brooks smile inwardly as he kissed her.

He was in love. Truly in love. Now all he had to do was win the object of his affection and quell the rumors that clung to him like dust to a cowboy's boots.

She pulled away and looked into his eyes. There was a wash of tears behind her obsidian orbs.

"Marisa? What is it?" Concern flowed through him.

"You are as crazy as a lovesick polecat." She sniffed.

"What?" Confusion raced through him. She had returned his kisses with the same passion he felt. "Why?"

"Why are you doin' this to me? You ain't—aren't—free. Why are you torturing me like this?" She jerked from his hold and smoothed a wayward curl with her palm. Her chin tilted up in the stubborn O'Bannion way that always signaled trouble.

"Yes, Brooks darling, tell us, why *are* you torturing her?" Violet Ashland stood staring at him with her cold eyes. "We both want to hear the answer to that one," she said as she walked toward them.

A strangled sound escaped Marisa's lips. She cast one last look full of hurt and longing toward Brooks, and then she stood and ran from the garden.

"Damn you, Violet!" Brooks stalked to her, murder in his heart as he grasped her upper arm. "What is your game?"

She shrugged and met his gaze, unblinking, unrepentant. "Sorry, Brooks, but it is necessary."

"Why? Why can't you just leave me alone?" He released her arm as if she were poisonous. "When you left with that English duke I thought I had seen the last of you." He turned away and dragged in a deep breath, determined to hold his temper in check, but the memory of Marisa's eyes burned his flesh like embers.

"And I intended to remain gone. Alas, the English bastard found a woman of comparable beauty and greater fortune." Violet spoke matter-of-factly.

Brooks whirled back to her. "You don't seriously think I will marry you!"

"Of course not. In due time I will be the one who changes her mind, as is a woman's prerogative. Until then you will continue to be my fiancé, to keep my pride, my reputation and my chances of making a proper match intact and unsullied."

"You're a liar and a bitch!"

"Because if you do not, I will wire Daddy and he will call a halt to the merger and your family will be ruined." She smiled at him, a cold expression full of wrath. "So now that we have all that settled, let's return to the party. And, Brooks, please, no more of this foolishness about that little country mouse. It just isn't seemly."

His arms dropped to his sides. Should he laugh in her face? Or should he snap her swanlike neck in his two hands? Brooks shook himself. "Do you really think that scandal could destroy my family?"

She shrugged. "Perhaps not, but even a delay would upset your parents. Do you want to take that chance?"

When Brooks saw Marisa standing alone by a darkened window, the wary, pained look in her eyes clawed at his heart. He wanted to hold her, to comfort her. He longed to tell her the truth, longed to take her in his arms, take her to his bed.

Forever.

With a jolt he realized that was what he truly wanted. He wanted forever with Marisa. He wanted to marry her.

He loved her, the prickly parts and the soft feminine parts as well. If only he were free to convince her of it.

By midnight Marisa felt as if she could no longer hold back the tears. She longed to speak to Ellen, to ask her advice about leaving tomorrow. But Leland stood like a sentry at his daughter's side, discouraging all but Cyril, who smiled at Ellen and ignored Leland's dark scowl.

At least her friend appeared happy. Ellen's clear tinkle of laughter reached Marisa's ears where she stood by a tall carved column. She blinked and realized she was near the front entry. She could slip away and nobody would be the wiser. Patricia was deep in conversation with a portly gentleman with thick chin whiskers, and Brooks...

Brooks stood straight and tall across the dance floor, with Violet clinging to his arm. Marisa glanced up and her breath caught in her throat. From where she stood it had almost appeared that Brooks was watching her. But that was just foolish fancy.

She turned and took a step toward the door, but ran smack into a young man in a tailored gray uniform. He touched the brim of his hat, apologized and went to the liveried butler. After a moment of conversation the butler pointed directly at Brooks. The young man nodded and made his way through the crowd to Brooks. Marisa watched while Brooks opened the cable he was handed.

A wide smile broke across his handsome face. She allowed her eyes to linger there, memorizing every aspect of that smile, while her heart bled.

Brooks held the paper in trembling hands and reread the message: "Merger finished. Father advises to do your worst." In Rod's usual terse style he had set his brother free.

Brooks tipped the delivery boy and turned to Violet. He whispered something in her ear. Marisa watched the blond beauty's face contort as if in a rage. She tried to move away from Brooks, but he clamped his hand on her arm.

Possessively?

With no regard for her lovely gown or the crowd, Brooks appeared to drag Violet Ashland through the tangle of dancers, past the long table set in silver and crystal, to the entryway where Marisa stood.

"Marisa, darling." His voice was as smooth as summer rain. "Miss Ashland has something to tell you."

Marisa searched his face, and when she could find no answer there she looked at Violet. Tears shimmered in her cool blue eyes.

"Tell her," Brooks demanded. "Tell her, or I swear I will shout it for all to hear."

Violet looked at him and her eyes were full of hate. Marisa didn't understand.

"I lied," she whispered.

"Louder," he ordered.

"I lied—about the engagement. I broke it off nearly two years ago."

"What?" Marisa whispered.

"She lied, sweetheart. We are not engaged. God help me, I can't believe I ever wanted to marry this creature, but I had given her a ring. But practical Violet wanted more than what I had to offer. She jilted me, and that is when I came to the Territory—and met you."

Marisa swallowed hard. "You mean…"

"I mean that I love you, only you, and now there is no obstacle between us."

"Let me go," Violet muttered. "People are beginning to stare."

Brooks glanced around the ballroom. "So they are. You had better hurry, Violet, if you intend to salvage any shred of your reputation."

She turned away and was soon surrounded by a crowd of women with fluttering fans.

"She will lie again, of course," he said easily. "By morning a story will have been concocted that paints me as a royal bastard."

"Don't you care?" Marisa asked.

He turned to her and smiled. The warmth of it flooded over her. He reached out and pulled her to his chest. "Not one damn bit, not as long as you know the truth."

"Are you…sure?"

"What I feel for you is a passion so strong, so hot and deep, a lady with no more backbone than the likes of Violet could not affect it."

Marisa blinked and the shimmering wash of tears lessened. "What the hell does that mean? I never understand what you are saying. Damn it, can't you speak plainly?"

He grinned at her. She was an enigma. Emeralds winked seductively at her smooth slender throat while curses trickled off her tongue. "It means, little lady, that you are mine. You always have been, and you always will be."

He reached out and traced the outline of the necklace with the tip of his index finger. "This feeling I have for you would scorch the skin off the kind of woman you think is a lady. I have a longing inside me that burns so blisteringly hot, only a woman with grit could ever dream of standing up to it, much less answering it with a craving of her own."

She shivered as his finger continued to draw an invisible line.

"I need a woman with backbone. I want a woman with a special kind of fire. I need you. Only you can quench this thirst I have." He slipped his hand around her neck and rested his palm against her nape as he drew her closer. "And by all that is holy, I will have you, Marisa O'Bannion."

He twirled her in a wide circle while waves of his deep warm laughter rippled over her. Marisa let the strains of the music and Brooks's strong arms guide her. He directed her through the maze of couples without ever allowing his gaze to leave her face. She swallowed hard, trying to ignore the thrumming of her pulse in her ears, trying to ignore the flutter inside her middle.

"A penny for your thoughts." His voice rubbed over her body like satin against freshly washed flesh.

"I was trying to decide if you meant what you said, or if you were funning me again."

The melody ended, but he did not release his hold on her.

"I meant every word, Marisa." He slipped his arm around her waist and escorted her toward a long table.

Among arrangements of fresh fruit and flowers, and trees made from oranges, there were several liquids in silver bowls. Ice cubes floated on top of something bright pink, next to slices of lime and slivers of lemon.

"Ready for a drink?" he asked.

Marisa's mouth suddenly felt as dry as desert sand in August. She couldn't seemed to find her voice, so she nodded.

While Brooks used a ladle to fill two cups, she scanned the crowd.

"Clair looks lovely tonight." Her soft brown hair was held in place by a garnet-studded tiara and complemented by the crimson velvet gown she wore.

"Mmm. Mother did not want her to attend, but Clair felt she has been cooped up too long. You are the loveliest woman here tonight," Brooks said as he placed a cup of punch in her hands, lingering to fold his fingers over her own.

"Brooks, Marisa, how wonderful to finally see you both," Clair said as she reached them. Her cheeks were flushed, her pale eyes brighter than normal. She fanned herself vigorously. "I need a cup of punch."

"Allow me." Brooks ladled liquid into a clean cup.

"Clair, you look a bit feverish," Marisa said.

"Now that you mention it I do feel somewhat warm." Clair took a sip. "That tastes good. Maybe I need to rest." She gave Brooks a beseeching look. "Could you find me a chair?"

"Consider it done." He turned away and went in search of one.

Marisa watched his wide back, encased in fine black cloth, until he was out of sight. Only then did her pulse return to anything near a normal cadence.

Brooks found a chair and his mother simultaneously. She was in a small sitting room off the ballroom.

"Mother? What are you doing in here?" Brooks scooped up a chair by the back.

"I just needed to take a breather. I have smiled until my jaw is aching."

"Did you get the endowment?" Brooks was sure she had or she wouldn't allow herself a respite.

"Yes. Thank the Lord, I don't know how much longer I could be charming to that man with his cigar smoke curling about my head." She glanced at her son's hand. "Who is the chair for?"

"Clair."

"What?" Patricia sat a little straighter. "Is she ill?"

"She says she is a little warm."

Patricia was instantly on her feet. "I knew she was overdoing it. With Rossmore out of town she hasn't had anybody to make sure she is taking proper care of herself. I told her not to come."

"Perhaps you should come and attend to her," he said with a wide grin. Being a prospective grandmother was a position Patricia was going to relish, that was obvious.

As soon as they found Clair and Marisa, Patricia reached out and felt her daughter's forehead.

"Clair?" She moved her palm to Clair's cheek. "Are you ill?"

"No, of course not. I think I have just underestimated the effect my condition would have on me. I find I tire easily and need so much extra rest."

"Of course you do. You are more delicate now. You must take care of yourself. Remember, an ounce of prevention..."

"I think you are right. I nearly yawned in Commodore Butler's face." Clair grinned mischievously.

"We must get you home at once." Patricia stood up. "I'll call the carriage, if Marisa would collect our wraps."

Brooks was a little amused at his mother's reaction. Images of how she would spoil the child upon its arrival flashed through his mind.

"You'll do no such thing," Clair protested. "I will not allow you all to cut your evening short on account of me. I refuse to budge an inch." She folded her arms beneath her bosom and pouted prettily, an expression Brooks had watched her practice when he was just a child.

Patricia glanced at Brooks.

He shrugged. "Don't ask me to get involved...."

Patricia worried her bottom lip.

"Not an inch, Mother," Clair repeated, and turned her nose up.

"Oh, very well." Patricia looked from Marisa to Brooks, and a tiny smile began to play at the corners of her mouth. "However, I am tired myself, and since Rod and Donovan are out of town as well, there is no reason in the world why I can't come home with you, Clair. You should not be alone in that big, rambling house." Patricia smoothed her skirt and gave Brooks a triumphant look.

"Brooks, please call the carriage. I am taking Clair home. I will be staying at her house until Rossmore returns from Australia. May I rely on you to see Marisa home and keep her company until I return?"

A wicked grin spread across his face beneath the mustache. "Of course, Mother. I will make it my special mission to see she is kept from being lonely."

Slivers of moonlight painted the trees and lane an electric blue. Marisa pulled the wrap closer about her shoulders, suddenly chilled not so much by the temperature, but by the knowledge that she and Brooks were alone as they approached the front door of the brownstone.

Of course, they were not truly alone—Tilly was asleep in her room off the kitchen. But Marisa *felt* alone. Every step up to the door seemed to remind her of that fact. When Brooks closed the door behind them, the sound echoed through the empty house. He grinned at her and she felt the impact of his smile arc across the space between them like a bolt of summer lightning. Her heart starting skipping beats inside her chest.

She felt as if she were expecting something...the way she felt when she looked at packages under the Christmas tree, or when her favorite mare was in foal.

Anticipation.

It sizzled through her veins and heated her body and mind to a fever pitch.

"Will you join me in a nightcap?" he asked as he slid her wrap from her shoulders.

"A nightcap?" she repeated, feeling more awkward than she could ever remember. The delicate gown of taffeta was poor armor against his devastating charm.

"Uh-huh. A nightcap—a drink to relax you for sleep." His eyes roamed over her face and across her cleavage in a way that was possessive and downright sinful.

"Yes, I'll have a nightcap with you, if you'd like," she murmured.

He trailed his fingers along her neck. "Good. I think we should talk, Marisa, about our future."

"Future?" Marisa shivered, suddenly wishing she had the wrap back.

"Yes. But first I'll light a fire. You seem a little cold." Brooks grinned at her before he moved to the hearth. He took a spill from the container on the mantle and busied himself. In seconds vermillion and ebony curls of fire licked the seasoned logs. A warm glow filled the room along with the faint attar of smoke and the silvery moonlight.

The masculine, wood-paneled study was Donovan's favorite hideaway, but there were signs of Patricia's feminine influence in all the right places. Overstuffed, comfortable furniture was strategically placed. A soft, inviting sofa done up in Wedgwood blue and cream was directly in front of the fireplace, just far enough away to be safe from flying embers. And a thick cut and sculpted wool rug covered the polished wood floor.

"Sit down, I'll pour you a drink." Brooks gestured toward the sofa with one hand.

He poured sherry into two stemmed crystal glasses and gave one to her. She thought he would sit down with her, but instead he circled the sofa and positioned himself directly behind her.

She was staring out between the heavy velvet curtains at the moon, trying to think of something to say, but he began tracing the line of her jaw and neck with the tip of his finger, taking away all thought.

"Marisa." Brooks's voice caressed her. "I want you tonight."

She sipped the sherry. The fiery liquid slid down her throat. The flames were consuming the log now, a little like his lust was engulfing her. The smell of gardenias wafted through the warm room.

She cleared her throat and shifted slightly beneath his hands. "Show me," she whispered. "Show me how to love you."

"I will show you things and make you feel things you cannot imagine, my love."

While he was standing behind her with the sofa between them, he put both his palms on her bare collarbones. He began to knead the muscles of her shoulders and neck. Within minutes he felt some of the tension leave her body. "But right now, drink your sherry. We have plenty of time—all night and all of our lives."

After she had drained her glass, he took it from her, noticing her hand trembled a bit when their fingers touched. He gently tilted her head back on the stuffed cushion and rubbed his fingertips against her temples.

"That feels so good," she murmured.

"I intend to make you feel good all over." Brooks pulled the long hairpins from her heavy hair. The strands uncoiled, falling like a dark cascade over the back of the sofa, down to the floor. He finger-combed it, feeling the weight of each precious strand slide through his fingers like a skein of silk.

Marisa was a conflict of emotions. One part of her had never felt more alive, more feminine. Strange things were happening to her, and Brooks was the cause of them all.

Brooks shed his tuxedo coat, tie and boots. Then he came to the front of the sofa and knelt before Marisa. She met his eyes.

Brooks picked up one of Marisa's slippered feet. He slid off the satin shoe, then positioned her instep on his thigh. Warmth from her foot telegraphed up his leg to his loins. While he studied her face, his fingers expertly kneaded the ball of her foot. He caressed her toes, massaged her arch and lovingly worked his hands along the delicate symmetry of her small ankle.

"Do you like this?"

"Um-hmm." She licked her lips and drew in a shallow breath. Her lashes dipped down for a moment as if she might doze off, but then they lifted, and her gaze locked onto his own with a vibrant intensity that made his gut contract.

He wanted her with every fiber of his being.

An image of her body, smooth and unclothed, flashed before his eyes, but he pushed it aside and quelled the smoldering heat in his blood. Brooks was determined to make each sensual activity an execution in pleasure, to taunt and tease Marisa until she was mad with wanting him.

With deliberate slowness his fingers invaded the tender spots between each toe. When he reached her smallest toe, a moan of delight escaped her lips. She shuddered.

He drew his finger up the length of her sole toward her angle.

She jerked.

"Aha, you are ticklish. I am learning more about you every day." He kissed her arch and slowly released her foot. Then he picked up the other one. With infinite care he administered the same attention, delighting in the way she relaxed and drifted unconsciously toward him, chuckling when he found a particularly sensitive and ticklish spot that made her squirm. When he had stroked, rubbed and cosseted both her feet, he slid his hand upward and grasped one calf.

He stilled his hand upon her silken skin. "Do you want me to stop?" He counted three ticks of the clock pendulum while he waited for her answer.

"No."

"Good, because I want to show you what I feel for you. I want to worship you with my body."

Chapter Fifteen

His sure fingers sought out the garter on her thigh. He could've flipped up her taffeta skirt, to see where his hands were resting, but that was not what he wanted. Brooks wanted his exploration of her to be mysterious and slow, not hurried or shocking to her in any way. He wanted to touch her skin, feel her flinch beneath his palm as he scouted and memorized every inch of virgin territory. Each new section of her body was a tantalizing exploration as his hands blazed a path to Marisa's heart and soul.

Halfway up her supple thigh his searching hand encountered stiff lace and ruffled satin. With gentle yet deliberate movements he pulled the elastic garter downward. Then he slipped it off her delicate foot. Brooks rubbed the material, still warm from her flesh, against his cheek. It carried a faint odor of gardenias and womanly musk. He stared into her eyes.

She shivered.

"I want you to remember each minute, every individual touch of this night." Brooks's voice was like the purr of a cat.

The fire added a magical glow to the room. Marisa felt

as if she were moving through a dream. The entire night felt unreal. First there had been Brooks's stunning declaration of love and the startling revelation that Violet was not his intended. Then, when her body had felt charged with the electricity of it all, he had given her the sherry, which brought on a calming lethargy. Now there was the sizzling sexual awareness he awakened with each touch of his fingers, glance of his eyes and word from his lips. It was the culmination of all she had hoped for—and all she had feared—since the day she'd met him.

Sitting there, watching and feeling his unceasing advance up her body, was both the hardest and easiest thing she had ever done. Hard, because it went against her very being to submit to his will, but easy because it felt so right. She wanted to be dominated by him in some primal way she didn't fully understand. She must've shuddered because he stopped what he was doing and sat back.

"Are you frightened of what is going to happen between us, Marisa?" His voice was gentle and strong.

"Yes. No. That is, I imagine what goes on between a man and a woman is not much different than horses."

The rich, throaty sound of his laughter sent shivers down her spine. "I'd like to think I am a bit more romantic than that," he teased.

"That wasn't exactly what I meant."

"Shh…no more teasing, not now." He slid his hand beneath her skirt and leaned toward her again. Slowly, so slowly that she thought her heart might stop beating from the anticipation of it, he starting rolling her stocking down toward her toes.

A lump formed in the back of her throat. It was as if he had become a part of her in some strange way. She watched his hands appear from under the folds of her gown.

She glanced up and their eyes met in a hot liquid gaze. She licked her lips and swallowed.

He smiled as if to reassure her.

There was a tightening of her middle and a deep gnawing need suddenly uncoiled inside her. It sprang up unbidden, without warning, from a secret place she never knew existed.

"Brooks?"

"I know, Marisa. It feels like all the air has gone out of the room, doesn't it?"

She nodded in agreement.

"You can feel every drop of your blood being pumped through your heart?"

She nodded again.

"And you think you will die if you don't have...*something?*"

"Yes," she answered thickly. "Oh, yes."

"Does it feel as if you are burning with fever? A fever so hot it will burn you from the inside out?"

"Yes." She sighed. He understood, oh dear Lord, he did know how she felt. "What is it, Brooks?"

"It's love, darling." He kissed the inside of her ankle. "I am going to show you every wonderful bit of it tonight." His fingers grazed over her thighs and moved upward.

She shivered.

"What are you thinking?" His warm hand sought the top of her other stocking beneath the layers of taffeta, lace and ruffles. She felt the scrape of his knuckles against the soft flesh on her inner leg when he started rolling the stocking downward.

She shivered again, and then sighed with contentment and leaned back on the overstuffed sofa.

"I love you, Marisa." His words sent chills skipping

over her flesh. He lifted the stocking in the air and tossed it on top of her shoes. Then he stood up, grasped her fingers and pulled her to her feet.

A log on the hearth popped, showering the air with a spray of sparks.

"Brooks?"

"Yes?"

"Teach me how to kiss." Marisa saw his mustache twitch. For a moment she feared she had said the wrong thing, but then he took a step nearer and placed his hands on either side of her jaw. Warm fingers wrapped around her neck and met at her nape.

"Tilt your head." His gaze never left her face.

She did as he instructed.

"Now part your lips, just a bit."

Again she followed his orders.

"Now do whatever feels right." He brushed his lips against hers. It was no more than the flutter of butterfly wings against her mouth, but something seemed to explode inside her. Her knees turned to liquid. Marisa grabbed hold of his strong shoulders to keep from falling.

Deep inside his chest the sound started. A growl rumbled out, vibrating her with its intensity. Stimulating her with its primal meaning.

"Honey, you are so sweet." He held her face away and stared into her eyes. "I swear you taste like sugar cookies." He nibbled along her ear and suckled her lobe. "I'm going to put emeralds on these pretty little ears, emeralds to match your necklace." He turned her around and unclasped the necklace, now warm from the heated fire of her passion. He placed it on a nearby table and stepped in front of her. "Marisa, I want you to know how much I love you."

Her throat tightened and she could not answer him. She

had no response to such a declaration. He frowned and searched her face as if he were looking for a reply in the depths of her eyes. Then he sighed.

"Do you trust me?" He cupped her chin and tilted her head up to deposit kisses to each of her eyelids, her nose, and finally to suckle gently on her bottom lip.

"Yes, Brooks." How could she not? Hadn't he proven himself by saving her life? Twice?

"That's my girl, my lovely Marisa, *my Missy.*" His voice vibrated with possessiveness. It made her shiver beneath his gaze. "Cold?" he asked.

"No... I don't know," she admitted.

"I know how you feel and I know what to do about it." He kissed her once more, then he began to gather the thick folds of her skirt and raise it. He lifted it over her head. She had to shimmy a little to assist him. Finally the yards of heavy material slipped free of her body. With a swish the gown was added to the pile of stockings, garters and shoes.

She stood there in her chemise, corset and drawers, waiting to see what he would do next. She didn't have to wonder long. He bent his head and feathered kisses to her throat and the hollow of her neck.

"I am going to brand you, Marisa O'Bannion." He threaded his fingers into the thickness of her hair, lifting it off her neck and shoulders. "Brand you with kisses and mark you with my passion. I want you to know how deep my love for you runs."

He stood up and allowed her hair to fall back against her skin. "When you see how we are together you'll know what I have come to realize myself." With his thumb and index finger he tugged on the bow that held the top of her chemise. Slowly the satin unfolded and released its grip. Rough, wide hands pushed the gathered material open. Then he stripped it from her body and tossed it onto the growing pile of her clothing. "We were meant for each other."

She felt something hot burst inside her chest at his words.

Meant for each other.

"God, you are lovely." He deposited kisses to the mounds of her breasts above the stiff corset edge. His fingers plucked at the laces and soon the corset was removed.

Now she stood before him naked to the waist. Her heart was pounding so hard she was sure he could hear it, see it in her flesh as it thumped.

"Oh, Marisa." He ran his hand over one breast, down the curvature of her belly, and as he slipped the last knot free, he slid his hand inside the top of her drawers.

Her breath drew inward in one sharp hiss. The sensation of his fingers kneading her flesh, above the hair that covered the most sensitive and pulsing part of her, was almost more than she could stand.

"Do you understand what I am trying to say, Marisa?" he asked while he slipped his other hand behind her, supporting her back. "My passion for you is so strong, so hot, it would burn a lesser woman. You are the only one for me, Missy, and I am going to prove it to you tonight— and every night."

Within minutes he had her lying on the thick wool rug. Her head was resting on a satin pillow, her backside cushioned by the velvet-and-satin patchwork throw he had snatched from a nearby easy chair. The crackle of the fire and the steady tick of the clock pendulum were the only sounds.

"Brooks?"

"Yes, love?"

"I want to see you."

His mustache turned up at the corners. It was a wicked grin, one that made her breath catch and her heart skip a beat.

"I thought you'd never ask, darlin'." He stared down at her. "Will you do the honors, or shall I?"

"You do it." She brought one arm up and rested her head on it. It was a pleasure for her to watch him reveal himself to her.

First he shed the shirt. The little jet studs clinked as he tossed them on the table. The glow of flames skipped over the well-defined muscles of his chest, along the scar on his arm and down the flat expanse of his belly.

She sighed in appreciation.

He undid the top of his black gaberdine trousers. They skimmed along his body, exposing powerful thighs sprinkled with a growth of dark curly hair.

Marisa's middle contracted.

At last he took off his drawers, and there before her was the long rigid proof of his desire.

Her heart thumped erratically. "You look like that roan stud my brother Shane bought," she said as her eyes roamed over his pelvis.

One brow arched. "Stud?" He placed his hands on his hips and grinned down at her. She was a puzzle, this lovely woman-child who had captured his soul. "Are you calling me a stud?" He chuckled.

"You look like one, but I can't say for sure until…"

He laughed again, and covered her body with his own. "Ah, Marisa, why did it take me so long to realize how very much I love you?"

He did not wait for her to answer; instead he kissed her. Marisa rose up to meet him. And as his tongue probed her mouth, he slipped between her thighs and held himself there, rigid, tense and ready. She felt a giddy sense of fulfillment as she lay beneath him in the half-dark room.

"It may hurt for just a minute or two." Brooks's voice was harsh and husky with controlled lust. He kissed her again, nearly devouring her with his passion. The fire was burning low, casting long gray shadows over the lovely rise of her breasts, the cleft of her thighs, the spot where their bodies pulsed nearly, but not quite, together.

"I'm ready," she whispered. "Remember, I trust you."

He sighed deeply and then his body and hands began to show her the meaning of magic.

Chapter Sixteen

When the big clock chimed four times, Brooks gathered Marisa's clothing along with his own. He tied them into a bundle, deposited them in her lap, then picked her up in his arms. He strode buck naked from the study into the hall and toward the stairs.

"What if somebody comes in?" she whispered against the warmth of his chest.

"I'd have a heap of explaining to do." He paused halfway up the stairs and looked at her with one brow raised. "We'd probably have to get married right away—no discussion, just a quick trip to the preacher."

Marisa smiled in spite of herself. "Do you want to marry me?"

"How can you even ask after what we just did?" He started climbing the stairs again, shaking his head in astonishment with each step. "I *love* you and I loved you to prove it."

What they had shared was wonderful and frightening and almost more than Marisa could comprehend. Earlier, when his breathing had been coming in harsh rasps, he had paused on stiff, powerful arms above her, to stare into her eyes with such longing that she had felt like she really did *belong* to him.

"Missy?" He used her old nickname with intimate ease. "Don't you know yet how much I care?" He nudged open the door of her room and stepped inside.

"I have an idea." The feeling was so new she wasn't comfortable speaking of it. Even thinking about it gave her butterflies.

He put her on the edge of the bed and took the bundle of clothes from her arms. "Then I guess I'll have to demonstrate again." He tossed the clothes onto a chair by the window.

"What?" she asked as he gently forced her to lie back on the bed.

He slid one hand up her leg toward the juncture of her thighs. "I still have a couple of hours before dawn to thoroughly convince you."

Brooks kissed, caressed and tasted every inch of her body, and still he was not satisfied. It came to him, as the first fingers of light traced uneven lines across the horizon, that he would never get enough of loving Marisa.

Not in a million years of pleasuring her.

She had dozed off, curled into the crook of his arm after their last shattering coupling had exploded between them. He held her still, snuggled up against his body like a precious treasure. He knew he should rise and return to his own room, but he was loath to leave her for even a moment. He kissed her forehead and she smiled in her sleep.

He wondered if she dreamed, and if she did, was it of him? Or did she dream of her life in the Territory, of wild rides across the unfettered expanse during fresh spring mornings and glorious sunsets?

She murmured and her eyes fluttered open. Sleep and

the softening effects of being well and truly loved turned her eyes a smoky gray.

"I fell asleep," she said through a yawn.

He marveled at how lovely she was. The thin shaft of light played on the strands of dark hair splayed across the white pillow cover.

"I was dreaming," she added with a shy smile.

"Of me?"

Her expression altered and he knew in his gut she was debating about whether to tell him a lie or the truth. He saw in that flicker of time that Marisa would lie to spare his pride. It was a realization that warmed him from the inside out. She did have a gentle concern for his feelings, even if she did not love him as he wished for her to.

"Well, I…"

"Marisa." He raised himself on one elbow and studied her face. "I never want you to lie to me. No matter what, even if you think you are sparing my feelings, always tell me the truth. And I swear I will do the same for you. There will be no lies between us."

"All right."

"Swear it."

"I swear it, Brooks." She levered herself up on her elbow in turn so she was face-to-face with him. "I wasn't dreaming of you."

He chuckled at her serious expression. "What were you dreaming of? Not another man? My pride couldn't take it.…"

"You are so consarned silly." She giggled. "I was dreaming of riding. I miss it so much, Brooks." Her voice was wistful. She flopped down on her back and stared at the ceiling.

He reached out and cupped her firm breast, then laved his tongue across her nipple. She leaned into his caress in a way that made his loins tighten. "Would you like to go riding?" He nuzzled her neck as he spoke.

"Here? In New York?" She giggled. "You are silly."

"Yes, we could rent some horses and ride in Central Park. It's not the Territory, but I think you would like it."

She scampered up on her knees, her dark hair hanging over her breasts and trailing down on the rumpled covers. "Could we?"

"Of course. There is only one thing."

She frowned and sat up straighter, the wild O'Bannion blood making her wary, cautious to agree to any terms unless she knew what they were.

"What?"

"You will have to ride sidesaddle." He chuckled as her brows shot upward.

"Well, if that isn't the damnedest thing I ever heard of. Sidesaddle?"

He made himself a promise right then and there. If it took the rest of the day, pulling her into his arms for clandestine couplings along the bridal paths, he was going to get her to accept his proposal of marriage.

The morning sun was bright and warm when Brooks returned to the brownstone. He had left Marisa bathing, a task he would've been happy to help with, except that he had to attend to something while she was occupied.

He smiled and drew the small, velvet-covered jeweler's box from his vest pocket. He snapped it open and looked at the ring. Sunlight reflected off the gold and diamonds, but the dark sapphire seemed to absorb the light, bend and splinter the rays until they turned to twilight mist.

"Like Marisa's eyes," he mumbled to himself. He returned the box to his vest and opened the front door.

He was so happy, it was hard to keep from singing or

whistling with joy. He had it all planned out. They would ride to a secluded spot near the lake, and after a picnic and some ardent kissing he would propose—again.

"And I swear, Marisa, you will say yes to me today."

The rented dapple gray mare tossed her head and nickered. The sunlight filtering through the thick alder boughs turned her pale mane to liquid silver as Marisa levered the reins and kept her mount under tight control.

"Marisa, I don't like the way she is acting. Let's go back and get you a gentler mount." Brooks frowned at her from beneath his fashionable bowler. The shadow from the brim created a dark slash above his blue eyes.

"Don't be silly, I can manage this little mare." A shaft of light shimmered on a carefully sculpted ebony curl and turned it inky blue. The jaunty, iridescent feather in her riding hat swayed saucily when she shook her head.

Brooks could not help but admire how well turned out she was, and how beautiful she remained whether in boots and chaps or satin and velvet.

"I've been riding since I was a baby."

"You have been riding *astraddle* since you were a child, not sidesaddle," Brooks corrected, reminding her of how awkward she had found mounting with one stirrup. "There is a big difference between a Western saddle on the open prairie and that thing you are perched on. Here in Central Park, you'll be meeting riders at every corner. Your mare may spook. She has a wild eye."

Marisa ducked her head slightly, watching him from under the narrow brim of her hat. "I'll be careful, I promise."

He smiled. How could he refuse her anything when she looked at him like that? "All right, we'll go easy. But at the first sign of a problem she goes back to the livery and we find you a gentle old plug with a sway back and Roman nose.''

"You wouldn't dare!" She smiled broadly.

His gut flip-flopped. He urged his brown gelding alongside the spirited gray and leaned over his saddle until he could deposit a kiss on Missy's lips.

"Uh-huh, just as I thought," he said.

"What?" she asked, knitting her brows together.

"You still taste like sugar cookies." He kissed her again. It was the merest grazing of flesh, but it left him burning for more.

A blush stole up her face. "You say the goll-dangedest things, Brooks." His love flowed over her in a hot wave each time she looked at him. It stunned her to admit it, but she loved him, too. She made herself a silent vow that today she would tell him how she felt.

"Am I forgiven for being foolishly in love and moved to saying silly things?" he teased.

"This time." Marisa moved slightly in the sidesaddle. "But you better not make a habit of it, or when we get home Clell will josh the hide right off you."

When we get home. Her words rang in Brooks's ear and gave him a tingling sensation. He would've questioned her about it, but the nimble-footed mare danced impatiently. Marisa gave her a loose rein and the animal exploded, taking off over the verdant turf in a blur. Brooks found himself staring at Marisa's straight slim back as her horse galloped away.

He kicked his horse, and within moments he was matching his mount's pace to the dapple gray mare's. The lumpy gunnysack he had tied behind his saddle bumped rhythmically against the animal's flank—not very fashionable, but the kernel of his battle plan was within that sack.

Brooks touched his finger to the brim of his hat when they cantered by another couple sedately walking their horses along the path. As soon as they rounded a bend, out of sight, Marisa veered off the pebbled path and took the mare over a small hillock. She cut through a dense stand of trees far away from the level meadow. When she had ridden a short distance she pulled up the mare and turned to smile at Brooks. A soft glow seemed to fill her dark eyes. He worshipped this wild, free-spirited woman.

"Ah, Miss O'Bannion, I think my family and I have done the world a great disservice."

"How so?"

"You were a natural heartbreaker in boots and chaps." He allowed his eyes to travel over her form, so artfully clothed in the riding habit of plum velvet. "But with the addition of all the feminine wiles my cousin and mother have taught you, there is not a man alive who could withstand your charms."

"Not a man?"

"Well, not this man," he admitted gruffly.

Marisa flashed him a flirty grin. "You might just be sweet-talking me to get me back into bed."

Brooks tipped his head back and laughed heartily. "I might be, but I'm not. Besides, would I have to sweet-talk you?"

She smiled and cast her eyes downward. "Maybe not."

The gray snorted and pranced nervously, but Marisa controlled her easily with a small movement of her tiny gloved hand.

"I am glad to hear it because I have brought something to ply you with. For dessert I was planning on having your sugar-cookie kisses." His lips curled into a smile.

"Lead the way." She tossed her head and grinned at him.

He loved her spirit, her beauty, and most of all he loved the way she was comfortable with her own sexuality. Marisa had been untutored and innocent, but now the mystery and delight of making love was as natural to her as breathing. He smiled at the thought of spending his life with her, and all of his nights.

"Follow me." He guided his horse through a dense growth of brush. After a few minutes the foliage thinned and they entered a small meadow, surrounded on three sides by the cover of trees and trailing vines.

"It is pretty as a picture." Marisa slipped to the ground. She tied the restive mare on a long lead where she could graze. Then Marisa turned to watch Brooks.

He took the gunnysack and opened it. Then he drew out an old woolen blanket, a tall green bottle and a round of cheese wrapped in gauze. When he looked up, Marisa was still staring at him. Some smoldering emotion lay deep in her eyes.

"What is it?" He stood up and walked to her.

"I have to tell you something."

His heart contracted. She was so serious a lancet of fear sliced through him. "Smile when you say that or I will begin to worry." He slipped his hands behind her nape and drew her to him. He kissed her, hard and long, willing her to say she was his—praying she was not going to reject him. When he released her, she drew in a shaky breath.

"I love you, Brooks," she said simply.

I love you. The words hung in the air like perfume. They wound around his head and heart.

He pulled her into a passionate kiss, hoping he could show her what those words meant to him.

An hour later the wine bottle was barely touched, the fruit whole and the cheese still wrapped in its gauzy covering. Marisa, however, had been peeled, bared, sampled and devoured. Brooks had undone her habit and lathed hot kisses across her breasts to the tune of buzzing honeybees going from blossom to blossom. Now the two of them lay curled together, satisfied and disheveled. Her skirt was shoved up around her smooth thighs as the sun traced an arc low in the westering sky.

"I guess we'll have to get married now."

"Why?"

"Didn't Ellen tell you?" His brow furrowed in mock despair. "It is an old New York City tradition. Once a maiden is deflowered among the flowers there is nothing else that can be done." He clicked his tongue and shook his head from side to side. "What a pity...."

"Oh, you!" She collapsed into giggles until he parted the front of her habit again and kissed the swell of her bare breast.

They both turned serious as their passion flared.

Marisa was drunk on happiness. Brooks had proposed no less than a dozen times in Donovan's study and at least that many more times today, each proposition of marriage more outlandish than the last.

"Marry me," he murmured into her mouth as he kissed her now.

"How many times are you going to ask me?" She sat up and pulled her habit closed. He was disappointed to see her luscious flesh disappear beneath the plum velvet.

"I'll ask until you say yes." Brooks sighed and grabbed his coat from the bush where he had flung it. "But perhaps I have been going about this the wrong way." He fished something out of the pocket and turned to Marisa. "Maybe you are the traditional type of female. Perhaps you prefer the old-fashioned way." His expression was serious as he positioned himself on one knee beside her.

"Miss O'Bannion, would you do me the very great honor of consenting to be my wife?" He flipped open the box. Sunlight glittered off the stones. "To have and to hold, in sickness and in health…?"

Her eyes snapped from his face to the ring and back again. "Oh, Brooks." She sat up and leaned over the box, staring at the ring. "Oh, oh, Brooks. I am going to cry."

"Now are tears a yes or a no?"

She looked up at him with eyes awash. Her bottom lip trembled. "Oh, Brooks…"

"Marisa, I love you. Will you marry me?" His eyes rolled up toward the treetops and his voice was teasing. "I mean, after all, I have this ring and I have developed an appetite for kisses that taste like sugar cookies. And after the way you have shamelessly seduced me, my reputation will be in tatters. It would be a crime for me to have gone through all this for nothing, that great proposal wasted. Besides, the ring might not fit another girl…."

She hit him on the shoulder with the palm of her hand. It was like striking stone. "Oh, you!"

It made his heart contract with love to have her teasing him.

"God knows why you want me, but…I love you, Brooks, that is a fact. If you are sure, then I'm willing."

"I'm sure."

"Then I'm willin'."

He crushed her to his chest. A hot, tight lump was in his throat and he had to swallow several times before he could breathe. For a moment he thought that he might actually break down and cry himself, so great was his joy.

"I'll do my best to make you a good wife."

"Just be yourself, honey, that is all I want. Just you and your love."

"That you will have for the rest of my life, Brooks. I swear it."

They allowed their mounts to walk aimlessly, picking a random path through the foliage. The afternoon sped by while they looked at each other with passion and love in their eyes.

Finally, Marisa pulled up on the reins and the gray reluctantly came to a halt.

"When would you like to be married?" she asked abruptly. Her mood had changed, shifted like mercury in the blink of an eye while Brooks had not been watching.

He smiled. "Tomorrow—today—now. This very minute would not be too soon for me."

Even white teeth flashed against the dusky smoothness of her skin. "What will your family say? Will they think you have picked a silly girl from the Territory?"

He reached across the short distance between them and laid his gloved hand upon her arm. "They might think of you as exasperating, stubborn, willful, and let's not forget reckless, but never silly."

She tilted her head and slanted him a look of mock irritation. "Do you think we were wrong not to have waited—I mean, for our wedding night?"

Brooks suppressed the urge to grin. He had never known a more passionate woman. He thought it was probably due to her upbringing in the Territory. She had none of the prudish attitudes of other women he had known. Marisa was a sensual, sexual woman, at ease with her body. But she had given him a gift beyond imagining because she had wanted to come to the marriage bed with her virtue intact. She had told him that last night after their first searing encounter.

"I don't know if I could've waited. I might've died from the discomfort, and then you would've been a widow."

She struggled to keep from giggling at his contrived expression of pain and agony. "I couldn't be a widow unless we got married first, you ninny!"

"Oh, right." He looked at her and felt a tug on his heart. "It makes me proud and happy that I was your first." His expression turned more serious. "But what is more important, Marisa, I will be your only lover. You are stuck with me, forever." He rolled his eyes heavenward. "Do you hear that, Lord?"

"You are awful. God may strike you dead right here and now."

"Probably, but I will die a happy man." They ducked under a low-hanging branch and emerged into a small meadow gilded with light. "I don't suppose you really would sneak away with me today, find an obliging judge and do the deed?"

"Uh, I think we did the deed last night." She winked.

"Don't tempt me, you vixen," he exclaimed. "We could find a minister and get the vows done."

"Your mother and father would be heartbroken."

Brooks frowned and sighed. "I suppose we do have to allow my family to help. Do we let our wedding become one of those horrible New York events? Mother has taken quite a shine to you. I hope you can endure her through the trials of preparing for a wedding. Thank God Clair is pregnant. At least that will spare us a small amount of the customary nonsense."

Marisa attempted to look sympathetic, but a smile tickled her lips. "It would mean a lot to your mother, I am sure. And I would like for Ellen to be my maid of honor."

The gelding lowered his head and clipped off a mouthful of grass. A squirrel peered at the animal from its perch on a low-hanging bough, chattering in irritation as the horse came too close to its territory.

"So be it. I will be the dutiful son and very impatient prospective groom. We will set a proper date in order to allow my mother to plan and fuss. And Cousin Ellen will be consulted and cosseted as you desire." Brooks swiveled slightly in the saddle and propped his leg on the horse's withers. The animal continued to graze around the bit in his mouth. "What shall it be, my love? A winter wedding? Or perhaps full summer when the roses are in bloom? Maybe Leland will forgive you by then. We could have the wedding in his rose arbor, after the repairs on his trellis have been taken care of, of course."

"I didn't mean to break his trellis."

He shrugged. "Oh, I am quite sure climbing on the rickety old thing was a complete accident...." He waggled his brows. "I mean, it was right there, more convenient than the front door and all...."

"Stop it," she ordered. She tried to ignore him and imagine a wedding in both settings. "The snow would be lovely, but it would make it difficult for guests."

"You are most sensible. What a wise wife I am getting. Then summer it is! The sooner the better."

She speared him with a frosty glance. "There are two more seasons in the year, Brooks."

His brows shot up toward his hairline. "Surely you are not proposing that we wait another whole *year?* Marisa, don't tell me you are thinking of *next* spring?" He slapped a hand over his chest in mock pain.

She laughed and shook her head. The action sent her

carefully arranged curls bouncing. "No. I am as anxious as you are, silly. How about this fall? We could be married in the autumn when the leaves are turning. I imagine the reds and golds in this park would be beautiful." She glanced overhead at the canopy of new spring growth.

"Fall...over four months from now." Brooks tapped his index finger upon his mustache. "All right, I accept. We shall be married in mid-October, and then, my lovely, I intend to ravish you on a regular basis throughout the cold winter months—so be warned."

"I think you have been ravishing me fairly regularly as it stands now." She leaned over the gray's neck to meet him halfway for a passionate kiss.

Abruptly she pulled away. She lifted the reins along with the riding crop she had insisted on carrying, intent on being outfitted properly. With a flick of her wrist she tapped the wild-eyed mare on the rump. The horse exploded in a ripple of sleek muscle.

"Race you back to the lake!" she shouted over her shoulder.

He laughed and kicked his horse, bringing the startled animal's head up. "If I win, I get five kisses!" Brooks was filled with admiration and a love so deep it was nearly frightening. She was everything he had ever dreamed of, and never expected to find.

And she had finally accepted his proposal. There was a ring firmly on her finger to prove it to one and all.

"Come on, boy, we have a race to win." Brooks leaned low and whispered encouragement into his mount's ear.

Marisa glanced over her shoulder. Brooks was finally gaining on the mare. She made a great show of trying to urge more speed from the animal, while she secretly pulled back on the reins.

She wanted to be caught. She wanted to have to pay

off the wager of five kisses. And she hoped that she and Brooks would lie in each other's arms once again tonight.

With each thud of the mare's hooves another burst of happiness warmed her chest.

She was engaged; she was in love. Life was just about perfect.

"Ha! I won," Brooks declared as he thundered passed her. He eased his horse to a stop and swung out of the saddle.

"Yes, you won." Marisa waited until he lifted his arms to assist her from the sidesaddle just so she would have the pleasure of feeling his wide rough hands on her body.

"After we walk the horses to cool them down, I expect my reward." Brooks leaned near and whispered into her ear. "And I have something for you."

"Another present?" Marisa raised her brows quizzically. "Hmm, I wonder if it is earbobs." She looked up at him and grinned mischievously. Now it was her turn to tease him.

"I see my dear cousin has been telling tales out of school." Brooks frowned.

"Actually, I heard this particular story from Cyril. He told me that one Christmas you practically saved the New York City economy by buying identical earbobs for all your, um, lady friends." Marisa's fine leather boots crunched over the early spring grass while she matched Brooks's long stride.

He sighed and shook his head. "I guess the folly of my youth is going to plague me forever. I bet good ol' Cyril loved revealing my sordid past to you." Then Brooks glanced down at her and tried to look melancholy. "Wait until I get him in the ring again."

"Now, Brooks."

''There is one thing you may be sure of. You are the only woman with my engagement ring on her finger.''

''As long as I am the last,'' she said, remembering Violet's confession.

He stopped walking and tipped her chin up with his gloved index finger. ''You aren't really bothered by these stories, or the past, are you, Marisa? Have no doubt, I have never loved anyone before you. What I felt for Violet was not love.''

''It doesn't matter what you did before, just what happens for the rest of our lives.'' She smiled and stood on her tiptoes to place a kiss on his chin.

He looped his free arm around her waist and kept her possessively close to his lean hip while they walked. A shiver of delight worked its way up her spine.

''Cold? We can go back if you are cold.''

''No, I'm fine.'' She absently tapped the riding crop against her skirt panel while she walked. ''Brooks, I love the gifts and the parties, but I don't want you to spoil me.''

''Too late.''

''I mean it. I don't want to forget how to take care of myself. I want to be…independent.''

He stopped and stared down at her in mock horror. ''Lord save me, have I just proposed to a Bloomer?''

''Don't tease.'' She bit her bottom lip and tried to think of a way she could make him understand. ''This is important to me. Since I have been here in New York I have seen women who, well, women who seem to have given up every little bit of themselves. All they do is stay home and make sure the servants keep the place tidy. They become so—so…'' She searched her mind for the right word.

''Dependant?'' he offered.

"Yes. I don't want to be like that. I love being a lady, but I can still take care of myself."

"I have seen you rope, shoot and cuss the hide off a mule skinner." He grinned when she blushed. "I am not likely to forget where you came from."

"Good, as long as you understand. I am not going to ever be one of those women who say 'yes, dear' and 'no, dear.' At least not all the time."

"I love you, Marisa. I love you because you are capable and independent. I don't want you to change. I adore you just the way you are right now."

"So would it bother you terribly if we didn't live here? I mean, after the wedding? I'd like to go *home*."

"I am glad to hear you say that." He clasped her hand and they walked side by side until they reached the edge of Harlem Lake. The horses were breathing normally and had begun to grab a mouthful of grass whenever the couple slowed enough for them to manage.

"Shall we sit?" Brooks pulled out a kerchief and wiped off a boulder that was nestled beneath an ash tree.

Marisa sat down and carefully arranged her skirt. Then she folded her hands in her lap and looked up at Brooks.

"You are a treasure, Miss O'Bannion." He tied the reins loosely to a slender bush. Then he returned to the boulder and knelt beside her on the damp turf.

"After all the ribbing I have taken over those damn Christmas earbobs, I shouldn't even give you these." Brooks reached into his coat pocket and withdrew another tiny, velvet-covered box. He opened it and took out a pair of emerald-and-diamond earbobs. Sunlight caught the faceted stones in the center and sent a rainbow prism of light across her plum riding skirt.

She giggled. "They *are* earbobs!" She felt tears well-ing up behind her eyes as she laughed. "And they match the necklace you gave me."

"I intended to buy them for you the minute I saw how that necklace looked around your pretty throat. Now my ring is on your finger, and my heart is in your hands. You are as good as branded, Marisa. And I have learned to think like your father and brothers. I don't take kindly to having what is mine rustled."

She threw her arms his neck and hugged him tightly. The feeling of his mustache scraping her cheek made her stomach clench and roll. Excitement telegraphed through every muscle in her body when she glanced at her hand where the sapphire and diamonds winked. A part of her still felt ill-suited to be the fiancée of this remarkable gentleman, but she was ready to take a leap of faith.

"Are you are as anxious to marry as I am?" he coaxed.

Marisa leaned into his embrace once again. "Yes, I am."

"Then I believe it is time I collected my bet." His voice was husky and low with passion.

"Five kisses?"

"Um-hmm."

She was only too happy to pay off the debt.

Chapter Seventeen

Lying on his back in the grass, Brooks watched the golden disk of the sun dip toward the west. "I suppose we should start back before the liveryman reports his horse stolen and we find ourselves residents of the penitentiary on Blackwell's Island." He stood up and stretched extravagantly. "Let's not wait until fall, Missy. Let's find a preacher and get married now—today." The prospect of waiting until fall to make her his wife suddenly seemed a terrible burden.

"Why?" She touched the side of his face with her bare fingers. "Are you afraid you will change your mind?"

"Not me, but maybe you. You have most of the eligible men in New York fawning over you." He tried to smile, but there was a strange sensation of foreboding he could not shake. "Sometimes I wish we had stayed in the Territory. Maybe if we were out West you would elope with me immediately instead of making me wait."

Missy smiled and rolled her eyes. "Those other men are all peacocks, Brooks. You know I don't take any of their folderol seriously."

"Not even Cyril?"

"Especially not Cyril. He smiles so widely that I am

always put in mind of a fox who has found the door to the henhouse open. Besides, Ellen is crazy about him.''

Brooks guffawed loudly and sat up straight. The gray mare raised her head and snorted at the sound of his laughter. "Ellen? You are joking."

"Nope. She has a real tender spot for him and I think he returns the feeling."

"Than all that nonsense with you…him…he was just—"

"Getting your goat, as the saying goes," Marisa said with a smile.

Marisa's rented horse rolled her eyes while the inside of her nostrils flared bright rose. She pulled hard on the lines, which were tied to a nearby bush.

"I don't like the way that filly is acting." A strange sensation crept up the back of Brooks's scalp while he watched the animal paw the earth. "She's got a wild look in her eyes that I just don't trust. Marisa, take my horse. I'll ride her back to the stable."

"Sidesaddle?" She giggled. "That would be a sight, now wouldn't it? She is just spirited. It feels good to have a well-bred horse beneath me."

"I'm serious, Marisa. Ride my gelding back." A sense of urgency gripped him as he brushed the grass from his trousers.

Marisa placed her hands on her hips, elbows akimbo. "Brooks James, I am capable of making my own decisions, and riding this horse. I haven't had your ring on my finger for more than two hours and you are already trying to make me…subservient." The word rolled off her tongue with some difficulty.

"I am doing no such thing." He shook his head in annoyance. "I don't want to see anything happen to you, that's all.'' In a quieter voice he added, ''I couldn't stand it, honey.''

''Nothing is going to happen to me.'' She kissed the tip of his chin. ''Now give me a leg up so we can get started back.'' Brooks reluctantly obliged, while he tried to shake off the feeling of doom.

Marisa tugged on her glove, but it would not fit over the stones of her engagement ring. With an exasperated sigh she stuck the glove between the front buttons on her jacket. The fingers poked out and flopped when she gathered the reins in her hand.

''Be careful. If she starts to give you any trouble, stop and we'll walk the horses.'' Brooks couldn't shake the uneasy feeling that had settled upon him. His knuckles were white on the reins while Marisa adjusted her seat and arranged the panel of her habit over the side pommel. He brought his docile gelding close to the mare, hoping she would calm, but her ears moved back and forth and she tossed her head with each high step. The bit jingled at every turn, making Brooks all the more aware of how jumpy he had become.

Marisa turned and smiled at him. ''I wish you wouldn't fret. There is nothing wrong with this mare, she just needs a good run.'' Her smile grew mischievous. ''And so do I.''

''Marisa, no. I'm asking you not to do it, for me.''

''You are worried, aren't you?'' She was genuinely surprised by the level of his concern.

''Yes, I am.''

She reached across the space between them and touched his arm. ''I am not a hothouse lily, but if it means that much to you I will keep her to a walk. Happy?''

''Very.'' Relief flooded through him like a warm current in an icy lake. "I promise I won't make a habit of asking you to comply with my wishes."

"That's good, because I don't plan on making a habit of letting you have your own way." She giggled and tossed her head. "It's not good for a man to have his own way too often, even Clell says so."

"Clell?"

"Yep."

"That old codger does nothing *but* have his own way, so how would he know?" Brooks shook his head and laughed.

"It's good to see you are relaxing," Marisa said with a wink.

All the way back she kept her word and made sure the mare was well in hand. The trip back took twice as long but was worth it. When they rounded the last bend in the bridal path, Brooks was not surprised to see the livery owner pacing in front of his barn with an anxious look on his face.

"Sorry we took a little longer than I planned," Brooks yelled. "The mare was a little shy."

A frisky ground squirrel darted from the area where the liveryman stored his grain. The animal stopped and sat back on its haunches as if surveying the land, then with a flick of its bushy tail darted straight toward the gray mare's legs. The ball of fur was bobbing like a cork on water as it deftly threaded through the maze of flashing hooves.

"Easy, girl." The hat on Marisa's head skewed slightly to the right. The feather dipped low in front of her eyes, obscuring her vision.

"Careful, Marisa," Brooks advised. He saw her draw in the reins and he relaxed a bit. But just when he was sure it was going to be all right, the dappled gray exploded upward like a rocket on the Fourth of July.

The scene before him unfolded in an exaggerated manner. It was as if time had been altered, each event taking place so slowly that Brooks could see every detail as it happened.

He saw the look of surprise sweep across Marisa's lovely face.

Guilt flooded over him.

He saw her hat come free and flutter to the ground like a bird with a broken wing.

Brooks mentally asked himself why he had not jerked the sidesaddle off and switched them.

He saw the mare's hooves hammer the hat into bits of ripped fabric and crushed feathers.

Marisa was too petite, too frail to handle a thousand pounds of startled fury. Why hadn't he done more to protect her?

And then, while his belly grew cold and heavy as a stone, he saw her thigh come away from the pommel. That was the moment when Brooks silently started trying to bargain with God. He promised a thousand things in the seconds it took for Marisa to fall to the earth in a flurry of ebony curls and plum velvet.

Brooks leaped from the gelding and rushed toward her.

I would give my own life for hers, Lord.

She lay on the hard-packed ground, all the color drained from her face.

Please, God, oh please, don't let her be hurt.

Before the bellow of impotent fear had left his throat, the mare shied once again. Just before Brooks reached her side, iron-shod hooves struck Marisa's body. Then the mare took off in a blur of gray, the stirrup slapping her side as she went.

Please don't let her be dead.

He touched the hollow of her throat with two fingers.

There is a pulse. Thank you, God.

She was alive, unconscious but alive. Her body bent at the waist in an unnatural position. He touched her cheeks, willing her to waken.

He looked at her small body, twisted and still, and willed himself to know what to do.

But he didn't.

"Where is the nearest hospital?" Brooks barked at the chalk-faced stableman.

"I—I don't think there is one close by. She isn't— dead?" The nervous man kept staring at Marisa's lifeless form with eyes wilder than the half-broken horse's.

"No. She won't die—she can't!" Brooks looked at her pale face and nearly cried out in rage and fear. "Think, man, think. Where? A physician's office, anything?" Brooks fought to control the panic rising inside him.

"The New York Hospital is on 68th Street and York Avenue."

Brooks glanced at Marisa and his belly twisted. "Hurry man, take the gelding."

"I'll hurry."

"I love this woman more than my life. Go, and ride like Satan himself is at your heels."

It seemed like an eternity had passed before the clang of a bell announced the arrival of the hospital wagon.

Brooks had gone from periods of praying to moments of dark despair when he questioned God, life and everything around him. But through it all he had remained crouched at Marisa's side as if his very presence could hold off the Grim Reaper.

He stood up when the wagon stopped beside him. Two men garbed in white jackets and trousers jumped out of the back, running with a canvas-and-wooden stretcher between them.

Brooks had covered Marisa's body with his coat and she had not moved since the fall. He dared not allow himself to think that she might not live.

She had to survive. She was his life.

He willed her to hang on, prayed she would regain consciousness, while the men prepared to place her body on the stretcher. Suddenly a wave of fear rolled over him.

"You'll handle her carefully, won't you?"

One man looked up and nodded; the other kept his eyes on Marisa.

"Because if you don't, I swear to God I will kill you."

That comment brought the other man's eyes up. He looked at Brooks, then nodded.

They slid her body onto the stretcher, and with practiced efficiency raised her between them.

"I'm riding with you." Brooks jogged beside the stretcher, watching Marisa for any signs of returning consciousness, any sign of pain. He had checked her head, but found no wound. That frightened him even more. Her injuries were internal.

Fear of what he could not see and what he could not fix threatened to overwhelm him. But he fought it off, thinking only of Marisa and what was best for her.

"There is no room in the back for all of us," one of the attendants said when they reached the wagon.

"Then one of you is walking, because I am damn well going with her," Brooks snarled. No more was said, but when the stretcher was loaded in the back of the wagon, one man, a swarthy fellow with a thick mustache, stepped aside and nodded toward the narrow bench that was fastened on one wall.

"God be with you, sir," he mumbled when Brooks impulsively grabbed his hand.

Brooks's eyes returned again and again to the black numbers on the round clock face as he paced the hospital corridor. His stride was in perfect cadence with the swinging arc of the old pendulum. He focused on a curved scratch on the old wall, looking for anything that might occupy his thoughts for a few minutes.

But it did not work. He thought only of Marisa and how long she had been suffering.

Twelve hours had ticked by since she'd been thrown. Eleven hours since she had arrived at The New York Hospital. Nine hours since Dr. Malone had responded to Brooks's plea. Six hours since Brooks had sent a frantic telegram to Marisa's family in the New Mexico Territory.

All that time had been marked by the silent clock on the wall.

Dr. Malone appeared at the end of the dimly lit corridor. Brooks rushed to meet him. "Is there any change?"

Doc Malone removed his glasses and dragged his palm down his lined face. "None. Come over here, Brooks, I want to talk with you."

Brooks followed the aging physician to a scarred wooden bench along one wall. "Spare me no detail."

Doc smiled wanly. "I never lied to Bellami and I will not lie to you." He sighed and tilted his graying head back against the wall. He closed his eyes while he spoke. "The young lady has shown no sign of waking. I've seen cases like this before. There is a chance she will open her eyes and be little worse for wear." He lifted his head, replaced his glasses and blinked several times. "Another possibility is that when she wakes she will be changed."

"How so?"

"We know so little about the workings of the mind. There have been incidents of people waking and being, well, just different. Sometimes they have lost blocks of memory. Sometimes their personalities have been transformed or, in the worse possible cases, they have lost their entire past and identity."

"I see." Brooks sighed. *Dear Lord, let Missy remain Missy.*

"No, I don't think you do, Brooks, but it does not matter. There is also another potentiality you must prepare for. She might not ever regain consciousness."

Might not ever regain consciousness? Brooks swallowed his fear. "Which of those options do you think will take place?"

"I just don't know, Brooks. I've examined her.... There do not seem to be any broken bones, but..."

"But what?"

"If she does wake up, her ordeal, and yours, may just be beginning." A cloud that might have been pity seemed to flit through his aging eyes.

"I want to know, Doc, whatever it is."

"All right. I have an area of deep concern. As I said, there are no obvious broken bones, but there is a massive amount of swelling around two contusions."

"Is that bad?"

"In this instance it is." Doc drew in a deep breath. His bony shoulders appeared to sag under an invisible weight. "The injuries are to her spine. If she wakes up and she is herself, with no change to her personality, she may still be facing the hardest situation in her life. She could be facing the prospect of partial or even complete paralysis."

Paralysis. "She might not walk again?" Brooks wanted to wake up and find this was all a hideous nightmare.

"It is a possibility."

Brooks inhaled the pungent, sterile smell of the hospital and focused on the problems at hand. Marisa needed care, and that was all that mattered at the moment. "Who is the best in this field of medicine?" He heard his own voice, oddly clear and composed.

Doc frowned. The skin between his brows wrinkled deeper. "Dr. Stanley Jakobs is good."

"The best, I want the best," Brooks insisted.

"This is not like hiring a mason or a carpenter. Opinions about physicians and their modes of treatment vary a great deal. Sometimes the doctor in vogue may not be the one with the most efficacious procedures."

"I trust you, Doc. Who do you personally consider the best in treating spinal injuries?" Brooks leaned forward and peered into Doc's eyes, as if he could will him to make the right choice.

"If it was my daughter in that room, I'd want Sonia Levy."

"A woman physician?" Brooks leaned back.

"Is that a problem?" Doc tilted his head and regarded Brooks seriously.

"No, not at all. In fact—" Brooks chewed the inside of his mouth and thought about Marisa's strong will "—in this case it could be a blessing." He stared at Doc Malone. "Can you reach her tonight?"

"I'll see what I can do. In the meantime, why don't you stretch out here and try to get some rest? I will leave instructions for you to be alerted if there is any change."

"I can't sleep."

"Fine, then just lie down and close your eyes for a bit." Doc stood up and waited for Brooks to comply.

After a moment Brooks sighed heavily. He leaned

against the wall. Doc watched the young man's face slowly relax. Within minutes he was breathing deeply.

Marisa opened her eyes, but felt like she was sloughing through thick sand. Her vision was blurring and she felt weak as a kitten.

''Here, have a sip of this,'' a disembodied voice said.

Strong hands helped her raise her head, and she felt cool, clear water touch her lips. It felt good, but swallowing was hard. She felt hot, dried out, as if she had been in the desert too long without water.

Marisa slumped back on something soft. She closed her eyes, while a headache thudded and pounded through her brain.

As if from a great distance she could hear people whispering and the sounds of things being moved, bedding being shifted. She could hear it all, but it was strangely disjointed and removed, as if it were happening to somebody else and not her.

Another spat of hushed voices and then she was alone.

Marisa tried to clear her head, but it seemed to get more fuzzy.

They have given me something.

The sound of a door closing roused Marisa from her laudanum-induced slumber. She fought to open her eyes, to focus, to participate in living. She had disjointed images of visitors; Brooks, Ellen, Patricia and other faces she did not know. Time had no meaning. Each time she woke, she never knew if hours or days had elapsed. Slowly, she began to stay awake longer, and she knew she was going to live.

A wavy form began to take shape beside the bed. As her vision cleared, she could see the person was female, slender and blond. A flash of deep green above and below told her the woman was wearing a hat that matched her suit.

"Ellen?" Marisa croaked.

A long pause made the pain in her head worse. She closed her eyes and stopped trying to focus.

"No, it is not Ellen. It is Violet Ashland."

The siren's voice brought Marisa's eyes open with a start. This time she willed herself to disregard the pain and focus on the face.

"What are you doing here?" Marisa demanded in a voice that was stronger than she really felt.

"I wanted to see for myself. So it *is* true—you had an injury." Violet smiled. "The news is all over town."

She's happy I'm hurt.

"I didn't believe the rumors at first—Brooks's family would tell me nothing—but the domestic help does talk, you know." She moved closer, and for the first time Marisa realized she was swathed in a white sheet and lying on a hospital bed. The knowledge made her feel doubly vulnerable.

"Just go away," she ordered.

Violet backed up an inch, but then stopped. "No. I have a few things to say to you. And I have been waiting until I was sure Brooks was gone so we would not be interrupted." She smiled again, and the expression was full of hate.

"Spit it out and then just *leave.*"

Violet's smile slipped a bit. "All right. I have been waiting days to see you. Actually, it was very lucky I picked today because I went to the chapel for a few minutes and when I came out your doctor—your *new* doctor—was discussing your case with Dr. Malone."

Marisa frowned. None of the names meant anything to her. She wondered how long she had been in the hospital.

"Will you just get on with it?" She was impatient to get up and find Brooks.

"You took a bad fall, but evidently the horse you were riding stepped on you." Violet frowned. "You don't remember any of this, do you?"

Marisa clamped her lips together. What she did or did not remember was her business.

"Suit yourself, Miss O'Bannion. Anyway, it seems you were hurt by the horse's shod hooves."

An image of lying in the grass with the gray mare over her flitted through her mind, but it brought pain with it, so Marisa let it go.

"The doctors are very sad. And it is a great pity." Violet looked sympathetic. "You will never walk again, Miss O'Bannion."

Chapter Eighteen

A part of Marisa didn't believe Violet, but in her heart she knew it was true. She willed her feet to move, so she could swing herself from the bed, but they did not respond. Hot stinging tears began to form at the back of her eyes, but she blinked them away.

I will not cry, not in front of her.

"So I decided to have a little chat with you," Violet continued. She walked close to the bed. "Lovely ring."

"My engagement ring."

Violet's blue eyes turned to ice. "It is time for me to be blunt, Miss O'Bannion. Brooks James has the respectability that I want. My earlier—shall we call it a slip of judgment?—cost me in this city. I want him."

"You can't possibly believe he wants you."

"Of course not, but after his behavior at the party I have even more reason to make our social circle think we are together. I have it all thought out. You see, I told everyone that Brooks and I had to postpone our plans because of a problem with you. Since you are related by marriage, it seems perfectly logical. Nobody except you, me and Brooks knows the real reason, and if you are sensible, nobody will have to know."

"I won't help save your reputation." Marisa turned away, staring at the white wall, willing this creature to leave.

"Really? And how about Brooks? Would you save him from humiliation? Surely you love him enough to do the best for him."

Marisa turned back. "Of course I want what is best for him."

"Then we have a common bond, Miss O'Bannion." Violet smiled again. "Because I am the best for him and I want him."

Marisa managed a snort of laughter. "You are a silly, spoiled bitch."

Violet's lips compressed. "Be that as it may, you cannot seriously believe that a *cripple* is what he wants?"

Cripple.

The word hung in the air like a rotten stench. It wrapped itself around Marisa's body and choked her, threatened to suffocate her.

"I can see that you are thinking about it. That's good, Miss O'Bannion. I want to leave you with a few more things to think about. Think about what it will be like for Brooks to push his bride around in an invalid's chair. Or consider how he will feel when he carries you across the threshold—forever." Violet *tsked* her tongue. "And I can't imagine a man like Brooks being happy about having a cripple for a wife in his marriage bed."

"Get out!" Marisa yelled. If she had been able to get out of the bed she would've beaten the hell out of Violet.

"Yes, I am through here." Violet adjusted her hat and gloves. "I am so glad we had this happy talk. And Miss O'Bannion, I do hope your stay in hospital is a short one. The sooner you return to where you belong the better, for all of us."

* * *

"Mr. James?"

The voice drifted to Brooks through layers of cotton and veils of fog.

He sat up with a shaking start. Sunlight blazed through the window at the end of the corridor. It had been night when he last talked to Doc.

"How long did I sleep?" Brooks asked the nurse who had hailed him as alarm ripped through him.

"The doctor would like to speak with you."

He focused on the freckled young woman in the crisp cotton pinafore. "Has there been any change?" Brooks lurched to his feet.

"I can't say, sir. You will need to speak with the doctor. Just go to that office over there."

"Thank you." Brooks ran his fingers through his hair and straightened his rumpled shirt. He was still in his riding clothes. He rubbed his hand over his jaws and felt a thickening beard.

A cold knot formed in his stomach as he walked down the hall toward the closed door. He forced himself to put one foot in front of the other, refusing to give in to the dark cloak of doubt and fear that hovered nearby.

He had to remain strong and confident for Marisa.

Brooks knocked lightly on the door. A woman's voice bade him enter. He stepped inside.

Sonia Levy was a middle-aged woman with iron gray hair and dark brows. She sat behind a battered desk. When she smiled Brooks noticed she had kind brown eyes.

Brown eyes, like Marisa's.

"Please, come in." She gestured to a chair in front of the desk. "Have a seat, Mr. James. Would you care for some coffee?"

"Yes, thanks, Dr. Levy," Brooks answered thickly. "I

am anxious to hear what you think about my fiancée's condition." Brooks had no time for idle chatter. "I brought her flowers," Brooks added awkwardly.

Dr. Levy's expression altered and she looked away, but not before Brooks recognized pity in her eyes. "As you know, I have already examined the young lady, Mr. James, several times."

"How is she? Is there improvement?" he asked eagerly.

Dr. Levy opened her mouth to speak, but a knock on the door interrupted her. She stood up and stepped out from behind the desk. Brooks noticed her uncommon height and the athletic slimness of her body. She opened the door and took a tray from the same young nurse who had roused Brooks. The smell of strong, freshly brewed coffee filled the small office.

"You look like you could use about a gallon of this." Dr. Levy smiled as she placed the tray on the desk.

"Not just now. I would like to discuss Marisa O'Bannion first. When did you last examine her?"

Dr. Levy returned to the chair behind her desk before she met Brooks's gaze. "Just this morning. She woke while I was in the process of examining her."

"Oh, thank God." Brooks ran a hand over his face. "How is she? Is she all right?"

"Yes, well, it does seem as if she has passed one milestone. She is alert, lucid, but that is all I can tell you, Mr. James."

Brooks's head snapped up and he frowned. "What do you mean?"

"I know no other way to put this, Mr. James. I have taken your fiancée on as a patient. She and I had a long talk today. Now my primary responsibility is for her health and welfare."

"As it should be." Brooks felt his belly twist into knots. That feeling of doom washed over him again.

"I am glad you agree. And I hope you will understand when I tell you that I cannot discuss my patient with you. Without her permission I cannot reveal any details of her health or care."

"She is my fiancée."

Dr. Levy managed a thin smile. "So you said. Today I did a more thorough physical examination and work up. I explained her condition in some detail. We discussed her options." Dr. Levy looked up and smiled. "She is a remarkable young woman."

"I have always thought so," Brooks agreed.

"I believe she understands what lies before her."

"Marisa is a strong woman. Whatever is ahead *we* will come through together."

"That's the issue I have been trying to get to, Mr. James. Miss O'Bannion does not wish you to know anything about her condition." Dr. Levy's eyes filled with pity again.

"What do you mean?"

"Miss O'Bannion has expressly requested that you *not* see her again while she is in my care or receive any information about her whatsoever."

Brooks was on his feet, across the room and reaching for the doorknob in a heartbeat. "I want to see her right now."

"Wait, please, Mr. James. There is more. She has asked me to give you this letter and begs that you will do as she requests." Dr. Levy opened the middle drawer of the desk and drew out an envelope.

Brooks stared at his name, written in Marisa's familiar bold hand.

A chill of fear seeped into his bones. "We are going to be married."

"I'm sorry, Mr. James, really I am." Dr. Levy reached inside her skirt pocket and brought out the engagement ring. It sparkled just as brilliantly as it had when he'd slipped it on Marisa's finger.

Before the accident.

"She asked me to return this to you and to tell you that she cannot marry you," Dr. Levy said softly.

"I don't believe it. I won't believe it." Brooks glowered at the physician. "Where is she? I want to see Marisa right now."

"I'm sorry, but I must respect the wishes of my patient. She specifically does not wish to see you, Mr. James. I know this must be difficult for you to understand." Dr. Levy nodded at the letter clutched in his hand. "Perhaps that will answer your questions. For your sake, I hope so." The doctor rose from the chair and stepped out from behind the desk. "I have rounds to make. Please, feel free to use my office as long as you like."

Brooks continued to stare at the sealed envelope. His heart contracted painfully in his chest. It was too much to consider that Marisa had changed her mind. She'd said she loved him, and had made love with him.

She'd given him her word, her promise of everlasting love.

There had to be another explanation, but as he stared at the dark ink, he could not imagine any reason strong enough to compel her to break their engagement.

"Unless she has changed her mind and she no longer cares," he murmured in a choked voice.

Brooks shoved the well-read telegrams into his shirt pocket. Clell had been as succinct in his reply as Marisa had been in the note she'd sent with Dr. Levy. From Clell's cable, Brooks knew that Hugh and Shane were trailing a bull and fifty heifers to Montana, Bellami and Trace were still on their honeymoon and Flynn was on some law business in the Arizona Territory near Tombstone. Only Logan and Clell would be arriving on the five-fifteen train today.

Brooks glanced at the huge clock face and to his surprise saw that it was after five o'clock. Within minutes he was engulfed by a crowd of people. Voices mingled in a humming murmur as he was pulled and pushed toward the arriving train. Numb from what he had read in Marisa's letter, he stood there waiting for Clell and Logan. When most of the people had left and he no longer felt as if he were suffocating in a sea of humanity, he looked up and saw them.

They both were wearing their Stetsons and both had trail-stained leather saddlebags thrown over their shoulders. They sauntered toward him in a loose-jointed gait that marked men who spent more time on horseback than on foot. A lump formed in Brooks's throat at the sight of them.

"Boy, you look like you been rode hard and put up wet." Clell slapped a wide palm on Brooks's shoulder.

"I feel like it, too." Brooks grimaced. He had not shaved and had barely eaten for the last several days. The reflection he saw in the mirror was of a shattered man. A man who had found love but unexplainably had had it slip away.

"How is Missy?" Logan asked as they made their way through the station.

"Marisa," Brooks corrected.

"Eh?"

"Marisa. She prefers to be called Marisa now." Brooks

rubbed his hand down his face, trying to focus, trying to sort his thoughts into some kind of order. He was exhausted both mentally and physically.

"Well, why in tarnation would she want to do a fool thing like that?" Logan asked.

"'Cause it's her name, you young fool." Clell's brows were deeply furrowed. "How bad is she hurt, Brooks?"

They reached the carriage that Brooks had hired, and climbed inside. Logan took the scenery in with wide eyes as the carriage rolled out of the station.

"I don't know how badly she is injured. They won't let me in to see her." Brooks nearly strangled on the words.

"What kind of damn hospital have you got her in? Take me to that consarned place. We'll take care of that nonsense in short order, by God." Clell tossed his saddlebags to the floor beside his boots.

Brooks leaned his head against the seat. He allowed his eyes to close against the pain of the bright sunshine. "I wish it was the hospital, Clell."

"What the devil do you mean?" Clell asked in a quieter voice.

"Marisa refuses to see me," Brooks admitted wearily.

"Did you two have another donnybrook?" Clell asked with a half grin.

"Not exactly." Brooks shifted in the seat and forced himself to meet the old cowboy's eyes.

Clell pressed on. "Why won't she see you? She's got to know you'd be worried about her."

"She should know it," Brooks said softly.

Clell narrowed his eyes and studied Brooks. "What exactly *did* go on between you two?"

"Oh, nothing much. I realized I was crazy in love with her, asked her to marry me and she said yes. That's all that happened.'' Brooks sighed deeply. ''We were engaged on the day of the accident.''

''Engaged?'' Logan repeated.

''Then why in Sam Hill won't she see you?'' Clell dragged off his hat and raked his fingers through his slightly thinning hair.

''I don't know. She was wearing my ring when she was thrown, but the doctor returned it to me with a note from Marisa that says she doesn't want to see me again. No explanation, just that she can't see me.''

''Have the driver of this rig take us to the hospital on the double. I'm gettin' to the bottom of this right quick.''

Marisa stared out the window and thought about God. She had never really given Him a lot of thought before. Oh, she was religious enough, but her relationship with God was comfortable and second nature. She always pictured Him as an indulgent father, nearby but never requiring a lot of her attention. Now all her attention was focused on God.

She realized that she had been leading a truly blessed life. God had been very good to her. She knew what it felt like to have the sunshine on her face, to feel the wind in her hair. She knew what it felt like to be spoiled and doted on by her brothers and father and Clell. And thanks to Brooks, she knew what it felt like to experience love.

The memory of his searing touch flitted through her mind each night when she was in that place between wakefulness and dreaming. She smiled when she thought of the hot, licking desire they had shared.

It was a memory she would always treasure. But that was all it would be—a memory. She sighed and adjusted the lap robe over her lifeless legs in an automatic gesture.

A knock on the door brought her head around. She felt

a mixture of happiness and dread when Clell strode into her room.

"Hello, lil' bit." He bent and hugged her tightly. It was the kind of hug that cut the air off in midbreath but felt too good to squirm out of. She clung to him, trying not to give in to tears.

He finally broke the contact and drew back enough to stare into her face. Rough, strong fingers pushed strands of hair away from her face. A gentle smile curled his lips.

"How are you, honey?"

She swallowed the lump that lodged in her throat. "I'm better—now that you are here." She ducked her head, unwilling for him to see her weakness. "Is anybody else with you? Pa and the boys?"

"Sorry, honey. Your pa and Shane are delivering some beef on the hoof, Flynn is workin'. They wasn't expectin' to have to come to New York."

He lifted her chin with a callused fingertip. "What is all this nonsense I hear about you makin' and then breakin' an engagement to Brooks?"

"I can't ever marry." She inhaled a ragged breath. "Not him or anybody else." She nearly choked on the truth of it.

Clell pulled a nearby chair close beside her bed. "Never is a mighty long time." He took her small hand in his. "Do you love him?"

Her bottom lip trembled and she looked Clell straight in the eye. "More than anything in the world."

"Then you can marry him. And it better be quick or he may just dry up and blow away. The poor boy is near starvin' himself to death worryin' over you. He looks bad, honey, real bad."

"Is he sick?" Marisa's heart contracted in fear.

"Lovesick." Clell stood up and stretched his legs. "Let

me go out and call him and Logan. We'll get this fool-ishness over with—''

''No!'' Marisa's voice cracked with emotion. She grabbed at Clell's shirt like a wild woman. ''I can't see him.''

Clell frowned. He had never seen her act like this. ''What in tarnation is wrong with you, girl?''

Tears threatened to spill over her bottom lids. ''I can't let him see me like this. I just can't.'' Her voice cracked again as she fought back the tears.

''Like what, honey?'' Clell stroked her face and tried to pry her fingers from his shirt. ''You look just fine.'' He reached out and traced the smudges under her eyes. ''You don't look like you been sleepin' a lot, but that is easily fixed.''

''I'm not fine. I'll never be fine.'' Her voice was high with barely restrained hysteria. ''Don't you understand? Can't you see?'' She suddenly released him and started pounding on her knees with her fists. ''Don't you see, Clell?''

''See what? I can't see anything wrong with you, honey.''

''I'm crippled!'' She looked at him with anguished eyes. ''I can't walk.'' Her voice was little more than a husky whisper. ''I can't stand. And as God is my witness, I will not saddle Brooks with a damn, useless *cripple* for a wife.''

Clell walked out into the hallway and for the first time in his life knew what a condemned man felt like. He glanced toward the hopeful, haggard face of Brooks.

A little part of him died when their eyes met.

''How is she?'' Brooks asked as he rushed forward.

''She asked to see you, Logan.'' Clell broke the contact and deliberately avoided Brooks's eyes. He wasn't sure

he could do as Marisa asked, but he knew he would because he had given his word. She had pleaded with him
in a voice dry as her eyes had been until he had given it.

Logan swallowed hard. He removed himself from the
windowsill where he had been lounging. Clell watched
him disappear inside Marisa's room.

"Tell me, Clell. How is she?" Brooks insisted.

Clell sighed and eased his body into a chair. A bone-
deep weariness seemed to overtake him as he searched his
mind for the right words. "She is recoverin', Brooks."

His answer would not satisfy the man staring down at
him.

"Clell, I consider you a friend. Now look me in the
eye and tell me." Brooks clenched his fists tightly against
his thighs, determined to maintain his unraveling control.

"She is awake and as stubborn as ever." Clell looked
up and managed a shaky smile. "She asked me to give
you a message."

"What?"

"She wants you to walk away from this hospital and
get on with your life. She said to tell you that it can't be.
She is not the woman you asked to marry you, not what
you thought she was."

Brooks contracted his fists harder. "Are those words
yours or Marisa's?"

Clell's eyes widened and he drew in a breath as if he
were going to shout, or spill his guts, but then he ducked
his head. "They are not mine," he said in a whisper.

"Why, Clell? Did she tell you why?"

"Yep, she told me." He sighed heavily.

"Well?" There was a sharp edge to Brooks's question.

"I gave her my word I wouldn't say, Brooks. But I will
tell you this. She has made up her mind, and no power
on earth is going to budge her. You might as well do as

she says. Get on with your life, forget you ever met Marisa O'Bannion.''

''I could as easily stop the sun from setting.'' Brooks raked his hand through his tousled hair. ''There has to be a damn good reason for her to change her mind.''

''There is.'' Logan strode toward them. His face was ashen and his eyes held a pain that Brooks had never witnessed in them before. Tight lines of tension bracketed his young mouth and eyes.

''What is it, Logan?''

''Logan, she doesn't want him to know,'' Clell warned as he took a step forward.

''Yeah, I know, but I wouldn't give her my word like you did, Clell. She asked for it, but I wouldn't give it.'' His voice cracked with restrained emotion. ''Near broke my heart to hear her beg me, but I couldn't do what she asked. It just ain't fair for him not to know.'' Logan's voice cracked. ''It ain't fair, Clell.''

''I know that.'' Clell nodded and swallowed hard.

''What? What has happened?'' A thousand imagined terrors flashed through Brooks's mind.

Logan drew himself up as if preparing to take a blow. ''She is crippled, Brooks.'' He met Brooks's gaze unblinkingly.

''What did you say?'' Brooks wasn't sure he had heard correctly.

''She is paralyzed. Missy can't move her legs.'' Logan sagged weakly against the wall as if the act of telling Brooks had sapped all his strength.

''Paralyzed?'' Brooks felt the cold blanket of dread wrap itself tightly around his heart. ''Marisa is paralyzed?''

''That is why she will never ever marry you,'' Logan said sadly. ''She means it, Brooks—she won't change her mind.''

Chapter Nineteen

"Try to move your toes, Marisa." Dr. Levy glanced up at Marisa. A frown puckered her forehead.

"I don't want to try," she said, lying flat on her back and staring at the ceiling. "Nothing helps, nothing changes. It doesn't matter, anyway."

Dr. Levy sighed and pulled the sheet up over Marisa's motionless legs. "You have given up."

Marisa hated to admit it, but Dr. Levy was right. She wasn't trying. But then what good did it do for her to try? She couldn't feel her legs, and she certainly couldn't move anything below her waist. Besides, she remembered how hard it had been for her, Clell and the rest of the family when Trace couldn't come to terms with his blindness. They'd had to stand by and helplessly watch him struggle day after day. No, she wasn't going to do that to her family.

I can adjust.

Marisa drew in a deep breath. The sooner she resigned herself to being a cripple, the sooner her lonely heart would begin to heal. And now that Brooks was out of her life, her heart felt almost as numb as her legs. Without his love she had no desire to try.

"You know, Marisa, your recovery depends on you."
Dr. Levy rubbed the furrow between her brows. "Everyone says you are a woman of fiery temperament and iron will. The fact that you won't fight worries me more than your injury. The swelling on your spine is lessening everyday. The bruise is all but gone."

Marisa turned her head and stared at the doctor. "Are you saying I will walk again?" she asked.

"No, I can't say that. But at this point it is a little early to decide your injury is permanent. There are many things we don't know about the human body. It could take weeks before you regain any feeling or mobility—even months...."

"Or?" Prompted Marisa.

"Or...you may never have any more mobility or sensation than you have now. But that is no reason not to try," Dr. Levy added quickly.

Marisa sighed. She would not cry. Tears were useless, just as struggling against her paralysis was useless. There was no point in trying to make Dr. Levy understand. Nobody could understand how she felt. She had never had to depend on anybody in her life. Losing her ability to walk was almost like being dead.

Worse than being dead because her heart still felt empty.

"Marisa, would you like to leave the hospital?"

She searched her mind for an opinion, but it really didn't matter where she was. The moment she'd taken Brooks's ring from her finger she'd stopped caring what happened. But then she thought of Violet's second visit. Miss Ashland had cautioned Marisa about returning home, saying it would be too easy for Brooks to reach her there, and that if she *really* cared, she would find someplace else to go.

Marisa turned to Dr. Levy. "No. I don't want to go home."

"Well, there is no reason for you to remain here," Dr. Levy noted.

Marisa pulled her thoughts from Brooks. "Is there some *place*, someplace where they take people like me— cripples?" The few times she'd left her bed she had been put in an invalid's chair and wheeled around by a nurse. She had felt people's eyes upon her back and seen pity on their faces when she'd turned.

"I wish you wouldn't speak of yourself like that," Dr. Levy said, and frowned. "There *is* a place not too far from here. With trees, animals and quiet. The facility was built for patients with special needs."

"You mean cripples?"

"No." Dr. Levy was growing impatient with Marisa's attitude. She needed something to shock her into *caring*. But what?

"My patients go there simply to rest." Dr. Levy smiled and patted Marisa's forearm. "To rest and to heal."

"Are you talking about a sanitarium?" Marisa asked.

"I suppose you could call it that."

She thought about Clell's and Logan's reactions. They would not be inclined to let her go anywhere alone. "Could my family come?"

"I don't see any reason why not."

"Then I'll go," Marisa answered. She had to hide from Brooks until he saw that what she was doing was for the best.

"Marisa, I want you to think about something else."

"What?"

"I need to hire another person to help with your rehabilitation. We don't seem to be making any headway."

"Why are you telling me this?" Marisa didn't care.

"Because I need your permission to bring another person in." Dr. Levy just wished she knew what kind of a person it would take to make Marisa want to get well. "Do I have your permission?"

"Sure, hire whatever nurse you want. I don't care."

Dr. Levy nodded and walked to the door. Her hand was on the doorknob.

"Dr. Levy, there is one thing I want." Marisa spoke before the door opened.

"Yes?" She paused, hoping that this was the turning point—that Marisa *wanted* something.

"I want this kept secret. I don't want anyone to know where I am going."

Dr. Levy nodded and felt disappointment fold over her. "Whatever you say, Marisa. You are the patient."

Brooks paced the corridor of the hospital, counting the uneven tiles, just as he had done for many long weeks. He had tried every way in the world to sneak into Marisa's room, but Dr. Levy had proved to be a formidable opponent. She had told him from the start that Marisa's care was her only concern and that he would have to find some other way of addressing the issue of their broken engagement.

He dragged his hands through his hair and tried to think of a way to see her. Strong, striding footsteps brought him around.

Logan grinned at Brooks from under the brim of his Stetson. "You are lookin' down in the mouth," Logan drawled.

"That's what losing the woman you love does to you."

Logan's smile widened.

Brooks grimaced in the face of such happiness, but then he realized that if Logan could smile, Marisa must be better, or at least no worse.

"How is she?" he asked hopefully.

"The same."

Hope died. Brooks fought the wave of melancholy that washed over him. "I see."

"No, I don't think you do, not yet." Logan pushed his hat back with the tip of one finger. "What would you say if I told you that you could find the woman you lost?"

"*Find* the woman?" Brooks's head snapped up and he focused intently on Logan's cheerful face. "What do you mean?"

"Say if a certain gal was goin' to take a trip—a secret trip—it would be nice of some fella who knew where she was headed to let another fella know, wouldn't it?"

The hair on Brooks's nape prickled. His stomach lurched at the possibility of finally speaking to Marisa face-to-face. "It would be more than nice."

Logan leaned against the wall, crossed his boots at the ankle and grinned. "I betcha if the time comes that I ever lose my lady love, somebody I consider a friend—like you, for instance, Brooks—would tell me what I needed to know. Wouldn't you?"

"You could count on it," Brooks said softly. "To my dying breath, you could count on it."

"I knew it." Logan rolled his eyes toward the ceiling. "You know, I heard a funny thing this morning...." He appeared to be tracing the outline of the ornate cornice with his eyes as he spoke. "Seems Missy, I mean Marisa, is goin' to some sort of sanitarium, a place called Hunter's Roost."

"I've heard the name," Brooks said.

"I understand the place is kind of secluded. It might be easy for a determined man to sneak in there without being seen. You know what I mean?" Logan's pale eyes slid over Brooks's face.

"I think I do," Brooks said with a small grin. "I think I follow your story real well, at that."

* * *

Marisa woke with a start. It took her a moment to get her bearings and remember she was in a train car. Both Clell and Logan were watching her with unguarded expressions of pity on their faces. She turned away from them and tried to banish the lingering memory of her dream.

The sensation of lying in Brooks's arms, feeling the heated desire of his kisses, had begun to haunt her. At first she'd taken comfort from the vivid recollections, as she sat immobile in her invalid's chair. But as the days wore on, the memories began to be more torture than comfort. Now she realized those recollections were her curse, not the blessing she had thought. No matter how determined she was, and how sure that she was right not to saddle Brooks with a wife who could never stand at his side, all she could think of was the look in his eyes and the touch of his fingers.

He was right. He had branded her with his love.

She would never ever be able to forget him. She choked back the pain and misery that clogged her throat.

I will not cry.

She had not shed a single tear for herself, and she wasn't about to start now. The sooner she came to grips with her paralysis, the better off she would be. Besides, what did it matter? Without Brooks in her life any kind of happiness was little more than a pipe dream.

Brooks sat huddled in the corner of his seat at the back of the train, watching, waiting. He was roasting in his disguise of muffler, coat and low-slung hat, but at least he'd gone undetected.

His eyes had never left Marisa since Clell had carried her into the car. There was a dull but steady ache in his heart. It was pure hell to be so near her and not be able to reveal himself.

Dr. Levy leaned over to adjust the lap rug across Marisa's motionless legs as he watched.

He wanted to be the one who cared for her. Brooks yearned to hold her, to comfort her.

She looked up.

He saw her face clearly in the spring sunshine slanting through the window. There was something unfamiliar about her eyes, something that clawed at his insides.

It was as if all the fire that had burned inside her soul had been extinguished. Not even tears were in those dark eyes.

For a moment she appeared to look straight at him. He held his breath, but her eyes slid away, and he realized she had not recognized him. He slouched lower in the seat and pulled his hat down over his eyes. He could not afford to be discovered, not yet. Logan had slipped him information about which train Marisa would be on. But not even Logan knew Brooks sat only yards away. It took all his control to keep from revealing himself. He forced himself to wait as mile after mile flowed by. He watched her from under the concealing brim of his hat while his hands itched to touch her and his body tightened with love.

Brooks loved the person that Marisa was inside, not just her legs, her hair or the color of her eyes.

If she would only talk to him he could make her understand. She was his soul mate, and if it took him until his last breath, he was going to prove it to her one way or another.

At a town so small it didn't appear to have a name, Marisa was carried off the train and loaded into a surrey with short black fringe hanging from the leather top. Clell carefully tucked the lap robe over her legs before he strapped their baggage to the back and climbed in beside her. Brooks watched every detail through the coal-streaked glass. Marisa never looked about, never changed her stoic expression.

As the surrey rolled away from the train, the axles bent down the tops of windflowers growing in the middle of the dirt road. This was not a mecca of activity.

He watched until the buggy disappeared from sight and only then did he leave the train, shedding his stifling disguise as he went. He stood staring at the spot where he had last seen Marisa, while his heart thudded painfully in his chest.

"Are you turning to stone?" a crackling voice asked in an accent that was pure New Englander.

Brooks turned to find a man so old his age was almost beyond calculating. He was perched on a stump, beneath the shelter of a million leaves. Sunlight dappled his features. Brooks was put in mind of a woodland gnome. The man's fingers were as knotted and burled as the root he was whittling. Curled slivers piled at his feet.

"You need to hire a buggy?" the old man asked, with only a cursory lift of his eyes.

"To do what?"

"Follow that gal you was a-watching, I'd figger."

Brooks grinned. Here was a man Clell would appreciate. "Maybe. How far is it to Hunter's Roost?"

"Hunter's Roost?" the man said derisively. He stopped whittling and looked at Brooks. One eye had a milky core in the center. Brooks realized the old man was almost blind. "It was Hunter's Roost when it was only a bird blind for a-hunting. I don't know why they call it that now, with all those people sitting around just a-waiting to die."

"Is that what you think they are doing up there?" A knot of worry formed in Brooks's gut. Was Marisa worse than Logan had told him? Had she been more injured than anyone had revealed to him?

Was she dying?

"Seems like to me. If'n they'd get up and move around I warrant they'd all feel a sight better. A body that don't keep busy might as well get planted, I always say." He bent his head and went back to whittling. Relief flooded through Brooks when he realized it was just the old man's personal convictions that made him say what he did and not some portent of doom regarding Marisa.

"How far is it to the place?" Brooks asked again.

"Depends."

"On what?"

"On whether your a-walking or a-riding."

Brooks grinned. He was enjoying this exchange. "What would be the best way if I didn't want somebody to see me coming?"

"Now that would best be done by taking the footpath. It curves around the lake and leads right to the back door."

"And how far would it be?"

"Not far. A quick man should reach the place 'bout suppertime."

"Thanks." Brooks hefted his valise and took off down the vine-lined path. He found himself whistling a hopeful tune as he hiked beside hedgerows and rabbit burrows. By suppertime he intended to find out why Marisa had broken their engagement, although he suspected it was due to her injury, and then he was going to get his ring back on her finger.

Chapter Twenty

Marisa sat with her back toward a hearth that was big enough to roast a full-grown steer in. The fire provided a pretty glow as she stared out the window and watched the blue sky turn to indigo and then finally black. Her chair was positioned near a table that was strewed with sea-shells, crystal vases and odd bits of New England–style bric-a-brac. The flames reflected off the glass and cast a prism of color on the polished wood floor.

It was quiet, just as Dr. Levy had promised it would be. Only the occasional pop and crackle of the fire broke the silence in the enormous room. After she begged them to give her some peace, Clell and Logan had gone exploring. The other patients were still in the dining hall in the other wing.

She was alone.

That was what she had wanted, wasn't it?

"You look pretty as a picture with that fire behind you."

Marisa stiffened. That rumbling, wonderful voice had to be wishful thinking, a product of her imagination.

It couldn't be Brooks.

She turned her head toward the small door that led to the exercise area.

It was Brooks.

Searing emotions ripped through her middle. She wanted to run to him, and at the same time to flee from his sight. She wanted to touch his face and kiss him, to hide away and never know the wonder of his touch again.

He stepped into the room.

His hair was peeking out from a shapeless cloth hat with a huge brim. The plaid coat he was wearing was a full size too large, but he looked wonderful.

She had been starved for a glimpse of him.

But she couldn't let him see what she had become.

"What are you doing here?" At least she was sitting in a normal chair and not an invalid's chair. Perhaps she could send him away without ever having to see pity in his eyes. She prayed she could salvage that small scrap of her pride.

"I came to talk some sense into you." He took another step toward her. He was wearing tall, lace-up boots with bloused pants tucked inside the tops. He smiled, but the expression didn't light his eyes. A pang of guilt sliced through her.

He was sad. Even though she had made the right decision about breaking their engagement, she died a little inside to know she had caused him pain.

"Then you wasted your time," she declared. Her eyes roamed over him hungrily. She wanted him to leave, yet she wanted him to stay. "What are you wearing?" Curiosity brought the words tumbling from her lips before she could stop them.

"Uncle Leland's gardening clothes." Brooks grabbed a handful of the tweedy material and held it away from his lean body. "I am in disguise. It worked—you didn't see me on the train. And nobody recognized me as I wandered around looking for you."

An icy finger traced a line down Marisa's back.

"When Clell carried you onto the train…I nearly went to you then. I was in the same car." He took another step toward her.

"Oh, God," she whispered, and dug her fingers into the chair arms. "You know…about me?"

"Yes." Another few steps. Now only a yard separated them.

"Oh, God," she repeated in anguish. "I never wanted you to know. You weren't ever supposed to know. Why couldn't you have just left it all alone?" She stared at the lap robe covering her numb legs.

"I love you, Marisa O'Bannion, not your ability to walk." He closed the last few paces and dropped down beside the chair. He put his finger under her chin, and with infinite tenderness forced her head up. "I love you."

She stared at him for a full minute. Then she drew back. "You had better stop loving me, because it doesn't make any difference. I won't marry you."

She wished she had not noticed the dark smudges beneath his eyes. He had not been sleeping well, that was obvious. How far would she have to push him before the volcano beneath the surface would explode and drive him from her in anger?

She had to do it. The sooner Brooks forgot about her, the better off he would be. "Don't you understand? I don't *want* to marry you."

He flinched as if he had been hit, but he remained on one knee beside her chair. His clear, pale eyes narrowed. "I *will* marry you, Marisa."

A muscle twitched in his jaw. His mustache barely covered the taut, determined line of his mouth. She had never seen him like this. Barely restrained violence hovered near the surface while he glared at her. She took a deep breath for courage.

"Maybe you didn't hear me, Brooks." She waved her hand in the air. "I am a cripple and I—I don't love you," she said, making sure not to look at his eyes, fearing she could not withstand what she might see in them.

He didn't blink, barely seemed to breathe. His hand still rested lightly on his bent knee. Suddenly he reached out and took her by both shoulders.

"Damn it, Marisa. You are mine. You have been mine since our first kiss. You'll be mine until the end of time." With that he yanked her close and claimed her mouth.

A thousand points of light exploded in Marisa's head. A thousand tiny daggers pierced her soul. Hot ribbons of passion and sorrow threaded their way around her breaking heart. She could not let him go on loving her, but she wanted to.

God forgive me, I want him to love me.

"Maybe you have no feeling in your legs, but you have feeling in your heart. Deny that kiss made your blood burn." He shook her. "Go ahead, deny it if you can."

A heated silence gripped the room.

"You can't deny it because you still love me." His eyes bored into hers and challenged her to lie once again.

"It doesn't make any difference," she whispered in agony. "I will not marry you. Now go away."

"We'll get through this together, sweetheart." He caressed the side of her face with one rough, wide palm as he drew her nearer.

Unconsciously she leaned into the strength and warmth of his chest. "There is nothing to 'get through,' Brooks. I am crippled. I will never walk again."

He drew back and looked at her through narrowed eyes. "Are you giving up?" Doubt rang in his voice.

"Just accepting the truth. I will never walk again, just as I will never marry you." Her voice was flat with conviction.

"I never would've believed it of you." There was a tone of disappointment in his statement.

"What?" She drew back from him, determined not to respond to his touch or the sound of his voice, even though she craved both.

"I would've denied it to the death." His voice was icy now. "I would've fought any man who dared suggest it, but now I see the truth, Marisa. You are a coward."

Coward.

The word hung like a foul stench.

If he had struck her she wouldn't have felt the pain any deeper. The accusation sliced so deep she couldn't draw her breath for three full beats of her heart.

"How could you?" She gasped. "How could you dare say that to me?"

"Honey, you have no idea what I will dare do or say. I'll try anything to convince you we belong together. And I am not leaving—not until you stop all this nonsense and let me love you, care for you."

"Then you are in for the fight of your life, Brooks James."

Clell and Logan heard the glass breaking as they left the dining wing. They ran down the hallway, meeting Dr. Levy as they came through the corridor that opened onto the great room.

"What has happened?" she gasped.

They could hear Marisa shouting at the top of her lungs.

"What on earth?" Dr. Levy exclaimed.

Clell opened the door, but then lurched to a stop, causing both Logan and Dr. Levy to bump into his back. They tried to step around him, but he put out a restraining hand to prevent them from entering the room. The sound of something heavy hitting the wall just beyond the door sent the three of them scurrying back a startled step.

"I have to get in there, my patient needs me," Dr. Levy said as she tussled with Clell.

"Hold on just a minute, Doc," Clell said. "Let's not be too hasty until we know what's goin' on." He glanced at Logan. "Sneak to the door and take a look."

Logan crept to the door and opened it a crack. "Brooks is, uh, having a talk with Missy, I mean Marisa." He chuckled when another object shattered against the stone hearth.

"Talk? It sounds as if they are tearing the place apart," Dr. Levy said. "Now let me pass."

"Well, the only one doin' any tearin' is Marisa. Brooks is just dodgin' and talkin'," Logan reported. Glass shattered against the door and Logan took cover for a moment. "And he's doin' all right so far. She hasn't hit him yet." Logan ducked back behind the shelter of the wall and eased the door shut.

"It's about damn time," Clell muttered under his breath.

"What? Are you both mad?" Dr. Levy tried to shake off Clell's hands. "That is a defenseless girl in there. She is sick! She is—"

"Is she sick?" Clell challenged. "Or has she just given up...until now?"

"I am not sure I know what you mean," Dr. Levy said.

"Listen, Doc, I've known that gal since she was born. The way she's been actin' lately just ain't natural. This is more like the real Marisa O'Bannion. If Brooks can get her all fired up like this some good might come of it."

Dr. Levy frowned. Her dark eyes searched Clell's face. "Let me see."

"Promise not to stop them?" Clell asked.

Dr. Levy sighed in exasperation. "I promise." She inched forward. Logan opened the door and she peeked around his broad shoulder. Marisa was grabbing every bit of crockery and china within her reach. As she threw she called Brooks James every name Dr. Levy had heard and added a few that were new.

Dr. Levy eased back into the dim hallway and stared at Clell in wonder. "You may be right, Mr. McClellan. If Mr. James can get her to show this kind of emotion, this may be what I have been searching for. This could be the key to her treatment."

Marisa had woken with a splitting headache. Now she was flat on her back, imagining mental pictures within the pattern of knots and swirls of grain in the bird's-eye maple paneling. A light tap on the door made her jump.

"Yes?" she rasped hoarsely. Her throat was raw from screaming at Brooks last night.

A uniformed nurse opened the door and stepped inside. "Dr. Levy is holding breakfast for you."

"I'd like a tray in my room." Marisa's heart was rawer than her throat. She couldn't face anyone. "I am not feeling very well today."

"Sorry, miss, but Dr. Levy gave strict instructions you were to come down to breakfast."

"But I don't feel well," she pleaded. It had taken all her energy to lie to Brooks. Now she wanted nothing more than to stay in bed and try to forget him, to forget life and love and all the pain it brought.

Just to forget.

"Sorry, miss." It was plain the nurse was not going to grant her request.

"Oh damnation," Marisa swore.

The nurse's brows shot upward.

She had forgotten Ellen's teachings once again, Marisa realized. "I'm sorry, I didn't mean that."

The nurse never looked her in the eye as she went about the process of lifting her. She dressed her in a soft blue cotton dress, dispensing with the petticoats and the corset. With amazing speed and efficiency, Marisa was soon in her chair with her hair brushed and tied back with a blue ribbon.

When the nurse pushed the invalid's chair toward the dining wing, Marisa noticed sunlight slanting through the canopy of trees. Heavy blackberry vines had lured a small flock of birds to the stone patio. Their happy twittering filled the high room and wafted out through the open door.

She resented them for being so alive.

Marisa was pushed to a long plank table. She didn't look around, not wanting to see the other patients this morning. Images of Brooks kept intruding on her thoughts as she stared at the food in front of her.

"Well, don't just sit there, your breakfast will get cold." Brooks's deep voice brought her head up with a start.

"You!" Marisa clenched her fists tightly together as she fought the unexpected burst of joy—and anger—that flared inside her chest. She didn't want to be glad to see him, yet a rebellious part of her was so happy she was stunned by the intensity of feeling.

She could not let him see it. She had to push him away. "What in hell are you still doin' here? I thought we had all of this settled."

"Not by a long shot." He crossed his arms on his chest

and stared at her down the long expanse of the table. He had shed Leland's oversize clothes. Now a plain work shirt and Levi's hugged his body as he casually leaned one hip against the back of a chair.

She didn't want to notice how good he looked in the rugged apparel.

Dr. Levy breezed into the dining room and drew her attention. "Marisa, how are you this morning?" Clell and Logan were with her. Suddenly the other patients were all leaving. Those who could walk left on their own power; others were wheeled out by uniformed staff.

A suspicion of betrayal twined through Marisa's mind.

"Which one of you told *him* where I was?" She glared at the trio. Last night she had not had an opportunity to question any of them, but now she intended to face the Judas who had led Brooks to her—and deal harshly with her betrayer.

"I did." Logan took a step forward. "And I would do it again," he added defiantly.

"Oh, if I could get out of this chair, I'd..." she threatened.

"Don't take it out on Logan." Brooks unfolded his arms and walked closer to her.

Every nerve ending sizzled, every inch of her craved his touch. She tried to deny the subtle change in her body at his nearness.

"If you want to tear into anybody, Marisa, then tear into me again. I can handle it. I can handle anything you care to throw." He focused on her face, daring her to deny the truth. "How about a cup? There is one right beside you." He set his jaw in a decisive way that made her want to run her fingertips over his face, to absorb his strength.

"I don't want anything to do with you," she blurted.

She had to stop letting her heart guide her. "I thought I made that clear. It is over between us, now just leave." Her heart lurched as she lied. "Go find yourself a city girl that can walk at your side. Violet Ashland wants the job, go to her."

"I don't want a city girl and I damn sure don't want a viper like Violet Ashland. I thought we had all that settled. I want you." One brow arched. "And I will have you."

"*I don't want you!* Now go away. I don't ever want to see you again." She tore her gaze from him and stared at her lap.

Please, God, help me send him away.

She could not stand much more of this. She was weakening. If Brooks didn't leave soon she was afraid she would admit how much she cared for him. That would be a disaster.

It would ruin his life.

Dr. Levy pulled out the chair next to Marisa and sat down. Her long navy skirt draped over the wheel of the invalid's chair. Clell and Logan turned and left the room. "I'm afraid you will be seeing a lot of Mr. James from now on, Marisa."

"Why?" Marisa shoved the material off the wheel.

"I have hired Mr. James to help out with your care," Dr. Levy said cheerfully.

"What?" Marisa reeled backward as if ice water had been tossed into her face.

"I had your full permission, if you will recall. It is done. Mr. James is going to assist me with your treatment. You might say he is going to be your own personal nurse for as long as you are here."

Marisa glanced at Brooks.

"Finish your breakfast, Marisa. We have a lot of work

to do." A glow of satisfaction and triumph gleamed in Brooks's blue eyes.

"Dr. Levy, you can't do this!" Marisa shivered at the thought of being with him every day. "You don't know what you are doing!" She turned, looking for Clell and Logan, but they had disappeared. "Get Clell and Logan. I want to go home."

"Sorry, honey, but I believe I just saw Clell and Logan going down the road."

"What?" Marisa's frantic gaze searched the road beyond the open doors. "They are letting you do this?"

"Yes, honey. They know I want only the best for you. They are taking the buggy back to the station." Brooks winked at her. "I suggested they enjoy the city while you and I are working."

"I won't do it. I won't have you here." Marisa glared at him. She felt small and helpless.

"Sorry, honey, but you don't have a lot of choice." Brooks slipped into the chair beside her. "Now will you eat, or will I feed you?"

"You wouldn't dare."

"Oh, but I would."

She wanted to slap him.

Chapter Twenty-One

Brooks stood waist deep in the warm water as two nurses eased Marisa into his arms. Steam rose up from the stone-lined bath.

"This is the craziest thing I ever heard of." Water crept up her thin cotton shift, turning it nearly opaque, while little clouds of steam swirled around her face.

Brooks nodded to the nurses, and they left without uttering a word. Now there was only the steaming pool, heated by a huge furnace underneath the stone floor, and the strong arms that held her captive.

The arms of the man I love too much....

"It's not as crazy as you think. There have been good results using water therapy. I told you before, honey, we are going to get through this together."

Marisa willed herself to ignore the way his shirt was becoming plastered to his wide, muscled chest like a second skin. "There is nothing to get through, Brooks. I am a *cripple*. And I don't want you to see me like this."

"So you keep telling me." He positioned her on one of the stone steps built into the side of the pool. Then he moved to her feet and started rotating one of her legs through the water as if she were kicking in a great circle.

"Go away, please. Just leave me in peace, Brooks." She felt helplessness mingled with angry frustration.

She was trapped. Trapped in a body that would no longer do her bidding.

There was nothing she could do but submit to him. She couldn't get up and walk out. But damn it all, if he would just let her go she could *crawl*.

"This isn't fair," she grumbled. "Let me go."

"Life rarely is fair, darlin'," he agreed. He continued to perform the ritual of moving her leg through the steaming water.

His patience was more infuriating than his stubbornness.

"No, I don't mean that. I mean it is not fair for you to keep me here. I am practically a prisoner now that you have charmed Dr. Levy into doing what you want."

Brooks looked at Marisa and grinned. "'Charmed'?" He shook his head from side to side and picked up her other leg. "I hardly think I charmed her. I have pleaded with her for weeks." Methodically, he repeated the movements. "And I had to prove to her that I was competent. She put me through a series of tests and training sessions before she would allow me to do this."

The knowledge that her doctor had not abandoned her care gave Marisa some comfort. And she couldn't blame Dr. Levy for letting the cat out of the bag—that had been Logan's doing.

"Oh, I wish I could punch you in the nose." She thrashed her arms, trying to reach Brooks with her hand, but the distance was too far. Warm waves lapped farther up her body, soaking her chest and wetting the ends of her hair.

"Good, that's good. Keep trying to move," he encouraged. "I'll tell you what, honey. You be a good girl, do your exercises, and if you still want to punch me in the nose, I'll let you."

"Really?" Marisa glared at him through narrowed eyes. "When? That is something I would enjoy."

He laughed aloud. "All right. How about right after dinner?" It felt so good to see some of the fire returning to her spirit. He stopped moving her leg and began to massage her muscles as Dr. Levy had instructed. The outline of her breasts kept distracting him. The dusky rose nipples beneath the clinging wet shift drew his eyes like a magnet.

Marisa stilled.

He glanced up at her to see if anything was wrong. Their gazes locked in an unexpected current of longing.

"Don't look at me like that—not now—not when I am like…this."

"I love you," he said softly.

"I don't want you to," she whispered, and glanced away. She tried to watch only his fingers as his hand kneaded her flesh.

She flushed and drew in a ragged breath, hypnotized by his hands and his continued declaration of love. Sure fingers worked their way up her leg, past her knee, beyond her thigh.

She remembered the night he had undressed her. His hands had been hidden beneath her skirt. She remembered the way it had felt….

The sodden fabric of her shift clung to her skin. She couldn't feel what he was doing, but she could see it. His palm slid over the slight swell of her belly.

"You are so beautiful, Marisa. I have missed you so much."

"Stop it, stop torturing me." Her voice was full of pent-up passion.

"I am not torturing you, Marisa. I am trying to show you that I love *you*. I don't love your ability to walk. I— love—" he punctuated each word with a kiss to her belly "—you."

Something thick and hot threatened to choke off her breath. She wanted to curl into a little ball and hide from the emotions that were clawing at her insides, trying to break free.

"Marisa, I know you can feel this. Maybe not here—" he touched her hip "—but you can feel it here." He laid his hand over her heart. "And your heart is the most important place to feel anything. Your heart is where I want to be."

"Oh, Brooks, just go away," she whispered. "Please leave me alone. You are making this harder—please stop."

"No, I won't stop until you admit that you love me and end all this nonsense about breaking our engagement." He moved closer to the stone steps and slid down beside her. Waves lapped over them both as he put his hands around her waist and lifted her body. He eased her down until she was straddling him beneath the steamy water.

He gazed up at her face, only inches away from his own. "Say it, Marisa—say I love you."

Images of how they had coupled in love and passion assaulted her. She remembered the feeling of his body inside her, the way she had responded to his lust and how she had answered it with her own need.

Without conscious thought, she reached out and wrapped her hand around the nape of his neck. She drew herself close and parted her lips. A feeling like an electric shock surged through her when he kissed her. Slowly she pulled away and rested her head on his strong shoulder.

"All right, I love you. Damn it—damn you! Is that what you wanted to hear? I love you. But as God is my witness, I will never marry you."

"Why?" He nuzzled her cheek as he held her against him. His hand stroked big circles on her back. "Why should this change anything between us?"

"Are you crazy? It changes everything. I can't allow you to marry a woman who can't even stand at your side, much less make love to you." Her words were strangled by the image of Violet's poisonous smile.

Brooks tilted up her head and forced her to face him. "Honey, I wouldn't care if you crawled on your belly to the altar. It has taken me too damn long to realize how much I care for you. I am not going to lose you now."

"You don't know what you're saying." Hot tears were suddenly streaming down her face. It was the first time she had cried. She cursed herself for weeping in front of Brooks, for allowing him to see how weak and frightened she was. "Life would be unbearable for you. You would come to hate me for allowing you to saddle yourself to a cripple."

"Marisa, you said you trusted me. Was that a lie?" His voice was smooth and strong.

"No. I do trust you," she sobbed.

"If you trusted me and yourself and the good Lord, then you wouldn't fight me so hard. Can't you trust me enough to know my own mind? Trust me to love you and to take care of you."

"I don't want you to be my caretaker—I wanted you to be my partner in life." Wrenching sobs shook her body.

"Can't I be both?" His voice rolled over her like the curtain of steam surrounding them. It leached away her will to oppose him.

"It wouldn't be an equal partnership," she sobbed. "It wouldn't be fair to you."

He kissed her salty tears. "Fair? I should've known an O'Bannion would be determined to be fair. Oh, honey…do you think any of this has been about fairness?" He was silent for a moment. "All right, Marisa, see if you think this suits your sense of fair play."

"What?" She sniffed and lifted her chin a tiny bit, trying to be strong and *fair*.

A warm rush of love burst through him. "I'll make you a deal. You agree to let me help you. If you see any improvement, no matter how small, you will marry me."

She narrowed her eyes and stared at him. "No. That is still not fair."

He frowned and thought some more. "All right, how about this. If you can move your legs you will marry me."

"No."

"Then what would suit your sense of fairness?"

"If I can stand at your side. Only then will I marry you."

"All or nothing?"

"That's about it."

"How long will you give it?" His brows had knitted together in a frown.

Her own brow furrowed as she thought about how long she could endure without breaking. "No more than six weeks. Any longer just wouldn't be—"

"I know—" he cut her off "—*fair*." He smiled at her stubbornness. "All right, honey, you've got a deal. Six weeks it is." He prayed six weeks would be enough.

"That's not all, Brooks."

"What now?" A chill ran up his spine.

"If there is no improvement, you must agree to go

away and forget about me.'' Her voice was flat with determination.

He stroked strands of damp hair back from her face. ''I will go away and leave you alone, darling, but know this—I will never stop loving you. And I will never, ever forget you.''

Marisa regretted her decision almost immediately. The look of hope in Brooks's eyes tore at her soul every day. She didn't want him to hope and she wasn't sure she could live with his disappointment.

Even though she longed to believe there was a chance she might recover the use of her legs, doubts nagged at her. And Violet's face came to her in dreams, taunting nightmares that broke her heart.

Days had gone by and nothing had happened to make her more optimistic. Today she was lying on her belly on a thick padded bench with a sheet over her nude body. Brooks gently rubbed her back and kneaded her flesh with hands that made her pulse quicken.

''That feels good,'' she admitted.

''I'm glad you like it.'' He gingerly touched the skin around the faint bruise on her spine, where the mare had struck her. The flesh was still slightly discolored in an area larger than his splayed hand. The darker imprint of the horseshoe was just barely visible on her soft skin.

''Does that hurt?'' He gently rubbed over the bruised area, wincing each time the image of her being trampled by the horse rushed through his mind.

''No.''

He shrugged off the cold chill of disappointment. He would be strong enough and certain enough for both of them. ''Now for your legs.'' Brooks slid the sheet up over her back and folded it upward to expose her slender, well-shaped legs. "You are a tempting sight, Marisa."

"Don't tease me," she whispered.

"I am not teasing. You are more sensual than you can possibly imagine." The dusky twilight added a measure of romance to their ritual. He swallowed his desire and focused on the task of rubbing her legs.

Marisa assumed he was still rubbing her body, but when his hands had crossed the invisible barrier at her waist she ceased to be aware of his magical touch.

In a way it was a kindness.

Each time she felt his strong fingers, warm and pliant against her flesh, she cringed inside. How she yearned to know the pleasure of his lovemaking again.

"Can you feel that, honey?" His deep voice rumbled through her. The timbre made her belly quiver.

"No." She turned her head and stared out the wide, six-over-six windows. In the dusk a timid doe was creeping toward the flowering shrubs at the edge of the stone patio.

Brooks smiled when he saw the look of wonder flit across Marisa's face. He was grateful for the momentary distraction of the deer. Each day when he stroked and rubbed Marisa's body the way Dr. Levy had trained him to do, his own body became taut and hard as stone with his passion for her.

He wanted her. It was as simple and as complicated as that.

His desire had not diminished because of her accident. If only he could make her understand. And he wasn't sure what she would think of him if he revealed his yearning.

Would she be disgusted with him?

He lifted her leg at the knee and rotated her ankle in his hand. There had to be some way to get over this awkwardness between them. He searched his mind for a way to let her know that he still found her attractive. Her injury had not changed his perceptions of her one bit.

While he rotated her ankle in his hand, there was the slightest bit of resistance in her normally unresponsive muscles. He frowned, wondering if he had imagined it, since his mind had been wandering. He stroked the delicate bones of her foot.

A muscle in her instep twitched.

Hope flared inside his chest.

"Are you sure you can't feel anything?"

"I'm sure." Marisa lifted her head and turned enough to look at him. "Are you ready to admit you were wrong?"

"About what?" He eased her leg down and grasped her shoulders to help her turn so she could face him. He wanted to shout the news to her, but decided he shouldn't say anything until he discussed it with Dr. Levy.

"About our deal. It isn't making any difference." She looked up at him with sad, serious eyes. The twilight made them look bottomless.

"Are you trying to get out of our agreement?"

"Well…" she began.

He cocked a brow and folded his arms across his chest. "I thought O'Bannions always kept their word."

"We do," she snapped. Her chin elevated in that stubborn way he liked so much. "I have never weaseled out of a deal in my life."

"Glad to hear it, because I have not even begun to make you work." He leaned down to plant a kiss on her defiant little chin.

She swore she wasn't going to respond, but even as she made the silent vow her arms raised and she clung to him.

The hair curling beneath her fingers felt so soft, so alive, it brought a lump to her throat.

Brooks cupped her breast beneath the sheet. He caressed her, warming her flesh with his own palm. "Honey…I want you," he whispered as he nipped at the lobe of her ear.

"You can't want me anymore."

"Oh, but I do." He raised his head enough to look at her. Passion turned her eyes a smoky gray. "You want me, too. I can see it in your face."

"Damn it, stop teasing me." She turned her face away, but he gently grasped her chin and pulled it.

"I am not teasing. A man can see these things, Marisa. You desire me as much as I do you. Life is still worth living. There are a thousand ways we can love each other, darling."

She blinked back tears. "How?"

He grinned. "I was hoping you would ask." He wrapped the sheet around her body and scooped her up in his arms. "The exercise pool is empty this time of night. We will not be disturbed."

"We are going back into the water?"

"Uh-huh, but this time not to work, my love."

An hour later Marisa's head was spinning from Brooks's intoxicating kisses. He had told her that making love was as much a state of mind as it was physical.

She could not deny it.

Her blood simmered in her veins each time he touched her. He held her against him, half sitting, half lying on the stone steps, and she felt complete sexual fulfillment.

"You see, my love, we can touch each other, love each other in so many ways."

"But it is not the same—for you," she murmured between ragged breaths.

''Perhaps not, but that doesn't mean it isn't just as good, just as fulfilling.''

He captured her lips again. As the moon rolled overhead and cast silvery shadows through the wide windows, his love managed to breach the loss of feeling in her lower body.

Chapter Twenty-Two

The following day dawned bright and glorious. Brooks was happy to see bees buzzing from one tuft of clover to the next. The summer air was alive with a warm humidity and lazy energy.

He loaded into the buggy a thick blanket and a wicker basket full of ham, chicken and anything else he thought might tempt Marisa. When he had everything hidden from sight he walked into the common room.

Several patients were playing cards and one silver-haired lady was embroidering a pillow top. His heart contracted painfully when he saw that Marisa was just as he had left her, staring into the cold hearth as if the weight of the world lay on her delicate shoulders.

When they were busy with her regimen of therapy and exercise, she was like her old self, but the moment they stopped, she retreated to a place she would not share with him. There was a private place inside herself that she protected with silence and a thick icy wall.

He knew it was because they had seen no real improvement. One tiny muscle spasm that Dr. Levy had said could've been a reflex was not enough. Marisa would not let Brooks get any closer. Three weeks had flown by, and though he hated to admit it, the specter of doubt was beginning to hover at the edges of his mind.

She turned her face to look up at him when he reached the side of her chair. "Are you sure you want to go for a buggy ride?" she asked.

There were smudges beneath her eyes and her cheeks were a little hollow. Even the pretty, pink-checked frock didn't bring much color to her face.

"Fresh air is what you need. You are a wild girl from the Territory, never meant to be cooped up. A buggy ride will put roses in your cheeks." Brooks tried to sound cheerful, but it wasn't easy when he read so much sadness in her eyes.

She tried to smile, but the wan curving of her lips cut deep into his soul. He picked her up, savoring the delicious weight of her body in his arms. He took her outside and put her in the front seat of the buggy. The little cart horse pawed restively as Brooks made sure Marisa was secure.

"Comfortable?"

"I'm fine, thank you." She grabbed hold of the iron support that ran from the top of the buggy down to the frame.

"I will drive slowly, and I promise I'll take good care of you."

Marisa stared at him for a moment. "I know you will, Brooks. I know you would sacrifice your own life and happiness to take care of me." She turned and stared straight ahead at the horse's rump.

His chest tightened.

In her own, not too subtle way she was reminding him of their deal. That unless she could walk she would never marry him. He had to find a solution, and he had to find it quickly, for time was rapidly running out.

At first Marisa just sat unmoving in the buggy, but as they traveled along the gently rolling mountain road, she found herself noticing her surroundings. This country was so different from the Territory. Everywhere she looked there was something green, or a trickle of water. It was soothing and yet incredibly exhilarating. She found herself craning her neck to see around the next curve in the road or through an unexpected break in the thick canopy of trees overhead.

Wildflowers added splashes of color in the rolling green carpet. Forest birds chirped and bravely swooped in front of the buggy as they violated their privacy.

"It is beautiful up here," Marisa murmured.

"The proper setting for you." Brooks clicked his tongue. As the horse picked up speed, the wind blew through Marisa's hair. She closed her eyes, held tighter to the iron rail and allowed her mind to take her far away. For one split second she actually thought she could feel the vibration of the wagon through the soles of her feet. But when she opened her eyes the sensation disappeared.

Fancy that—wishful thinking.

She would've given in to the feeling of helplessness, except Brooks had stopped the buggy in a place so wondrous she could only stare.

A waterfall plunged into a pond with so much power the water below the cascade churned with white foam. Slate gray rocks glistened, having been polished to a high sheen from the force of the water. Grass grew in thick abundance at the edge of the pond, dotted with white daisies and yellow buttercups.

"This looks like heaven." She was transfixed by the strength and beauty of the waterfall.

"I have a surprise for you. If you don't mind waiting for a few minutes."

"I could watch this all day."

Brooks wrapped the reins around the iron foot rail and jumped down. While Marisa was distracted with the water, he removed the blanket and basket. A huge willow was nearby and he chose a spot beneath its dripping branches to spread out the blanket and position their picnic.

He returned to the buggy and went to Marisa. "Are you ready for the rest of my surprise?"

"That depends." Her voice was wary.

Marisa's hands went instinctively to his shoulders when he grasped her waist. He held his position, not moving her from the seat but not removing his hands. He felt suspended in time while she gently but firmly kept her grip on his shoulders.

"I promise it is not a ring, like last time," he said.

A flicker of embarrassment flashed across her face, and he knew that was what she had feared, what she had been dreading.

"I will not offer you a ring again unless the terms of our agreement are met. You can trust me to keep my word, Marisa."

She smiled.

For the first time in days the action brought a light into her eyes. "You are teasing me again."

"Me? Never." He slipped one arm under her legs and lifted her out of the buggy. A bird trilled a happy song nearby and he heard Marisa sigh.

She smiled at him again. "Don't bother to act innocent. I know what kind of thoughts go on in that head of yours."

"I wonder if you really do." A cloud crossed her eyes and he decided to change the subject, determined to recapture the easy feeling that had been between them. "I got a letter from Ellen today," he said.

"Really? How is she?"

"I don't know. I haven't opened it yet. I thought we would read it together, after lunch." He settled Marisa on the blanket. When her gaze fell upon the basket her eyes filled with unshed tears. She blinked rapidly, as if trying to drive them back to their source.

"What is it, Marisa?" He dropped to his knees beside her.

"I know what you are trying to do, but it will only make things harder."

"How can you say that?"

"There are only three weeks left until the end of our bargain." She said no more, knowing that he would understand what she meant.

"God is not going to let me down. Besides, it is a beautiful summer day and I am with the woman I love. I intend to enjoy every single minute." He reached out and with the tip of his index finger captured a teardrop that had escaped. "Now, no more tears. Let's open Ellen's letter and hear the gossip of the city."

She sniffed. "All right."

He ripped open the envelope and unfolded two pages. Ellen's precise hand covered both of them, front and back. "She is in a chatty mood, it appears."

"Unless there is something private, would you read it to me?" Marisa leaned back against the willow tree. Her motionless legs were stretched out in front of her, the toes of her boots peeking out from under her skirt.

"I have no secrets from you, love." He winked and held up the page. "Dear Cousin," he read. "I hope this letter finds you and Marisa well. I am feeling more my old self. Cyril has been stopping by and taking me for strolls in the park. I believe the daily visits are working miracles. Brooks, please tell Marisa that she must hurry and get well in order to fulfill her half of the bargain.''

He glanced up. ''What does she mean?''

Marisa sighed and closed her eyes. ''It was just a silly promise I made.''

''Oh.'' He gazed at the letter and read more. ''By now I am certain Marisa has taken back your ring—''

''Stop,'' Marisa said. ''Don't read anymore—please.''

He folded the pages and stuffed them back inside the envelope. ''Tell me about your promises. It appears you are the one with the secrets, darling.''

She studied him with smoky gray eyes. ''Swear you won't tease me?''

''I swear on my honor.'' He held up his hand as if taking a solemn oath.

''When we first left the Territory the most important thing in the world to me was becoming a proper lady. I put such stock in fine manners and knowing which petticoat to wear....'' Her voice trailed off.

''Go on.''

''Ellen and I made a bargain. She would teach me how to be a lady and I...''

''Yes?''

''I would teach her how to ride.'' Her lids lifted and she stared at Brooks. ''Just foolishness, on both our parts. I wanted to be a lady so badly.'' Her voice was flat and dry, almost devoid of emotion.

He reached out and stroked her cheek with one fingertip. ''It doesn't matter if you are a lady, or if you can walk. None of that matters to me.''

She grasped the finger tracing a line around her jaw. ''I know, but it matters to me.'' She glanced at the churning water in the clear blue pond. ''It matters that I can't walk. And it matters that I can't dangle my feet in that water.''

''Who says you can't?''

She frowned at him. ''What do you mean?''

''Let me show you.'' He moved to her feet and lifted the edge of her skirt. Nimble fingers unlaced one high-topped boot and tugged it off, then he reached up under her petticoat and found the top of her stocking. Slowly he rolled it down.

''You know what I miss the most?'' she whispered.

''What, honey?''

''I miss you tickling the bottom of my feet.''

''Like this?'' He deposited kisses across her instep and on each toe.

Her foot jerked.

They looked at each other, afraid to move, afraid to speak.

''Did you do that?'' he finally asked.

''I'm not sure. I think I... I'm not sure.'' Her heart beat a little faster.

Brooks shoved up her skirt and quickly removed the other boot and stocking. With his index finger he drew an invisible line on the sole of that foot.

''Could you feel that?''

''No. Nothing.'' Disappointment flooded through her. Until that moment she had not realized how hopeful that tiny jerk had made her.

''Let's try it again.'' Brooks ran his finger down her other foot. Again there was a small amount of movement. He looked up at her.

A bright smile flashed across his face.

''Dr. Levy said I might experience some reflexive movement. It could be nothing.'' Even while Marisa was cautioning him, the stubborn flame of hope had been ignited in her own soul. She couldn't let Brooks know it, though, not unless she was truly getting better. "Brooks, you can't get your hopes up."

"Too late. I think this calls for a celebration." He stood up and gathered her into his arms. With sure strides he brought her to the edge of the pool. The crashing noise from the waterfall made conversation impossible, but when Marisa looked at his face, she knew.

He was happy.

Probably for the first time since her accident. He grinned at her while a cold spray of mist covered his dark hair and mustache. Droplets of water turned to jewels in the summer sun. She couldn't help but laugh even though a tendril of fear still clung to her heart. It was crazy and irresponsible, but she allowed herself to think there was a slim hope for a future with Brooks as he gently placed her feet in the churning pool and sat down beside her.

Marisa dreamed of walking in knee-deep snow. Her feet and legs were so cold they were numb. She searched for shelter, but no matter how hard she tried, she couldn't find a place to get warm. Her feet and legs ached from the frigid temperature.

She was freezing....

Marisa woke with a start. The moon hung like a fat yellow pearl in the night sky. The curtains fluttered in front of the open window.

She touched her throat. Sweat had pooled in the hollow of her neck. Damp strands of hair clung to her face.

I'm not freezing, it's hotter than blazes in here.

It was puzzling that she would dream of ice and snow when her room was warmer than the desert in August.

A frisson of pins and needles suddenly shot from her lower spine to her toes and back again. She levered herself up and stared at her legs in doubt and wonder. They were contorting, cramping, the muscles twitching and pulling.

And with the strange reawakening of her limbs she had the sensation of being wrapped in ice.

"Oh dear Lord," she whispered. She was determined not to marry Brooks until she could stand at his side. But would she ever be able to do that?

"Can you feel this, Marisa?" Dr. Levy prodded the sole of Marisa's foot with a pin.

"Not really."

Dr. Levy pulled the sheet down over Marisa's bare toes and tucked it under the mattress. She stood up, and as usual, her brows were pinched together in thought.

"Describe the sensation to me again."

"One leg feels like a million red ants are crawling over me. The other is sort of like having your foot go to sleep in church."

"Hmm…"

"What does it mean? Am I getting better?"

"I'd like to give you assurances, Marisa, but I can't. The sensations you are experiencing could mean the swelling in your spine was only temporary and feeling is returning to your limbs. Or…it could mean nothing. It is just too early to say. We need to observe this for at least another month."

"That long?"

"At least. If you are recovering, it is important to keep exercising those muscles. Right now is the most critical time in your recovery. You are going to have to work twice as hard as before, but we simply can't rush things."

"I understand," Marisa said. Now hope warred with her determination to spare Brooks. She had sent for Dr. Levy secretly, not wishing to give him false hope.

"Dr. Levy?"

"Yes?"

"I don't want you to say anything about this to Brooks."

Dark brows rose. "Why am I not surprised?" The doctor's words were tinged with sarcasm. "Is there any part of your care that I am allowed to share with him?"

"Do you think I am wrong to try and protect him?" Marisa levered herself up in the bed and frowned at the doctor.

"Wrong? I don't know if that is the right word. Mr. James is a grown man. I think perhaps you are doing him a disservice."

"The only disservice I could do him is to agree to marry him. And if you can't be sure about my legs in less than a month.... Our agreement ends in three weeks."

"Ah, yes, the agreement. I heard about it. Utter madness that you would risk love and happiness on such an agreement. I suppose this means you intend to stick to it—rigidly?"

"You don't understand. If I give in about the time limit, then Brooks will pressure me to give in on other things. No, I have to make sure we keep our word exactly as we made it. I have to be able to stand on my own two feet beside the man I love or I won't marry him. I won't settle for less and I won't allow him to, either. He deserves better than that."

"You love him very much, don't you?"

"More than my own life, Dr. Levy."

"All right. I will say nothing to Mr. James, but I hope you know what you are doing, Marisa."

"So do I, Dr. Levy. Believe me, so do I."

Chapter Twenty-Three

Marisa clung to Brooks's shoulders. Steam swirled around their faces and obscured her vision. The saturated muslin of her shift floated up around her waist, tying itself in knots as he walked through the water, carrying her to their usual spot on the stone steps.

Dr. Levy had taken a short leave from her duties in New York after she had sent word to Patricia and Ellen that Marisa desired no visitors. For the last week Dr. Levy had obliged her by coming to her room after Brooks left her and went to bed in his own room. Marisa had frequently pleaded fatigue and any other excuse she could think of in order to get back to her room. She and Dr. Levy stayed up late each night, trying different exercises, hoping for some indication that the prickly sensations in Marisa's legs were more than just wishful thinking, but so far little had happened to restore her faith that she was going to fully recover.

"A penny for your thoughts, pretty lady." Brooks kissed the tip of her nose.

"I was just thinking that summer is nearly over." Her eyes flicked across his face.

"I haven't forgotten, Marisa. I know we have exactly fourteen days left."

She stopped avoiding his eyes and looked at him. Her gaze locked onto his own with an intensity that nearly rocked him backward in the warm water. "And you still believe?"

"I have always believed in miracles." He grinned at her wryly. "You fell in love with me, didn't you? If that isn't a miracle, then I don't know what is."

"Oh, Brooks." Her voice cracked with emotion. And as if they had a will of their own, her arms rose and reached out for him.

"If I only had your strength." She kissed him—hard. All her longing and tentative hope was wrapped up in that one kiss. She clung to him and the strength of his belief, wishing she could have the same unshakable certainty in their future.

"You are stronger than anyone I know, Missy O'Bannion."

She looked up at him and smiled. "You haven't called me Missy for a long time."

"I thought you preferred Marisa."

"I thought I did, too, but maybe the truth is I don't know what I prefer. I think I never appreciated what it was to be a happy girl growing up wild as a weed in the New Mexico Territory. I thought I would be happier being a lady named Marisa. But look what has happened."

"You know what I think?" He toyed with a wet strand of hair that floated near his hand.

"What?" Absently she curled her fingertips in the whorls of damp hair on his chest.

"I think you can be both. I think you can be strong, feisty Missy and still allow me to care for the lovely lady inside you."

She stiffened slightly at his words. "Brooks, nothing has changed. Our agreement still holds. If I can't stand beside you in front of a preacher—"

"Don't." He pressed his fingers to her lips. "Don't say it, don't even think it. Just keep believing that miracles can happen."

He positioned her on the stone steps and began the ritual of rubbing and rotating her limbs.

He shoved his hands beneath the water and slowly began to inch her shift out of the way. The firm texture of her thighs and the way her skin slipped like silk beneath his fingers excited him. He was unwilling to think that Marisa could never again share in this pleasure.

She had to recover. This woman was his life. He refused to imagine they would not be together until the end of time.

Marisa leaned her head back against the hard lip of stone. Her heart ached with love for Brooks, but she could not weaken.

Especially not now.

She closed her eyes and tried to block the pain she felt each time she saw love shining in his blue eyes. In all the weeks she had been here, the specter of self-pity had hovered near the edge of her consciousness. She had managed to keep it at bay, but now, with the slight glimmer of hope so near, it folded over her in a dark, cold wave. If only she had listened to Brooks. He had told her the filly was wild-eyed and she could not handle her in that sidesaddle.

Why hadn't she listened? Why had her vanity been stronger than her good sense? Why had this happened to her?

As she sat there, guilt ridden and miserable, with the gentle waves washing over her waist, she fancied she could feel the slight abrasive scrape of the stone bottom of the pool against her left heel.

It was a silly idea. Brooks had been vigorously rubbing that foot in his strong hands. She squeezed her eyes tighter, determined to stop torturing herself with foolish notions, but the sensation of rough rock against her heel persisted. Marisa opened her eyes and looked down at her limbs. Brooks was not holding her left foot as she had thought. Her heel was resting beneath the water on the bottom of the pool, just as she had imagined.

Felt.

A shudder of hope rippled through her. Could it be?

A part of her wanted to shout out the question, to ask Brooks, to involve him in this moment, but the cautious side of her remained quiet.

What if this was nothing? The tiny tremor of movement she had experienced before had not come again. What if she raised his hopes higher than they were? She could not stand to see the look of pain and disappointment in his eyes. Their agreement was firm and it had to endure. If she could not stand at the altar, she would not marry him. The truth of it all clawed at her, made her want to cry out with frustration, but she forced herself to remain quiet while Brooks continued to massage her other leg.

He released her right ankle. As her foot slipped beneath the water, she had the sensation of being tickled. When her toes came to rest at the bottom of the pool, she felt the distinct scratch of the stone tiles against her flesh. Marisa's thoughts were racing ahead, hoping Dr. Levy would be able to tell her something more definite about her condition now.

"Brooks, I am tired. Would you take me back to my room?"

"Are you sure you don't want to work longer?" The hopeful note in his voice condemned her for wanting to quit.

"I'm sure. I am very tired and would just like to go to my room." The look of disappointment that flashed across his face as he climbed from the pool nearly changed her mind. She almost told him what was happening, but fought the impulse. She allowed herself to look at him, to savor his body with her eyes.

Water sheeted off his clothes and drew her gaze. Desire seeped through her. She could not let him know how much she wanted him, not until she knew what the future held for both of them. It would only make it harder for him to leave her if she didn't improve any more. She forced herself to look away from the tantalizing sight of his body and reminded herself that Dr. Levy was waiting to come to her room. Perhaps tonight they would see something encouraging about her condition.

Brooks woke from the dream hard as a post. He lay still, eyes wide open and staring into the dark. His breath came in ragged gulps, while the memory of what he had envisioned hammered at his heart.

He wanted Marisa so badly his body ached. During their therapy sessions his groin tightened and throbbed with wanting her.

"Damn me," he swore. What kind of man thought about such things when the woman he loved was suffering? As much as he hated to admit it, he was after all, just a man. His flesh and his heart didn't seem to follow the same path. Maybe that was what made men and women so different. A woman's desire was all wrapped up in emotion, logic and her own style of reason. For a man it was purely physical. Brooks fought to control his body's natural hunger while the memory of making love to Marisa haunted and taunted, crashing over him in ways that crumbled his resolve.

Even though his soul and heart loved her beyond reason, his traitorous body yearned for physical release. It tore his heart to little pieces each time he caught the look of hopelessness in Marisa's dark eyes, and it shredded his soul to want her when she could not walk.

But maybe she felt the same kind of conflict when they were together. Maybe that was why she had suddenly curtailed their periods of massage and exercise. Even though he understood her need to be away from him if that was true, another part of him withered and died each time she asked to be wheeled back to her room.

A frustrated hiss issued from between his clenched teeth. He tossed back the sheet and rose from the bed. The room was hot and sultry, so he threw open the window and leaned out to inhale the still night air. But he noted little change in the temperature surrounding his nude body. There was no breeze, no relief. It was hot, torrid in a way that only exacerbated his lust and torment.

An owl hooted and his attention was drawn upward through lacy fingers of branches to the night sky. The vista wasn't the velvet-and-diamond tapestry he had learned to love in the Territory, but it was beautiful just the same. A slender arc of light flashed across the darkness.

"A falling star."

And even though it was about the stupidest thing he had ever done, Brooks made a wish upon it. He wished that Marisa would realize that he loved her—the woman she was inside—and that she would let him commit to her for the rest of his life.

"Try harder," Dr. Levy urged. "With the returning sensation you are experiencing, there must be at least a minimal amount of movement. Try again.''

Marisa bit down on her lip and willed her foot to rise from the mattress. Her upper torso trembled and shook from the effort. Beads of sweat formed at her temples and across her upper lip. This was the hardest thing she had ever done. Harder than roping a half-grown steer, harder than walking across the heat-scorched llano when her horse pulled up lame. She was ready to cry out in desperation and defeat when the image of Brooks flashed through her consciousness.

He had never given up. Not once.

Her foot jerked upward.

It was only a fraction of an inch, uncontrolled and spasmodic, but for a moment her nerves and muscles responded to the commands from her mind.

''I did it.'' She slumped back into the pile of pillows, as exhausted as if she had run miles. ''I made it move.'' A smile wreathed her face.

''Yes, you did.'' Dr. Levy's voice was oddly thick.

Marisa levered herself back up and looked at her doctor.

''Are you going to cry?''

''Me? Of course not. I never cry. It's not professional. I would never allow myself to get emotionally involved with my patients,'' she said gruffly. ''Now why don't we stop for the night? You need to get some sleep. If you are going to get back on your feet, we can't let you become exhausted.'' Dr. Levy yawned when she thought Marisa wasn't looking.

Marisa frowned. ''I only have two weeks left. That is not very long to get back on my feet. I need to work longer.''

''All right, Marisa,'' Dr. Levy said tiredly. ''Have it

your way, but I don't know how long we can keep this up.''

Brooks woke to the sound of pounding rain. He had slept badly, plagued by carnal thoughts and diminishing hope. When he pulled on his clothes and went to find a cup of coffee, his mood was dark. It did not improve when the sun retreated farther behind a veil of gray, foreboding clouds.

He stared at the dismal sky. It seemed a portent of bad things to come. But he shoved the pessimistic feeling aside and forced himself to brighten. He loved Marisa and she loved him. As long as they shared a bond like that, anything was possible.

He entered the dining hall to find Clell and Logan, dripping wet, sitting at one of the long tables nursing cups of coffee.

'''Bout time you got up. All this soft livin' is ruin' you,'' Clell said. Logan grinned at Brooks's shocked expression.

''Not that it isn't good to see you two, but what are you doing here?'' An uneasy feeling was crawling around inside Brooks's belly.

''Missy sent for us,'' Logan said cheerfully. Clell shot him a dark gaze that clearly said, *For once would you just shut the hell up and quit spilling the beans?*

Something thick and choking formed in the back of Brooks's throat. ''Missy sent for you?'' He took a step nearer and focused on Clell's face. ''You can't take her now. We still have another week.''

''Settle down, Brooks. She didn't say nothin' about comin' home.'' Clell gave Brooks a slight, reassuring smile. ''Don't go gettin' all het up just yet. I ain't even had a chance to talk to her or the doctor.''

As if on cue, Dr. Levy walked into the dining area. Her face was drawn and she looked tired, but she smiled and extended her hand to Clell. ''Thank you for coming, Mr. McClellan.''

''Ma'am, I wish I could persuade you to call me Clell.'' He smiled and pulled out a chair for Dr. Levy to join them at the table. Rain beat against the panes of glass and ran down in thready diagonal rivulets. ''How is Marisa?''

Dr. Levy glanced at Brooks and then Logan. A frown creased her forehead. ''I wonder if you would mind excusing us for a few minutes, gentlemen?''

Logan's eyebrows shot up. He flicked an uneasy glance toward Brooks. ''Pardon, ma'am?'' he said.

''If you don't mind…''

''Dr. Levy, is there something going on with Marisa that I should know about?'' Brooks asked abruptly. ''We had an arrangement.''

''Mr. James, I am fully aware of your arrangement and I believe it has been highly beneficial for Miss O'Bannion, thus far. However, at no time have I ever stopped being her physician. My loyalty and responsibility still lies solely with my patient.''

''What exactly are you saying?'' Fear, protectiveness and anger all mingled within Brooks's chest.

Dr. Levy sighed and rubbed her palm over her face in a gesture of fatigue. ''I am not saying anything, Mr. James. I simply would like to talk to Mr. McClellan privately.''

Brooks glared at the doctor, then he heard the scrape of chair legs and realized that Logan was standing beside him.

''Come on, Brooks. Let's go find us some eggs and bacon. We ain't wanted here.'' Logan scowled at Clell and Dr. Levy with eyes so much like Marisa's it made Brooks's belly tighten.

He fell into step beside Logan and went toward the kitchen, allowing himself one backward glance at Clell.

As soon as Brooks disappeared, Clell turned to Dr. Levy. "What is this all about? Is Missy worse?"

"Not at all, Mr. McClellan. She is showing remarkable improvement. I am sure that her paralysis has been caused by swelling and pressure surrounding her spinal cord."

The cold bands that had been around Clell's heart for months loosened. He inhaled deeply, feeling a happiness so profound it was painful. "Well, what is all this nonsense about sending Brooks and Logan away just now? Logan should be told. And why is Brooks's jaw draggin' on the ground? This is the best news he's bound to have heard in a month of Sundays."

Dr. Levy shook her head and sighed. "He hasn't been told."

"What?"

"You know Miss O'Bannion better than I do. She is a very stubborn young woman."

"Cussedly bullheaded, you mean." Clell snorted.

Dr. Levy managed a smile. "Well put, Mr. McClellan. At any rate, she has once again demanded that Mr. James not know about her improving condition. She has forbidden me to tell him about her regained feeling."

"Why would she do that? Isn't she goin' to be cured?"

"I wouldn't go that far. She has some returning sensation, limited movement. The work Mr. James has done keeping her muscles in tone has saved her from an overly long convalescence, but I cannot say how much more she will improve. She hopes to enlist your help now."

"My help?" Clell was stunned and confused.

"Yes. With hard work and dedication... I simply cannot say how much more she will accomplish but there is a chance—"

"How big a chance?"

"I am not a gambler, Mr. McClellan. I cannot give you odds. All I can tell you is that Miss O'Bannion is determined to recover. And that is half the battle."

Chapter Twenty-Four

"Missy, why do you have to be so consarned stubborn?" Clell's voice rang with exasperation. For the last hour he had tried threats, promises and plain logic, but his young adversary had refused to change her mind about her plan.

"Call me Marisa. I am using my given name now."

"Marisa, Missy, what does it matter what I call you? You are being pure-D muley about this." He raked his gnarled fingers through his hair and flopped down in a chair. "Why don't you want to tell Brooks that you are gettin' better?"

"I've explained to you a hundred times, Clell. I *can't* let him know. I know exactly what he would do." She inhaled deeply and levered her upper body into a more comfortable position in the invalid's chair. The wicker felt like iron bands against her back and shoulders.

"Our agreement was that if I had any improvement, I would marry him. But I can't marry him unless I am able to stand. I won't—I can't do it." She speared Clell with a gaze. "You have got to help me."

"What do you want me to do?" he asked tiredly.

"Dr. Levy has been helping me at night, but it is too

hard on her and me both to work half the night and all day, too. I can barely keep my eyes open." Marisa yawned. "She is worn-out and so am I. There is a small cottage on the other side of the lake. We could go there and work—privately. The lake will not be as warm as the pool, but we could do it."

"What are you going to tell Brooks?"

"I am not going to tell him anything. If you agree to help me, then we will leave now."

"Just sneak off like a couple of chicken thieves?" His voice was ripe with disapproval. "In the rain?" He gestured to the rain-slicked glass of her windows.

"I don't want to think of it as sneaking off." She frowned. "And the rain is not something I planned. We will just have to work around it. Will you help me? Please?"

"Ah, hell, you know I will. I been helpin' you since you were knee high to a banty rooster. I ain't about to up and stop all of a sudden." Clell managed a shaky grin. "What are we goin' to tell Logan?"

"Nothing!" Marisa snapped. "Don't you dare let one word slip about this."

"You still ain't forgiven him?" Clell glanced at the floor. The truth was he had not completely forgiven the young rascal either, but he understood why Logan had done what he did.

"No, I haven't," she whispered. "He never should've told Brooks. Things would be so much easier if Brooks had never found out where I went." She folded her arms across her chest and scowled.

"Easier for who? You or Brooks?"

She looked up and her eyes filled with tears. "That isn't fair, Clell. You know I love him."

"I know you do, honey, but you have got to quit makin' the decisions for him. He is a grown man."

Marisa could not allow herself to consider that Clell might be right. She was afraid if she let herself see Brooks's point of view for one instant she would weaken.

"Just this one last time, Clell, I promise. It really is the best way to handle everything."

"I have my doubts about that," he whispered. "Just how do you plan to get to this cottage?"

"Dr. Levy made sure the buggy that brought you and Logan waited for us," Marisa said sheepishly.

"The two of you must've been pretty damn sure I would agree."

"I've always been able to count on you. I knew I still could." Marisa bit down on her bottom lip to stop it from quivering.

Clell cleared his throat and wiped his hand beneath his nose. "Don't go all maudlin on me." He stood up and inhaled. "All right, tell me what to start packin'."

"Thank you, Clell."

"Don't go thankin' me. We ain't managed to get clean away yet. And I have a feelin' this time you may be pushing Brooks too far."

The air smelled fresh and clean. Dr. Levy had asked Brooks to leave Marisa alone for the entire morning so she could visit with Clell and then get some rest. But now, as the afternoon sun was peeking weakly through a thin veil of clouds, he was anxious to get to work. There was a clock in his head, ticking off the time he and Marisa had left on their agreement.

He strode down the hall to her closed bedroom door. It was quiet inside. Perhaps she was napping. He leaned close and put his ear to the door. Not a sound could be heard within.

Brooks raised his knuckles and knocked, but there was no response. He waited for a few minutes and then he knocked again.

No answer. He put his hand on the knob and turned.

The door swung open to reveal an empty room. The bed was stripped and every personal item of Marisa's was gone. A tendril of fear wrapped itself around his heart.

Brooks entered Dr. Levy's office with all the finesse of a runaway stallion. His jaw ached from being clenched so tightly. He took a belligerent stance, his legs wide apart, in front of her desk.

"Where the hell is she?" His voice held the wrath of a jilted lover.

Dr. Levy's dark brows shot upward at the sound of his voice. "I assume you mean Miss O'Bannion."

"You're damn right that is who I mean! Where is she?" Anger coursed through him.

Dr. Levy inhaled a deep breath and rearranged a pile of papers on her desk.

"And don't give me that song and dance about patient privilege. I have had it up to here with that nonsense." Brooks raised his palm over his head. "I love Marisa O'Bannion, and by all that is holy I am going to have her as my wife."

"She has left the clinic," Dr. Levy said in a voice that was not quite as calm and assured as she would've liked.

Brooks leaned down and put his palms on the desk. "Where did she go? There haven't been any buggies around for days, except for the one that brought Clell and Logan."

A flicker of something crossed her eyes.

"Ah, so she did use that buggy." Brooks concentrated on Dr. Levy's face, trying to read her thoughts. "You are the most conscientious of physicians. You would not have let her go alone, or very far, for that matter."

Dr. Levy stood up. She smoothed the folds of her navy serge skirt, then straightened the front of her shirtwaist. "Mr. James, I can't tell you anything about my patient."

A wide grin broke across Brooks's face, and for the first time since he had discovered the empty room, a feeling of peace settled over him. "You already have."

"What on earth do you mean?" Dr. Levy clasped her hands together, but not before Brooks saw the slightest tremble of her fingers.

"I spent some time out West, Dr. Levy. One of the many things I learned from that old codger Thomas Mc-Clellan is how to read a man's—er, a woman's—eyes." He winked. "And how to track. I will just follow Marisa's trail."

Brooks strode into the common room, looking for Clell and Logan. He spotted Logan by a window, sitting patiently while Judge Smith, one of the other residents, slowly dealt two hands of cards.

"Where is Clell?" Brooks glanced at the cards Logan picked up. They were good, probably good enough to win the hand.

"Dunno. I thought he might be with you." Logan plunked down two cards. "I'll take a pair, Mr. Smith."

The older man clumsily managed to get two cards from the deck. He had suffered a stroke. One side of his body had been affected. When he glanced up at Brooks and smiled, only half of his face responded.

"I am getting better," the judge said.

"Yep, Judge, you'll be dealin' monte by the time I

finish with you," Logan joked. "I told you playin' poker was good medicine."

"Why did you think Clell might be with me?" Brooks watched the deft movements of Logan's work-hardened hands while he tried to get back to the problem of Marisa's whereabouts.

"I haven't seen him, Missy or you this morning. I figured the three of you had gone off together."

"Why?" A finger of suspicion drew a line down Brooks's back.

"'Cause Clell's saddlebag is gone. He packed up this mornin'."

"So that's who took her," Brooks mused, as thoughts of anger and betrayal warred within him.

Logan looked up, his dark brows pushing together in a frown. "Took who?"

Brooks grimaced and sighed. "My intended has once again left me."

Logan grinned broadly and folded his hand, allowing the judge to win. "I swear, Brooks, the way that sister of mine acts, a body would almost think she *doesn't* want to marry you." Logan chuckled and shook his head. "Course, she did say yes once. Didn't she?"

Brooks gave Logan a scowl he hoped would silence the young scamp, but all it did was make him laugh even harder.

"I'm going to go find her."

"Need any help?" Logan asked.

"No." Brooks took a step and then turned back. "Judge, you once practiced law, didn't you?"

"Yes, I did." His answer was a little slurred, but easily understandable. "Why?"

"Oh, I was just thinking I may have to file a breach of promise suit if this keeps up."

Logan erupted in gales of laughter. His echoing chuckles followed Brooks through the dining hall and toward the kitchen, where he grabbed some food. He was determined he and Marisa were going to come to an understanding once and for all.

Decades of rotting leaves and brush padded the narrow wagon road, providing a soft carpet for Brooks to walk upon. He was barely aware of his surroundings as his thoughts focused on Marisa.

Logan's crack about Marisa not wanting to marry Brooks kept intruding on his thoughts. He finally forced himself to face the question that had been gnawing at the edges of his mind.

Did Marisa love him?

He thought so. Each time he kissed her and held her close there was a smoldering look of passion in her dark eyes that made his own body tighten in response. But was it love or was it only physical desire? Perhaps he had been fooling himself.

But then his thoughts returned to the day in the park, the day she had been hurt. She'd told him she loved him then. She had given him her word.

"And if there is one thing I can count on, it is the word of an O'Bannion," he muttered as he plucked a drooping sunflower from its sticky stem.

By noon Brooks had walked miles from the sanitarium. He stood on a low promontory and glanced around. The thick growth of trees and bushes prevented him from seeing much, but he heard water running nearby, and by following his ears found a creek not far from the road. He bent at the moss-covered edge and scooped water into his palm. The question of where Marisa was going kept nagging him. He was unfamiliar with the countryside, but he doubted there were any towns nearby.

Could it be that she and Clell were going to camp out? Surely not. Not with her in a wheelchair. But then where? "A cabin?" He shook himself and stood up.

In the end it really didn't matter, because wherever she went he intended to follow, even if it was to the ends of the earth and beyond.

Marisa looked out the small window at the vibrant valley that lay below. The cottage was simple, but the rooms were large and airy. It was easy for her to push herself about by grabbing the large wheels on either side of her invalid's chair and shoving them forward.

She and Clell had spent the morning working. The front porch railing was just narrow enough for her to grab on to, and with Clell's help she was able to hold herself up and more or less drag her legs along. It wasn't walking, but she was no longer flat on her back. Most of the feeling had returned to her legs, but she still wasn't able to do more than jerk her feet forward every now and then.

The last few nights she had woke to find her legs in a completely different position than when she went to bed. It was baffling, but then most everything about her dreams disturbed her because they centered around Brooks. In one scenario Marisa saw herself running to him on legs that were strong and sure. But in another she envisioned herself as a cripple, condemned to the chair, while Brooks dutifully cared for her, denying himself the possibility of a real life.

The thought made her shiver. That was why she was here. If she could not force her battered body to respond, if she could not be whole, then she was never going to see him again. Clell had warned her that Brooks would not allow it, but no power on earth could induce her to permit Brooks to sacrifice his chance for a normal life and happiness.

She loved him too much for that.

"I'm gettin' hungry enough to eat a bear. How about you?" Clell asked. His gravelly voice drew her attention away from the majestic view.

"I could eat."

"Good. I'll go chop up some kindling for the stove. How about you mixin' up some biscuits?" Clell was already getting the flour, bowl and other necessities together. He put them on the table where Marisa could reach them.

"They'll be heavy enough to use for doorstops," she warned with a grin. "You know the only thing I can make is coffee."

"I'll take my chances." The door slammed behind him before she had a chance to say more.

Marisa grasped the wheels of her chair. It took a couple of tries, but eventually she had the chair positioned at the table's edge. She could hear Clell whistling between the steady thunks and whacks of the ax. The familiar sounds reminded her of home.

Brooks stopped to have a bite of the apple he had tossed into his knapsack. He found a rock in the sunshine and stretched out his legs. The summer sun seeped into his bones and warmed him from the inside out.

He allowed his eyes to scan the country while he wondered what Marisa thought of it. It was about as different from the Territory as he could imagine a place being, but he thought she probably liked it.

"The trees..." he muttered to himself.

Marisa liked trees and water. The sound of a fast-running stream induced him to pull in his long legs and get up. He shoved aside blackberry vines and scrambled down a small rock-strewn ravine. At the bottom was a clear-running creek. Lichen and moss carpeted the steep bank.

He bent low and scooped up a drink. Then he heard a sound. At first he thought it was just an animal, but as he stilled and listened, he realized it couldn't be. The cadence was steady, definitely a man-made rhythm.

Brooks stood up and finished his apple. He tossed the core to a squirrel that had been watching him from the stump of a lightning-struck tree.

''Marisa O'Bannion, prepare yourself.'' He shoved his body through the dense growth while he followed the sound. ''We are about to have a reckoning.''

It took the better part of a half hour for Brooks to thread his way through the dense forest. He could've simply climbed back up and used the road, but the prickly side of his bruised ego wanted to come up on Marisa unannounced and unnoticed. He didn't want her to have any warning that he had found her. He wanted to make damn sure she knew how much her taking off had worried and angered him, and he wasn't going to take a chance that Clell might head him off before he did.

The back door to the cottage opened, sending a wash of fresh air over Marisa's bare toes. She wiggled them, savoring the joy of being able to feel the change in temperature, rejoicing in the fact that she could do so small a thing as move her feet. For a moment she stopped mixing the biscuits, wondering why Clell had decided to come in the back door, but she shrugged and pushed the question out of her mind. She worked the wooden spoon in the dough. The sound of determined strides on the floor behind her froze her hand. They were not Clell's footfalls.

"Damn it all to hell, Missy, when will you face your problems and stop running?" Brooks's voice roared over her.

She shoved the bowl away from her and turned the chair around as fast as she could manage. When she saw his expression she almost wished that she hadn't been in such a hurry.

His eyes were the color of a storm-filled sky. Anger had hewn his jaw into stone. His lips nearly vanished in a thin line beneath his mustache.

"You weren't supposed to find me." It was a stupid thing to say under the circumstances, but it was the best she could do.

He narrowed his gaze to slits as he advanced upon her. "I want some answers, Miss O'Bannion. And neither one of us is leaving this room until I get them."

Marisa drew in a sharp breath. It had been a long time since she'd seen this determined side of Brooks. Since she had been hurt he had bent over backward to be sweet and patient. The menacing man before her was anything but gentle.

Perhaps Clell had been right when he'd said this might push Brooks too far.

"Clell is outside," she warned, as if that information might somehow take away the fury she saw etched into each line of Brooks's face.

He stared at her—hard. "I'll let him know I am here if it will relieve your mind." He strode to the front door and flung it open. Clell was already there, alerted no doubt by the sound of Brooks's voice.

"Hello, Brooks. I didn't think it would take you long

to find her—I left a trail that a blind man could follow. But I'll admit this is a bit quicker than I expected."

"Missy and I have some things to get straight, Clell. I'd like for you to leave us alone for a while."

Clell leaned inside the door and glanced at Marisa. "You ain't goin' to beat her or anything, are you?" he asked with a half grin tugging at his lips.

"Don't tempt me," Brooks snapped. He flashed Marisa a dark look, then turned back to Clell. "She probably deserves a good spanking, but I am not her father. That is Hugh's domain, not mine. Rest easy, Clell. I only came to talk—this time."

"I'll be down by the creek if you need me," Clell said soberly.

"Clell! You aren't going to leave me with him, are you?" Marisa's voice was shrill.

"I warned you that you were pushing him too far this time, gal. You did the dance, now you've got to pay the fiddler."

Brooks closed the door and threw the bolt. He strode across the room until he was scowling down at Marisa. He folded his arms across his chest and nailed her with a cold gaze.

"Now, little lady, let's get down to business."

Chapter Twenty-Five

Brooks took a deep breath and focused on Marisa's face. Her eyes were wide and luminous. He was taking a big risk, he knew, but while he followed Marisa's trail an idea had come into his head that he just couldn't shake.

She had left because she had regained some feeling in her lower body. Just how much, he didn't know, but when he examined her latest disappearance, held it up to the light and picked it apart, the only logical explanation was that she had recovered some movement. If not, she would have simply held him to their bargain and sent him away. With each step through the woods his anger had dwindled as the truth of that took root and grew.

He was still disappointed in her for walking out, but he was no longer simmering with indignation. She was, after all, just being Missy. If the improvement was not enough to meet her expectations, she would do her damnedest to keep it from him. He watched her eyes and prayed he was not wrong. What he was about to do was the riskiest thing he had ever done in his life.

"You know, Marisa, when you first got hurt I thought you were a coward."

She flinched and gripped the arms of the invalid's chair

so hard her knuckles whitened. Her reaction hurt his heart, but he had gone too far to turn back now. The insult caused her eyes to flash in anger, though she remained silent. Brooks wanted to pull her up out of the chair and shower her with kisses and professions of love, but he forced himself to maintain the distance of less than a yard.

"I guess I misjudged you." He raised one brow and cocked his hip, trying to pretend he wasn't stiff with worry. The look in her eyes clawed at him, but he had to do it, had to force her to reveal herself. "You are not a coward."

Her brows rose and her lips parted as if she were going to say something. He hurried on, not daring to give himself a chance to change his mind.

"What you are, Marisa O'Bannion, is a lovely liar. You lied when you said you loved me. You lied when you agreed to marry me. And most of all you lied about our bargain."

All the air seemed to rush from the cottage. Brooks could feel his own heartbeat as they stared at each other. Her eyes narrowed to slits. Her hands made the wood of her armrests creak. And then, as he had prayed she would, Marisa O'Bannion exploded like a volcano.

"Of all the mean-spirited, chuckle-headed things to say. I love you!" She clenched her teeth together. "Oh! If I had a whip I'd flay the hide off you, you miserable, low-down, no-good..." The insults trailed off as she glared at him, evidently trying to think of stronger epithets to hurl at him. "I wish you would just go to Violet, for you deserve each other. And when you see her tell her that I *tried* to do what was best. I *tried* to send you away—" Her voice broke off into sobs.

"So that was it." Brooks came to her and knelt on one knee. "Violet came to see you."

"Yes. She said—well, it doesn't matter what she said."

"Oh, I can imagine. Let me see, it probably went something like this. You would be a burden to me. I would grow to hate you. I deserve a *whole* woman...." His gaze slid to her feet. "Is that about it?"

Marisa was tapping one foot like an angry cat flicks its tail. "Yes! Is that what you wanted to hear? She was right. Oh, I hated her for saying it, but she was right."

"No. She wasn't, Marisa." He touched her face. "I love you, and you could never be a burden."

"Just go away, I can't fight you anymore."

"Then why are you?" He laughed, amused that she wasn't aware of that tapping foot. He stood up, still laughing.

"Damn you! Double damn you! Oh, how I wish I could walk out of here."

"Then why don't you?"

She was operating on pure fury and adrenaline, not even thinking. And that was when Marisa put her two feet on the wood floor and pushed herself shakily erect.

Brooks swallowed hard. He stared at her face, still taut with fury and indignation. She supported herself on trembling legs. Then, as she became aware of what she had accomplished, the wrath melted from her lovely face. She looked down at her own feet.

Her lip began to tremble. "Brooks?" she whispered. "Do you see?" Her voice held all the wonder of life.

"Yes, honey." He took a step toward her, in case she might fall, but he didn't make a move to help her. "I see."

"Remember when I told you that the day would never come when I couldn't stand on my own two feet?" There were tears in her voice, but her eyes were dry and round with amazement.

"How could I forget? You were the prettiest thing I had ever seen. I think I fell in love with you on the day of Bellami's wedding."

Marisa glanced up. A shadow of doubt passed through her beautiful dark eyes. "But I was not even a lady. I didn't know how to act or talk or anything. How could you have thought I was pretty?"

"Honey, don't you understand yet?" Brooks shook his head in disbelief. "It has never been about the way you dress or talk. I love you. I love the woman inside that gorgeous skin of yours." He took slow steps toward her. "I...love...you."

"And I love you, Brooks James. I would never lie about that."

She let go of the chair arms and stood there, wobbly as a newborn colt, but on her own two feet.

He wrapped her in his arms and kissed her. All the fear and anger that had been dammed up inside him flowed away. This was the woman he wanted, and she was worth all he had to go through to get her.

The guests came from miles around. Some rode horseback, others used buckboards and some had even fastened runners to the bottoms of their buggies so they could cut through the thick snow that had fallen.

Hugh had sent a couple of cowhands into the mountains to bring back a pine tree. They had eaten more cookies than had actually made it to the green fringe of branches, but the tree was decorated and the house smelled of crisp winter air and pine fronds.

Members of the groom's family had arrived in Socorro by train more than a month ago. They rented a buggy and proceeded to the Circle B, to turn the O'Bannion ranch house into a den of happy chaos as preparations were made for the wedding.

Out of concern for the bride's health and her comfort, the decision to have the wedding at the ranch had been unanimous. And now, on Christmas Eve, as the hour drew near, a mixture of cowboy drawl, excited Spanish and cultured New York accents filled the adobe ranch.

"I am not sure we should have a veil," Marisa said doubtfully as Ellen and Patricia fluffed and arranged the gossamer fabric over her shoulders. "I am afraid it might get in my way. What if I stumble?"

"Then Brooks will be there to catch you, my dear."

"Aunt Patricia is correct, Marisa, you must have a veil." Ellen flashed a quick smile and then turned her attention to the tiny silk roses arranged around the scalloped lace panel on the front of her wedding gown.

"I don't want him to catch me. I want to be able to walk all on my own," Marisa said stubbornly.

"Surely you are using your cane." Patricia stopped fluffing and stepped around to look Marisa in the eye. "Everyone will understand—you should use the cane."

"No. We had a bargain. I would stand on my own two feet. And in my mind that means walking down the aisle, even if it is a short one through the parlor, to stand before the preacher."

There was no organ music. Marisa was glad of it, happy there was nothing, not even the notes of music to distract her as she concentrated on walking the short distance from the hall to the parlor.

She stared at the hem of her dress as her satin slipper appeared. Her grip on her bouquet was so tight she could feel the stems of holly cutting into her hands, but she was glad of something to hold on to.

Pick up the left foot. Concentrate. Bring it forward. Set it down.

Her progress was slow, deliberate and anything but graceful, but she felt a burst of pride and accomplishment as she slowly proceeded.

She drew in a breath and glanced up at Brooks. He was grinning from ear to ear.

"Take your time, baby, you are doing great."

Marisa nodded and allowed herself a glance at the guests, some standing, some sitting. Ellen was weeping softly into the shoulder of Cyril. Shane and Logan had spruced themselves up for the occasion and several of the neighboring girls were casting calf-eyes at them. Marisa grinned at her brothers and they both winked in return.

Hugh kept clearing his throat and Clell seemed to be swiping at his eyes a lot as she painstakingly took each step. Trace and Bellami kept looking at each other and smiling. Everyone had come home for Christmas except Flynn.

Three more careful steps, and at last Marisa was standing beside Brooks. He reached out and took her hand, squeezing it tightly.

"Dearly beloved…" The ceremony proceeded quickly.

A moment after Marisa and Brooks said "I do" there was a knock on the door.

"Must be a last-minute guest," Hugh said as he went to open it.

Then, covered with snow and carrying boxes and paper-wrapped bundles, Flynn walked in. He kicked snow from his boots as he set the parcels aside.

"Merry Christmas." He strode forward and swept Marisa into a big bear hug. "I brought presents for everyone." He carefully set Marisa back on her feet.

Brooks slipped his arm around Marisa's waist and drew

her against his side protectively. "Mighty kind of you, brother-in-law, but I have the best Christmas gift of all. Marisa. It took me a long time to win her. For the rest of my life I want this woman standing at my side." He beamed at Marisa.

A happy, rowdy territorial cheer filled the room as one and all agreed.

Epilogue

Marisa woke with a pair of firm buttocks pressed against her groin. She wiggled her toes and felt the hard muscular calf flinch beneath her digits. She lifted her leg and put her thigh over his hip. The warmth of his body, nestled against her body gave her a sense of security.

In this moment between wake and sleep where the hard edges of reality were softened, Marisa thanked God once again for sending her a man like Brooks and for all the blessings of her regained health.

She shifted her hips and nudged her pelvis against her sleeping husband. A drowsy grunt was followed by five curious fingers reaching back to caress whatever part of her flesh they happened to find.

This was the time she loved the best. In this half twilight world she was neither Marisa nor Missy nor even Mrs. James. She was simply a well loved woman with a man who had the good sense to appreciate all the facets of her personality.

"Are you awake?" she whispered into the nape of his neck.

"I'm getting that way." He drew her hand to his manhood, hot, hard and pulsing. "What did you have in mind?"

"Do we have time?" She grasped him and smiled at his spasmodic jerk.

"We'll make time," he growled, and rolled over, coming to rest above her body. He positioned himself between her thighs and slid into her.

"Brooks, we have to get ready for Christmas dinner…" she said into his mouth as he kissed her.

When he finally released her mouth, she gasped as he drove himself deep. "Let's not go." His breath was warm on her face.

"We have to…Lupe will come up and drag us out of bed—besides your mother is certain that Clair and Rossmore will be coming in from Socorro."

Then all thought, all ability to do anything but feel and respond to him, vanished as his lovemaking intensified. He quickened the rhythm of his thrusts and she clung to him, meeting him, joining him in a long ecstatic moan that wafted out over the snow-covered New Mexico prairie beyond.

* * * * *

Author's Note

While this was a work of fiction, the reality is that too many young adults are paralyzed each year. Spinal cord injuries claim many of our best, most of the injuries resulting from sports and athletics.

Research offers a way to combat the crippler, to bring back those who have been afflicted and put them on their feet once again. If you would like to take an active role in the battle or if you would like information about this worthy cause, please write to:

Christopher Reeve Foundation
Post Office Box 277 FDR STATION
NEW YORK, NY 10150-0277
or
Paralyzed Veterans of America
7 Mill Road
Wilton, NH 03086

Linda

Looking For More Romance?

Visit Romance.net

Look us up on-line at: http://www.romance.net

Check in daily for these and other exciting features:

Hot off the press

View all current titles, and purchase them on-line.

What do the stars have in store for you?

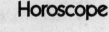

Horoscope

Hot deals

Exclusive offers available only at Romance.net

Plus, don't miss our interactive quizzes, contests and bonus gifts.

PWEB

Fill your holiday with...
excitement, magic and love!

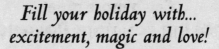

December is the time for Christmas carols, surprises
wrapped in colored paper and kisses under the mistletoe.
Mistletoe Kisses is a festive collection of stories about three
humbug bachelors and the feisty heroines who entice them
to ring in the holiday season with love and kisses.

AN OFFICER AND A GENTLEMAN
by Rachel Lee

THE MAGIC OF CHRISTMAS
by Andrea Edwards

THE PENDRAGON VIRUS
by Cait London

Available December 1998
wherever Harlequin and Silhouette books are sold.

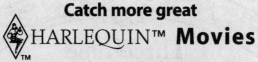 

MEN at WORK

All work and no play?
Not these men!

October 1998
SOUND OF SUMMER by Annette Broadrick

Secret agent Adam Conroy's seductive gaze could hypnotize a woman's heart. But it was Selena Stanford's body that needed saving—when she stumbled into the middle of an espionage ring and forced Adam out of hiding....

November 1998
GLASS HOUSES by Anne Stuart

Billionaire Michael Dubrovnik never lost a negotiation—until Laura de Kelsey Winston changed the boardroom rules. He might acquire her business...but a kiss would cost him his heart....

December 1998
FIT TO BE TIED by Joan Johnston

Matthew Benson had a way with words and women—but he refused to be tied down. Could Jennifer Smith get him to retract his scathing review of her art by trying another tactic: tying him *up?*

Available at your favorite retail outlet!

MEN AT WORK™

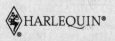 

COMING NEXT MONTH FROM

HARLEQUIN HISTORICALS